He cocks a brow and laughs.

"Are you serious?" he asks, and when I don't answer, he laughs even harder. "Oh God, you are. You can't sincerely believe I want to be seen with a witch. That's crazy, Manda."

Here we go. There's the Alex I've grown to hate. My pulse races. "Of course, we wouldn't want to hurt your reputation," I snarl through gritted teeth. "I'm curious, though. Are your hunter friends okay with the fact you were screwin' a witch?"

He cocks a brow. "I wasn't screwing a witch," he clarifies. "I screwed a girl who lied to me. There's a difference."

Wow. How the hell did we go from I-cheer-you-up-with-cupcakes to you-were-the-biggest-mistake-of-my-life in the blink of an eye?

I'm about to go ballistic on him when he makes a calming gesture. "All right, calm down, lil' avenger. I didn't mean to hurt you, but working with a witch is against everything a hunter believes. Jesus, I'd never hear the end of it if anyone knew."

Alex's apologies suck ass. "You're a douchebag, Alex, a first-class douchebag."

Knocking the sand off his trousers, he jumps up. "Yeah, you're right. But I'm a douchebag who bought you lemon cupcakes."

"No," I say as I get up. "You're a douchebag who thinks buying lemon cupcakes justifies being a douchebag."

Alex pulls a pair of sunglasses out of his jacket. "Chicken and egg, Manda."

Stomping away, I yell, "Egg and chicken, Alex."

Praise for Nadine Nightingale

"The varied texture of the narrative, produced by shifts between description, scene-setting, thoughts, dialogue, memories, etc., is rich and vivid and contributes much to the momentum and sustained interest. The characterization of Amanda has depth, while at the same time being entertaining and self-consciously played to the reader."

~Frank Egerton, Novelist

Karma

by

Nadine Nightingale

Drag.Me.To.Hell Series, Book One

Karma

Contact Information: info@thewildrosepress.com

Cover Art by *Debbie Taylor*

The Wild Rose Press, Inc.
PO Box 708
Adams Basin, NY 14410-0708
Visit us at www.thewildrosepress.com

Publishing History
First Black Rose Edition, 2016
Print ISBN 978-1-5092-0731-2
Digital ISBN 978-1-5092-0732-9

Drag.Me.To.Hell Series, Book One,
Published in the United States of America

Dedication

To my grandparents.
Your love and wisdom will always be with me.
See you on the other side.

"Even chance meetings are the result of karma…
Things in life are fated by our previous lives.
That even in the smallest events,
there's no such thing as coincidence."

~Haruki Murakami

Chapter 1

An electric hum charges the chilly air. The ghostly light of a bulb flickers. Seconds later, I gaze into Baphomet's onyx eyes. He lingers over a naked couple chained to his harpy feet, guarding them like a sphinx, imprisoning them like a warden.

"Oh my freakin' gosh! Is that…Is that the devil?" Redhead screams. The look on her high-school-queen-bee face is priceless.

I take a deep breath. "Yes," I say, swallowing the laughter that crawls up my throat. "It's the devil."

Redhead presses a palm against her chest. "Sweet baby Jesus. Does that mean I'm…I'm going to hell?" Her otherwise brown aura, indicating self-absorption, is gray. In other words, she's petrified.

The chick is obviously not the sharpest tool in the shed, and I doubt hell recruits stupid cheerleaders. I fake a smile and wave her question off. "Nah, don't worry. In the tarot, the devil represents desire and passion." I point to the card deck. "Draw another one."

Her delicate fingers fly over the cards, and she pulls the sixth major arcana card out of the pile. The lovers.

Redhead's sapphire eyes gleam. "I know what that means. He loves me, right?"

The devil and the lovers? That's as bad as a relationship can get. When her fingers accidently brush mine, I get a glimpse of how bad it'll be.

****

The fluorescent lights of the ER blinded Redhead. Closing her eyes, she reminded herself this was her fault. She should have never asked him about the other girl. She'd gotten a taste of his temper before and knew better than to challenge him. But that damn jealousy had gotten the best of her.

"Can you hear me?" the doctor asked, worried.

She wanted to answer, wanted to tell him she was fine, but she could hardly breathe. It felt like the air hit an invisible wall inside her bleeding nose. Parting her bruised lips, she gasped for oxygen, but the taste of sanitizer made her sick.

"Miss Rosewood, can you hear me?" The doctor's rich voice hammered through her brain.

She swallowed the pins and needles in her throat. "Yes."

"How did this happen?"

Every muscle in her body tensed. "I...I...fell."

****

I shake the brutal vision off. Every fortune-teller with a conscience would tell Redhead to stay the hell away from this guy. The thing is, if I tell her the truth, she'll accuse me of lying, and being called a liar is the doom of a clairvoyant. Luckily, I don't have a conscience.

"You guys are star-crossed lovers."

"Really?" she squeaks, like the dumb cheerleader she is.

"Yeah, course. Even Romeo and Juliet would envy you guys." If she doesn't hear the sarcasm in my voice, she totally deserves someone who'll beat the crap out of her. Besides, the whole Romeo and Juliet reference should put her on high alert. Yeah, I know, people think of them as the ultimate couple. But did they actually read the play? Let's summarize their fate: first Romeo wants Rosalind. Why? Because she's a nun, and guys dig things they can't have. Then Juliet, another forbidden fruit, comes along. Unfortunately, she's dumb enough to fall for his shit, and bada bing, bada boom, they both end up dead. Some call that romantic. I prefer stupid.

Her aura radiates fifty shades of red. Making an educated guess, I'd say she didn't get the hint. Hey, at least I tried.

Pleased, she pulls a hundred-dollar bill from her bag and puts it on the table. "You're amazing."

"I know," I reply flatly before shoving the money in my black lace bra. "Now get out and send the next one in."

The chick doesn't even mind my rudeness. "Thanks. Thank you so much." She sounds like a broken record, and I breathe a sigh of relief when the door slams shut behind her.

Waiting for my next client, I gather the cards. The foulness of the air bugs me a little. I hate rundown motel rooms, but they add to the mystery, and in my business, it's all about being mysterious. Harpers Ferry is my third stop in the last two weeks. Small town folk are good clients. They hunger for the perfect house, perfect husband, perfect kids. If they could, they'd even try to breed the perfect dog. No need to say this makes me perfectly sick. But beggars can't be choosers, and all I need is another five hundred bucks, and then I can kiss my old life goodbye.

A faint knock, then the door swings open. My next client is a middle-aged woman accompanied by her daughter. What kind of a mother drags her kid to a fortune-teller? I straighten and wave them over. The little girl is about ten, but she still sucks her thumb.

"Are you a witch?" the blonde angel asks, precariously.

I totally prefer the term Wise Independent Tremendously Charismatic Human, but before I get a chance to clarify, her mother interferes. "They said you could help us."

They? Who the heck are they? And did she just say help them? Who the hell does she think I am, Mother Theresa? "You want to know if your daughter will become the next Miss America, am I right?" A little sarcasm never hurts.

The woman steps closer. The flames of the black candles shed light on her wrinkled face. "Please kill my husband," she says, throwing a bundle of hundreds on the table. My guess is about ten thousand dollars.

"Lady, I'm a fortune-teller, not an assassin," I say, never taking my eyes off the money.

"You're a witch."

I cock a brow. "Still not an assassin."

"He hurts her," she whispers, pointing to the kid.

I know he does. I'd sensed her heartache the moment they walked in. I might tell lies for a living, but I tend to see the truth when no one else does. The aura of the little girl is a dark, muddy gray, evidence of a broken soul.

"Call the cops and get a divorce."

The woman pushes the little girl in my lap. "Please, I'm begging you. Help her."

Hazel eyes, clouded with misery and sorrow, look right through me. That son of a bitch robbed her of her innocence and left her drowning in self-hatred. Shivers run down my spine. Shit. I have no intention of bearing witness to the bastard's barbaric crime. It's a real shame visions don't ask for permission.

****

She stared at the gleaming stars on her ceiling. Her mother had put them there to keep the darkness at bay, but it didn't work. The room was gloomy. She knew the monster would come for her. It would look like her dad, but that was just a disguise. Her real dad would never do such things to her. He loved her. She thought of the puppy he'd once bought for her and the places he had taken her. A monster could never be so kind.

The creaking of the wooden door stopped her heart. She pulled the blanket over her head and started to count.

One, two, three.
The blanket pulled back.
Four, five six.
A wet kiss.
Seven, eight, nine.
"I love you, princess."

****

I push the fragile body of the girl away. Her pain. Her destiny. I don't give a shit about any of it. "Take your money and get the hell outta here."

The woman's jaw drops. "But—"

I hold my hand up. "Out! Now."

The little girl's gaze drops to her pink ballerina flats. Her disappointment floats through the dark room, leaving traces of hate and sadness in the air.

"You said she'd make him stop," she says as her mother hauls her to the door.

Don't. This is none of your business. Let them go.

Shit!

I heave a sigh. "Wait."

They spin around. Hope flickers across the mother's face. The woman makes me sick. How dare she call herself a mother? She knows what her husband is up to. Why on earth did she never try to stop him? I remind myself this isn't about her. It's about the little girl.

"What's your name?" I ask the kid.

"Jamie," she replies, voice weak and broken.

I wave her over. When she doesn't move, her mother grabs her by the wrist and pulls her toward me. Ruthless bitch. Can't she see her daughter is terrified?

Mother of the Year is probably expecting me to cast a spell or torment a voodoo doll. Yeah, you kinda get the wrong idea about magic when you've watched too many *Buffy the Vampire Slayer* episodes. But real magic doesn't come cheap. I wonder if the ruthless bitch is ready to pay the price.

I pull Jamie's rigid body closer and put my forefinger on her third eye. The kid is already damaged beyond repair, but what I'm about to do will kill a piece of her soul forever.

"Close your eyes, Jamie."

Chapter 2

The bus ticket in my bag, I barrel through the double doors of the Salty Dog Tavern. The place is a mess: empty glasses on empty tables, cockroaches picnicking on the decayed oak floor, and the smell a weird mixture of beer, rancid oil, and vodka. Call me sentimental, but I think it's appropriate to honor the end of my fucked up, always-on-the-road life, in a shithole like this.

Careful not to trample my crawling drinking buddies, I walk to the bar, grab one of the grungy barstools, and take a seat.

The fifty-something bartender greets me with a single nod. "What can I get ya, sweetheart?" he croaks. Poor guy should quit smoking.

"How about a glass of your best bourbon?"

He arches a brow, and I half expect him to ask for my ID. Instead, he says, "Best bourbon, huh?"

"I'm celebrating."

The bartender shrugs and pours me a glass of Jim Beam's Devil's Cut. "What's to celebrate?"

The ankh tattoo on my right wrist itches like crazy. I know what this means, but right now I don't give a shit about karma. "New York," I reply before I down the shot.

"Big town for a lil' girl."

I smile. People call me all sorts of names. Satan's

bride and stab-worthy bitch are my favorites, but lil' girl is a first. I tip the edge of my glass, and Papa Bear fills it up.

"Folks sayin' you're a fortune-teller. That true?" he asks, crossing his arms over his chest.

"Must be, if that's what they're saying."

"Folks also sayin' you're a witch."

For the love of God, what's wrong with the people in Harpers Ferry? Do they have a witch detector or something?

I keep my gaze on the glass. "Yeah, they must have seen me riding my broomstick at night. I'm telling ya, the way to Hogwarts is a dangerous path. So…" I bring the glass to my lips. "Here's to J.K. Rowling." The golden liquid wraps around my throat like a warm velvet scarf.

Papa Bear's husky laughter echoes through the empty tavern. One hand resting on his big belly, he uses the other to pour another shot. "Folks are goin' crazy after the McKenzie thing. But me, I ain't believin' such superstitious nonsense."

It's time to go. His aura might be soft blue, suggesting he really doesn't believe, but with the ankh tattoo itching, karma is about to bite, and I don't intend to wait for retribution.

I dig in my bag for an Andrew Jackson when I hear footsteps scuffling over the creaky floor. My right hand grows heavy, and the tattoo burns like freaking frostbite.

"Going somewhere, Amanda?"

I close my eyes and let my head fall back. Really, God? Alex Righteous-Ass Remington? Is that your way of thanking me?

Straightening, I take a deep breath and face him. Eighteen months no see, and he still wears the same worn-out leather jacket, along with completely ripped jeans? The guy needs a stylist. And a shave. Although, I have to admit he totally rocks the three-day beard.

From the corner of my eye, I see Papa Bear monitoring Alex suspiciously. Guess he doesn't like him either.

"Bourbon for my friend," I say before focusing my attention on jerk-face. "Good to see ya, Alex." His malachite eyes travel over me, slowly, drinking in my appearance. What can I say? I'm hot. Even Alex can't deny that.

"Cut the crap, Amanda."

No pleasantries? Fine by me. "How did you find me?" I ask, examining my freshly manicured nails.

"Tracked your phone."

I flash him a fake smile. "How very NSA of you."

Alex throws yesterday's newspaper on the counter. "Mind explaining this?"

"Don't know what you're talking about. Listen, I'd love to chat, but I have a bus to catch." I get up to leave, but Alex grabs my wrist.

"Quit playing dumb." Shoving the newspaper under my nose, he forces me to read.

HARPERS TIMES

Mayor's mysterious death shocks Harpers Ferry.

The popular mayor and founder of the Prevent Crimes Against Children (PCAC) foundation, James McKenzie, 41, died earlier this week at his idyllic Harpers Ferry home.

McKenzie, who supported at least a dozen charities, was well known for his fight against child pornography. He was found dead by his wife shortly after midnight Wednesday.

Detective Bucket of the Harpers Ferry police described his death as "sudden" and "unexplained."

"There was pure and utter terror on his face. He bled from the mouth and nose, and his hair was white as snow. I'm telling you, the man faced the devil before he died," said a source close to the County Coroner.

Officers searching McKenzie's house after the tragic death found no evidence of a crime. "It's an ongoing investigation, and all I can say is we're still waiting for the coroner's report," explained Detective Bucket.

A few hours prior to McKenzie's tragic death, the police responded to an emergency call from Jamie McKenzie, the ten-year-old daughter of the mayor. The little girl claimed her father was a monster and about to hurt her, said a spokeswoman of the Harpers Ferry police.

"The little girl said the witch promised to stop him, but only if she called the cops," said the 911 operator who responded to Jamie's emergency call.

According to the responding officers, Jamie was safe and sound when they arrived. James McKenzie claimed his daughter had watched a horror film that scared and confused her.

McKenzie's wife was admitted to the local hospital after suffering a mental breakdown. Jamie McKenzie is now with her grandparents.

"Our prayers are with his family. James was a hero, and we will all miss him," said his neighbor Charles Kenwood, 64.

I push the newspaper away. The ankh tattoo

burning like a newly-burned brand, I face Alex. “Sounds like the son of a bitch got what he deserved.”

“Did you kill him?” His grip tightens around my wrist.

“Would you believe me if I said no?”

Alex shrugs. “Try me.”

I wrench free from his grip. “I didn’t kill the bastard. Happy? Are we done now?”

Alex runs a hand through his messy, dark brown hair and sighs. “Try again.”

Taking a deep breath, I turn to Papa Bear, who’s eagerly eavesdropping while polishing his glasses with a filthy towel. “More bourbon, please.” Papa Bear is about to pour when I stop him. “Know what? Just pass me the bottle.” I need more than a glass to handle jerk-face. The old fella looks a bit startled, but he does what every good bartender would do—he serves.

“Amanda,” Alex says impatiently.

“Alex,” I mock him.

His eyes grow darker. Balling his hands into fists, he closes the gap between us. “Last chance. Did you, or did you not, kill the fuckin’ mayor?”

“Why does everyone think I’m some kind of assassin? I mean, I get it. I totally rock the Scarlett Johansson slash I’m-a-super-sexy-absolutely-lethal-Russian-spy look, but dude, I’m a professional liar, not a serial killer.” I take a large sip of the fiery liquid, hoping it’ll drown the anger building inside me. I don’t even know why Alex’s accusations bug me. By now, I should be used to it. Let’s face it. I would never have come this far if I had given shit about other people’s opinions, so why the fuck should I care about Alex’s?

“That’s my point,” he says. “You’re a liar. Nothing

you've ever said is true, so why should I believe you now?"

I know exactly to what he's referring, but no way in hell I'm going there. I'm done playing his games. With the grace of a ballerina, I rise from the barstool.

"Where do you think you're going?" His rich voice echoes through the empty tavern.

"I have a bus to catch, Alex. So if you're not here to kill me, you'll have to excuse me." I wink at Papa Bear and walk toward the double doors when two strong hands grab my shoulders and yank me backward.

What the fuck? I spin around, heart racing. "Dude, are you off your meds, or did you finally lose your weed virginity?"

Hands still on my shoulders, he keeps me from bolting. "We had a deal," Alex hisses.

"Ah, I didn't violate any of your stupid rules, because I didn't kill the fuckin' mayor." I roll my eyes as a dry laugh parts my lips. "You can't sincerely believe I would jeopardize my own life for a spoiled brat. Dude, you of all people should know me better than that."

Alex pulls me close. His hot breath tingles on my skin. "You're right, Amanda. I do know you. So tell me, how much did they pay you?"

"Screw you!" I try to break free, but Alex won't let go.

He digs his fingers into my soft skin. "I knew you couldn't be trusted. I should have never let you walk."

"Now what? Are you going to burn me at the stake?" Mental note: learn to keep your mouth shut. I bet he has a supply of green wood in his trunk.

A crooked smile tugging at his lips, he releases me.

"You have no idea how badly I want to see you burn, but I'm not here to kill you."

What? "You didn't come because of the article?"

"Nope." Alex steps back. His shoulders sink, and for the very first time since he walked into this shithole of a bar, his gaze drops.

This ain't good. Whatever it is that haunts him changes his aura into a dark blue mess. Meaning, he's scared of the truth. "What's going on, Alex?"

Alex's eyes drift to Papa Bear. Judging from the look on the old fella's wrinkled face, I'd say the Salty Dog Tavern has never seen more action. "I need your help," Alex whispers.

Wow. Did Alexander Remington really just ask for my help? I bet hell just froze over.

"It's Jesse. I think he's in trouble." He sounds desperate.

"What kinda trouble are we talking about?"

He arches a brow. "Careful, Manda. One might think you actually care."

The truth is I do care about Jesse. He's like the little brother I never wanted. Plus, if it wasn't for him, I'd be dead by now. Alex would have killed me the day he found out I was a witch. I narrow my eyes at him. "Where is he, Alex?"

"He was working a case in California, and I haven't heard from him in days."

"He was working a case alone? Why?" This situation got weirder and weirder. Jesse and Alex are inseparable, and even though Alex is a complete jerk when it comes to me, he'd never let his brother work a case on his own. Can't say I blame him. Working for the Paranormal Analysis Unit of the FBI, hunting down all sorts of evil, is a dangerous gig. Hunters don't always come out on top.

Alex frowns. "If we're done with the Q&A session, I'd like to go. It's a long way to California."

My jaw drops to the cockroach-inhabited floor. "Are you fuckin' insane? California? I have a bus ticket to New York and a freakin' dorm room at New York State University waiting for me."

Alex's burst into laughter. "NYU? You?"

Crossing my arms, I close the gap between us. "What's that supposed to mean, jerk?"

"Nothing." Covering his mouth with one hand, he tries to hide the mischievous grin that's curling his full lips. "Just didn't know they offered degrees in witchcraft."

Enough is enough. I sucker punch him in the ribs and walk toward the door when I hear a metallic clicking. I know that sound too damn well. "Put that gun down, son before you shoot someone," Papa Bear croaks.

My back still turned toward Alex, I shake my head in disbelief. "Really? You're going to shoot me in the back? That's pretty low even for you, Alex."

I feel the vibration in the wooden floor as he approaches me. "It's either California or a bullet to your brain. Your choice."

The air around me is chilly and thick. Papa Bear murmurs something, but I can't hear him. I'm too busy concentrating on my heartbeat. It's slow, but steady. Hand pressed against the door, I close my eyes and consider my options. Option number one: I ignore the gun pointed to my head and walk out. Most definitely get shot in the head and end up in a body bag next to the mayor's corpse. Option number two: I lose my room at NYU and help Alex find Jesse. Probably get killed in the process and end up in a body bag next to some Californian Barbie. Either way I'm screwed. Alex isn't the pretentious type. He'd shoot me in an instant. He's been waiting for this opportunity for way too long.

****

Minutes passed, but he didn't say a word. He didn't have to. I felt the disappointment, and disgust running through his veins.

"Are you going to kill me, Alex?" I said with a charming grin.

"You're a witch. A freaking witch."

Jesse took a step toward his furious brother. "She's your girlfriend, dude."

"I'm not his girlfriend," I said.

"She's not my girlfriend," he agreed.

Jesse gave me the shut-the-fuck-up-I'm-trying-to-save-your-dumb-ass look and rested a hand on his brother's shoulder. "Put that gun down, Alex. I know you don't want to kill her."

The air grew cold. "She's a witch, Jesse. A goddamn witch." His aura revealed a tornado of emotions. Muddy red, dark brownish-yellow, and charcoal swirled around him.

I got it; he was angry, stressed, and unforgiving. He felt betrayed. But what about me? He never told me he was a hunter. Never mentioned his job was to kill my kind. Granted, I had sensed it the second I laid eyes on him, but that didn't change the fact he, too, was a liar.

"You wanna shoot me?" I barked. "Then do it."

Alex's eyes widened. "You think I won't?" He sounded shocked.

"Shut up, Amanda!" Jesse hissed through gritted teeth before moving between Alex and me. "You banged her, and now you want to whack her, dude? You can't be serious!"

I thoroughly enjoyed the Alex Horror Picture Show, but it was time to get this over with. "You guys don't get it, do ya? I don't care if he shoots me or not. We all have to die one day, and it could be worse than taking a bullet from a hunter."

Alex's finger rested on the trigger.

Jesse desperately tried to talk some sense into him. "Don't do it, man. You'll regret this."

"She killed a man, Jesse."

Whoa! What? "Are you insane? I ain't killed nobody."

Alex's laughter echoed through the old house. "Right. Let me guess. A gremlin carved the sigil into the guy's chest after he slaughtered him like a pig."

My ankh tattoo burned like hell as I tried to make sense of his accusation. "Are you delusional or something?" My gaze darted to Jesse. "Seriously, what the hell is he talking about?"

The gun still pointed at me, he grabbed a few pictures from the table and threw them at me. "Recognize him?"

Shit, Mister Sinister? Damn, I had seen crime scene photos before, but this was a scene straight out of a Wes Craven horror flick. The pictures looked like a canvas of crimson red. Mister Sinister was positioned on a bed, his body twisted in an unnatural way. Eyes wide open, his expression reflected pure horror, and carved into his chest was a sigil I had never seen before.

I faced Jesse because there was no point talking to Alex right now. "Listen, I am a witch, a liar, and most of the time, a stab-worthy bitch, but I've never killed anyone in my entire life." I paused for a moment to study Jesse's expression, and when I realized he believed me, I continued. "Jesus, I'm a vegetarian."

Slowly, Jesse reached for Alex's gun. "I believe her."

Alex raised a brow at his brother. "Because you want to believe her."

"And you don't?"

"I want the truth, Jess. If she killed him, I'll kill her. End of story."

His attitude started to piss me off. "The guy was a first-class jerk, but I did not end his life. Understood?"

I knew nothing would change Alex's opinion about me, but Jesse believed me. I saw it in his eyes. "Let her go, Alex."

Alex's finger moved away from the trigger, then back to it. Away, then back. His dark blue aura turned red, then gray, and eventually back to blue. As if he mentally counted daisies; I'll kill her, I'll kill her not.

****

"Amanda!" His hoarse voice snaps me out of my trance-like state, and the memory fades into oblivion.

I sigh. "Yes, Alex?"

He presses the barrel of his Beretta against my back. "What's it gonna be?"

Careful not to make any sudden movements, I turn and give him my best fake smile. "I'll help you find your brother, but once this is done, I never want to see you again. Do I make myself clear?"

Alex puts the gun down and opens the door for me.

"Crystal. Now move."

Awesome. I love choices where you come out the loser either way. Bye bye, New York. Hello, hell.

Chapter 3

Merging onto Interstate 70, we are about to enter Indiana. It's only been a few hours, but I already have pins and needles in my legs. I hate road trips. Especially the ones where the driver abducts you and the whole scenario has Stockholm syndrome written all over it. "It's a fucking forty-one-hour trip, Alex. Why couldn't we fly? You know, like normal people."

Alex's eyes are fixed on the road. By now, he'd mastered the art of ignoring me. I have to admit his stubbornness is sort of impressive. There aren't many people who can ignore me.

Jeez, eighteen months ago *he* couldn't ignore me.

Understatement of the year; he couldn't take his freaking eyes off me. But now that he knows what I am, it's easy for him to turn a deaf ear to the supernatural abomination next to him.

Letting my head fall against the black leather seat, I enjoy the last rays of the warm sun as Steven Tyler's rough voice quavers "Crying." I love this song. I reach for the radio, intending to turn up the volume.

Alex shoots me a killer look. "Hands off my radio," he orders, sounding like a drill sergeant.

Is he serious? "Dude, you pointed a gun at my back, dragged me on a fuckin' cross-country trip without telling me what's really going on, and holding me hostage, and now I can't even turn up the volume on the radio?"

Jerk-face keeps his eyes on the road, pretending I don't exist.

Red-hot, bitter anger flushes my system. Who does he think I am, one of his damn groupies who wets her panties when she hears his rich, deep voice? Yeah, wrong girl, pal. I am Amanda Bishop. No one messes with me, and no one ignores me. I grab the steering wheel and jerk it to the right. Bet he didn't see this one coming.

"What the fuck?" he yells, trying to keep his baby under control. "Let go, Amanda!"

But I don't.

The Mustang swerves from one side to the other until the jarring sound of brakes howls through the black beauty, and it comes to a halt.

Murder on his face, Alex glares at me. "Do you have a death wish or something?" It's the first time he's actually looked at me.

Mission accomplished.

Putting a hand on my hip, I grin. "Just don't like to be ignored." I pause and straighten. "Now, dude. You've got two seconds to tell me what the hell is going on with Jesse, or I will get out of this car and hitch a ride to New York. Fuck, I'll walk if I have to."

Alex reaches for the Beretta in his waistband, a hint of a smile in his eyes. "I'm going to—"

I hold my hand up Beyoncé-style. "What? Shoot me?" I laugh. "Go ahead; because I swear to God, it'll be the only way to keep me in this goddamn car."

His gaze roams my face, and when he realizes I'm serious, he bites his totally kissable lower lip.

"Kinda sucks when you're out of options, hm?"

My voice is impregnated with victory.

He eyeballs his skinned knuckles and lets out a sharp breath. “All right, a couple of weeks ago, Jesse heard about a bocor in Bakersfield. Word on the street was the guy could break contracts. I told him to stay away from him, but you know Jesse. He just doesn’t listen. Took off while I was sleeping, and I haven’t heard from him since. No call. No message. Nothing.”

Jesse ran off to see a voodoo priest? Talk about a death wish. “What contracts are we talking about?”

Alex frowns as his features tense. “The ‘I sold my soul’ kind.”

My stomach drops to the ground. “Jesse didn’t—”

“What, sell his soul?” He knits his brows and shakes his head. “No, he’d never do that.”

A heavy weight lifts off my chest. We knew selling your soul came with a “go straight to hell” card, and couldn’t be undone. But I’m still confused about why he would look for someone to break this sort of deal in the first place. “If he didn’t sell his soul, then why on earth is he looking for a bocor with said ability?”

Alex averts his gaze. “I don’t know.” His aura beams a bright pink. Bloody liar.

I cross my arms. “Try again.”

“It’s the truth,” he says, voice low.

The truth, my ass. Even if I couldn’t read auras, I’d know he’s not sharing all the info. “Not a good enough answer,” I bark. “So, last chance, Alex.” Enjoying the fact the tables have turned, I look him right in the eyes and start counting. “One.” My hand rests on the door handle. “One and a half.” I face the door, ready to get out of here. “Two.” I open the door, but Alex grabs my arm.

"Wait." His voice is in my ear. "Jesse is trying to save a friend."

I arch a brow. "A friend?" My disbelief is loud and clear.

Scrubbing his fingers through his dark hair, he nods. "They are pretty close, and when Jesse heard he'd made a deal with a demon, he was hellbent on saving him. I tried to stop him, told him he couldn't be saved, but he didn't believe me."

His aura changed into a soft blue. Meaning he's telling the truth. I still think he's holding back on me, but decide to cut him some slack. "Let's say I believe you. I still don't understand how I can help."

"You're a witch."

Why is everyone using this word as if it's the solution to all of the problems in the world? I cast him a sideways glance. "Yeah, but you're the one who works for the goddamn FBI, Alex."

"I tracked his phone, smartass. The last thing I got before it went dead was Bakersfield, and I thought you might be able to locate him there. You know, with your witch-mojo and all. Plus…" He leans forward and grins. "You're so above yourself, you'd even mess with a psychotic voodoo priest."

I shrug the comment off. "Compliments aren't your strong suit, hm?"

Alex's eyes soften. "Look, I know you hate me. I mean I almost killed you—"

"Twice," I remind him, holding two fingers up.

A muscle tightens along the curve of his jaw. "Yeah, whatever. Point is Jesse is your friend and the only reason you're still alive."

"He's a hunter, and I'm a witch. Makes friendship

sorta impossible." I squeeze my eyes shut and sigh. "But you're right. I owe him, and I always pay my dues."

Alex knows me well enough to understand I just agreed to help him. He starts the engine, and as the roaring of the Black Panther echoes through the interior, I lean against the cool window, wondering if I truly understand what the hell I just got myself into.

****

Alex's need to find the one person who'd stood by him his entire life turned into a dangerous obsession. Hitting the gas pedal full force, he raced down the interstate.

"Slow down," I ordered.

He ignored me.

Gazing out the window, I focused on Kylie Minogue's voice on the radio. She sang that creepy song about wild roses. The one that had always given me the chills.

"We have to hurry," Alex muttered under his breath.

"I know." Trees and fields faded into oblivion as the Mustang flew over the deserted interstate. I'm a sucker for speed, but we were moving too damn fast. "Please slow down, Alex. You're gonna get us killed."

"We have to hurry," he repeated as the radio decomposed into static.

A chilly draft caressed my cheek. Raw emotion flooded my chest, and a piercing pain stabbed through my heart. Something wasn't right.

"We have to hurry." Alex's voice was hoarse and distant.

My gaze went to the driver's seat, and an

unspeakable fear pulsated through my carotid artery. Alex was gone. The driver's seat was empty. What the fuck? I turned around, looking for Alex, but he was nowhere to be seen. Driven by an invisible hand, the needle on the Mustang's speedometer pointed at 140mph.

"Alex?" I screamed, terrified.

There was no answer. Just white noise blaring from the radio speakers.

"Alex, where the hell are you?"

"You have to hurry," a soft voice whispered like distant wind chimes. "Find the wild roses, Amanda."

I saw the imprint of a small hand on a breath-clouded window. It looked less Titanic *and more* Insidious, *which amplified my fear. "Who are you?" I yelled, but panic weakened my voice.*

I felt a cold touch on my thigh. The hair on my neck stood higher than the Empire State Building, and for a split second I refused to face whatever was with me in the car.

"Help me."

Swallowing fear, I turned to the driver's seat. Raven hair covered the scarred face of a little girl. She crawled toward me, body twitching and jerking in an unnatural way. "Help us,*" she whispered, reaching for my face.*

"Don't," I begged. The girl's pain was hard enough to endure from a distance. I wasn't sure I could handle it up close.

"You have to understand," she said and ran her chilly fingers over my temple.

Excruciating pain rushed through me as the worst feeling of all paralyzed me—helplessness.

****

"Manda!" A pair of strong hands chases away the cold. "Wake up."

Yanking my eyes open, I find Alex leaning over me with his fingers folded over my shoulders. "You okay?"

I don't know. *Am I?*

"Yeah," I groan and pull back. "Just get off me." I didn't mean to sound so harsh, but Alex's touch is dangerous, and after a dream like that, I don't feel like playing with fire.

Alex retreats to his seat, but watches me suspiciously. "Bad dream?"

More like the worst nightmare ever. Stretching my numb muscles, I roll my eyes. "Dude, if I need a shrink, I'll call Dr. Phil."

"Whatever." He shakes his head and throws a brown doggy bag in my lap. "Here, thought you might be hungry."

The smell of spicy vegetarian chili fries crawls in my nose as I open the bag. "Is it poisoned?" I ask, not trusting the fact that, all of a sudden, he's treating me like a human being.

He unwraps a burrito. "I wish," he mutters under his breath.

I shove a few fries in my mouth. "I always liked that about you."

He cocks a brow, and something close to shock fills those beautiful eyes. "What, that I want to poison you?"

I laugh. "That you're not afraid to speak your mind, Alex."

"Stop sweet talkin' me, Manda," he says and takes

a bite.

I frown. "Will do. If you stop callin' me Manda, that is." I hate nicknames. Granted, Manda is much better than Mandy, but when Alex accused me of slaughtering Mister Sinister, he had lost the right to call me that.

He shoots me a dirty look. "You are—"

"Awesome?" I shrug. "I know."

Chin low and jaw hard, he doesn't look happy. I anticipate a retort or one of his famous you're-an-arrogant-bitch speeches. Instead, he takes a large bite of his burrito and keeps quiet.

Gazing out the window, I realize we're in a remote area, surrounded by trees and fields. "Where are we?"

"Near Joplin," he murmurs, mouth full.

"Missouri?"

He gives me the are-you-serious look. "No, Arizona."

I frown. "You're so funny, honey."

Alex's lips curl into a half smile. "Stupid questions require snarky answers."

Arrogant asshole. "There ain't no stupid questions, dude. There are only stupid answers." After that, we eat in silence, not looking at each other. The whole road-trip-with-the-ex-lover-who-hates-you shit is more than just uncomfortable, and I bet the next Oxford dictionary features "Amanda and Alex in the car" as a new definition of awkward.

Twenty minutes and two sodas later, we hit the road. Trees and landscapes flit past us when the scent of incense pricks my nostrils.

"You smell that?" I ask, scanning the car for the source.

"Smell what?" he asks, fiddling with the radio.

"Incense," I reply.

He casts me a look that is a cross between delighted and concerned. "You sure you're okay?"

"Yeah," I assure him as "Where the Wild Roses Grow" blasts through the car. Déjà vu and not a good one. I switch it off.

"Hey," Alex barks. "What did I say about the radio?"

"Don't care." Haunted by the image of the little girl from my dream, chills ripple through me. "I hate that song."

Chapter 4

Crossing the border to Texas, half our trip is behind us with another twenty hours ahead. As the twilight's last gleaming fades into blackness, I feel limp. We've been in this car way too long, and I could really use a break from the Mustang and Alex.

Jerk-face is barely able to keep his eyes open. But even if I suggested a pit stop, he wouldn't listen. I guess some things never change. His inability to listen got us into this weird relationship—friends-with-benefits, you're-a-freaking-witch, and I-want-to-kill-you mess—in the first place.

****

A flickering street lamp provided the only light in a starless night. Knowing I was being followed, I zipped my faux-leather jacket, and picked up the pace.

My last client's heavy footsteps resonated through the desolate alley, and his fury pierced my back like a butcher knife. He probably wanted his money back, but the jerk could kiss my peachy little ass. I read cards. There is no money back guarantee in my business. Besides, it wasn't my fault he couldn't deal with the truth. Sure, it had to suck when your girlfriend cheated on you with your best friend, but he should have known a former beauty queen wouldn't waste her sweet chunk on a guy like him.

The stomping behind me grew louder. The dude

was beyond pissed. His raw hate flooded the night like a bloody tsunami. I knew right then and there I had to make a choice; I could either run or show some lady-balls and face the bastard.

Every fiber in my body urged me to flee. Running was for chickens, though, and I was anything but. Forcing myself to pause, I turned around quickly. "What do you want?" I asked, keeping my voice casual. Because the first survival rule on the streets was show no fear.

Mister Sinister stopped dead in his tracks. He clearly hadn't expected a face-off. His surprise quickly converted to anger, though. "You're a fucking liar, bitch! My girlfriend would never cheat one me."

My lips curled into a wicked grin. "Am I?" Hands on my hips, I took a step toward him. "Then why the hell are you so fuckin' mad?"

"Because you lied," he yelled, fisting his stubby fingers.

I should have kept my mouth shut, but a rush of excitement and a human's biological bodyguard, adrenalin, poisoned my system. "Wanna know what I think?" I asked, voice even.

He looked amused. "Go ahead, bitch. Hit me with your best shot."

"The reason behind your psycho act is that gut-wrenching feeling in the pit of your stomach which tells you I didn't lie."

His expression darkened. Muddy red and dark green swirled around him like a mad swarm of bees. He grabbed a fistful of my hair, and hauled me closer. "Taking people's money and feeding them lies that ruin their lives? How do you live with yourself?"

I thought about gouging his eyes out, but decided to stay calm a little longer. "Look, you're wasted, man. Why don't you go home, sober up, get yourself a new girlfriend, and while you're at it, find yourself a best friend who lives by the bro code instead of the ho code?" His eyes widened, and he let go off my hair. I turned, ready to walk away from the mess telling the truth had created, but his bulky hands yanked me back violently.

"Admit it! Admit you lied!"

Mister Sinister was about to wake the whole neighborhood. Although his lack of self-control entertained me, I'd had enough. Straightening, I grinned at him. "All right, I lied. Satisfied?"

He inched closer. His repulsive hands crushed my shoulder blade in a vicious manner. "No." He shook me hard. "Say it as if you mean it."

The guy was about to lose it, so I held my hands up in defeat and suppressed the blazing fire inside me. "Okay, buddy, calm down. Your girlfriend loves you more than any pleasure she could get from mind-blowing sex, and she'd never ever cheat on you." I put on my best fake smile. "Happy? Can I go now? 'Cause I really need to wash your disgusting touch off my skin."

The lie appeared to infuriate him even more. He leaned closer, and I felt his whiskey breath on my face. "You're a bitch! A fucking bitch!" A spark of crazy gleamed in his blue eyes. "And do you know what we do with lying bitches like you around here?"

My arms dropped to my sides. "Worship the ground they walk on?"

His grip tightened. "We screw the lies out of 'em."

My shoulder hurt like hell, and the firestorm inside me had turned into a live grenade about to blow him into bits and pieces. "Dude, I'll only say this once. Take your creepy hands off me. Now."

"Or what?" His voice was razor-sharp.

I ran my forefinger over his temple and down to his jawline. "I know they say hell hath no fury like a woman scorned." I closed the little gap still between us. "But, unlike you, most people never pissed of a witch."

The bastard's laughter echoed off the walls. "Cheeky. Think you can keep that attitude up once I'm done with you?"

Just when I decided Mister Sinister would become my guinea pig for the castration curse I had always wanted to try, a shadowy figure stepped out of the darkness. "Let her go," a deep voice demanded.

Black biker boots, ripped jeans, a worn-out leather jacket, and from what I could see, the body of a Greek god. Long story short, he was freaking hot.

I appreciated his concern, but he had this "I'm a super soldier who's going to save the world" thing going for him, and I certainly wasn't a damsel in distress. "Stay out of this," I said matter-of-factly.

Mister Sinister's mouth snapped shut. Confusion washed over his face, but he quickly pulled it together and faced the god-like creature. "You heard the bitch. Get lost."

My self-appointed savior moved nearer. The flickering streetlamp shed light on his striking face. Christ, even Damon Salvatore of The Vampire Diaries *would have envied this guy. "Hands off her. Now."*

Mister Sinister's cheeks flushed with fury. "Mind your own fucking business, pal."

That was just great. I was caught in the middle of a freaking testosterone battle and couldn't even use magic. My day had gone from bad to hell.

Stalking toward us, the hottie cocked a brow. "I'm not going to say it again. Let her go, asshole."

Anxiety blossomed in my stomach as I got a glimpse of Captain Righteous's golden aura. That, and the heroic attitude, turned all my alarm bells on, and I felt the overwhelming urge to run.

I was so mesmerized by the feeling something wasn't right about this guy, I didn't even realize Mister Sinister lay on the street with a bleeding nose until a husky voice brought me back to reality. "Are you okay?"

I didn't answer, and not because his malachite eyes took my breath away, and he had the most handsome face I'd ever seen. I knew why my alarm bells had gone off. Captain Righteous was no superhero. He was a freaking hunter, and I was his favorite kind of prey.

****

The little trip down memory lane ends when Alex's irritating yelling snaps me out of it. "Manda!"

"What?" I hiss.

"We have to take a break. I'm tired, and it's irresponsible to drive like this."

I laugh my ass off. Irresponsible? Jesus, who talks like this? "Of course," I say, swallowing the laughter. "We wouldn't want to run down a cactus, right?"

He frowns. "Quit being a smartass and shut up. Will ya?"

I'm too tired to put up much of a fight. "Whatever, Alex."

He parks the Mustang in front of a shitty motel.

"A fucked-up motel," I bark. "That's such a cliché."

Unimpressed, he shrugs. "You can always stay in the car. Maybe the coyotes will keep you company. Or better, do me a favor and tear you into pieces."

I open the door and stretch my battered legs. "Animals love me."

He slams the car door shut behind him. "At least someone does," he mutters before heading inside.

Leaning against the Mustang, I wait for him to book our rooms. Seriously, the guy is a first-class jerk. Why in God's name did I screw him in the first place? Because he's a *hot*, first-class jerk.

Ten minutes later, Alex returns. The problem is he only has one keycard. Chasing after him, my six-inch knee-high boots leave an angry impression on the dry ground. This isn't happening. God would have to fucking hate me to do that. "What do you mean they only have one room left?"

Checking the room number on the keycard, he stops in front of a red door. "Exactly what I said."

I put my hands on my hips and shake my head. "I'm not going to sleep with you."

A mischievous grin on his full lips, he cocks a brow. "Guess we're finally on the same page."

I roll my eyes. "Shut up. You know exactly what I mean."

Alex unlocks the scarlet door with the number thirteen on it and lets out a frustrated sigh. "We can share this room, or you can spend the night in the car." Running his hand over the wall, searching for the light switch, he looks over his shoulder at me. "Your call, Manda. Do whatever you want. I. Don't. Care."

I glare at the squiggly, black thirteen on the door. I don't believe in bad luck, but it might be time to reconsider.

The light from the fixture overhead glides over two dirty beds with ill-favored flower sheets, a 1950s TV, and curtains from the 70s that give the room its fucked-up flair. This might be Norman Bates's cup of tea, but it sure as hell ain't mine. I shoot Alex a death glare. "Did the room come with complementary kitchen knife, shower curtain, and a *How to Become a Psycho Killer for Dummies* handbook?"

Alex throws his bag on the left bed. "I told the guy at the desk you carry that stuff in your vanity case."

I fold my arms across my chest. "You're such an ass."

"Says the stab-worthy bitch," he murmurs, heading to the tiny bathroom. "I'll shower and catch some sleep. We'll hit the road in a couple of hours."

A hot shower sounds tempting, but one look at the monstrosity of a bathroom destroys all my fantasies. I am used to beat-up motels, but the crimson stains on the white tiles make me want to puke. Either someone got killed in here, or the last resident used her sanitary pads to paint the freaking walls. Gross.

"Hey." I seize hold of Alex's shirt. "Sure you want to take a shower in there?"

Alex pulls away, shoots me one last evil glare, and slams the door in my face.

Guess that means yes.

The water turns on. Moments later, hot steam wafts through the brittle door. Holding my breath to block the foul smell, I scan the room and spot a cockroach on the nightstand. Gosh, I need a drink. Or ten.

Chapter 5

Sitting on a barstool inside the Titty Twister—yes, someone actually named a bar in the middle of nowhere after the one in Tarantino's cult vampire flick, and no, no one bit me or did a snake dance—I gulp down my third tequila shot.

Alex was still in the shower when I hauled butt to the bar across the street. I even left him a note that said something like, "Gone to drink you pretty." Not that he deserved one, but I figured he might go all Sigourney Weaver aka Ellen Ripley on my ass if he thought I ran.

In need of more booze, I wave the cute, inked bartender over. "So," I say, leaning on my elbows. "What's a girl gotta do to get another drink around here?"

He places his hands against the counter and cocks a brow. "I guess you just have to be nice to the hot bartender."

"Oh, really?" I lift my brows to my hairline and scan the bar. "You better call him then. 'Cause I'm dying for another drink."

I'm-sexy-and-I-know-it flinches. "Ouch, that hurt."

I shrug. "You'll get over it."

He grabs the brown tequila from the shelf behind him and pours two shots. Shoving one toward me, he keeps the other for himself. "To you, sweetheart," he says, raising the short glass.

I down the tasty poison and wipe my mouth. "Do you always drink with your customers?"

His lips curl into a cocky grin. "Only if they're as pretty as you."

I make a face. "Seriously? That's like the second worst pick-up line I've heard in years."

"Yeah? What's the worst?"

"I'm Wolverine, and my boner is adamantium-laced," I reply.

Mister I'm-sexy-and-I-know-it throws his head back and laughs. "Gotta write that one down," he says, shoving another shot toward me. "I'm Bay."

"Amanda."

A genuine smile touches his eyes. "Nice to meet you, Amanda."

I look him over. Shaved head, gunmetal-blue eyes, brawny, inked arms, and an "I'll give you an unforgettable night and disappear from your life forever" aura, he's definitely a guy after my own heart. But today, I just don't feel it. I could tell myself it's not because of Alex, but lying to others is so much easier than lying to myself.

Leaning against the counter, Bay puts a bowl of nuts in front of me. "You're not from around here, are ya?"

"Let me guess, my accent gave me away?"

He points to my boots. "Nah," he says, an impish grin tugging at his lips. "The Gucci boots did, angel."

What's wrong with my boots? They'd cost me a freaking fortune. "What about you?" I ask, popping a handful of nuts into my mouth. I expected them to be stale, like most bar food, but they were delicious. "Are you a Texas cowboy?"

"Nope, I'm a true-bred Mainiac," he confesses, voice filled with pride.

"You're what?"

He laughs. "I'm from Maine."

I kinda like this guy.

His gunmetal-blue eyes meet mine. "Tell me, what's a pretty girl like you doing in a crap hole like this?"

Chewing on the nuts, I shrug. "Figured the Titty Twister would be the ideal place to get shitfaced before I head to a safe house in Mexico."

"Safe house?"

"Oh, didn't I mention I robbed a bank?"

Bay's jaw drops, and his eyes go wide. "You what?"

Damn, if a guy like Bay believes that crap, I must be a better liar than I thought. His benumbed expression is hilarious, but I let him off the hook before he calls the cops. "Jeez, relax. I was just kidding. I'm on my way to Bakersfield and checked into the motel across the street for the night."

Bay's eyes narrow and he takes a step back. "Bakersfield, huh?" He looks curious and surprised at the same time. "Don't tell me you're one of those prying journalist chicks."

I'm not the *Gossip Girl* type, but my gut tells me this could be interesting. "What if I am? Is there a story for me in Bakersfield?"

Bay runs a hand over his shaved head and knits his brows. "You're screwing with me, right?"

"Trust me," I say, my gaze traveling to his crotch. "You'd know if I was screwing with you."

He bites his lower lip and swallows hard. "I bet I

would."

I smile and pop more nuts in my mouth. "About Bakersfield…you were saying?"

Bay squints. "Haven't you seen the news lately?"

"Would I ask you if I had?"

He studies me closely. "I guess not."

Bending over the counter, I shove my two girlfriends under his nose. "Why don't you bring me up to date?"

Bay's cheeks flush a bright red, and he has a hard time taking his eyes off my boobs. "Y-You…" he stutters, "haven't heard of the disappearing kids?"

Leaning back, I slide a finger over my neck. "No, but I bet you'll tell me all about it, am I right?"

Bay looks at me as if I'm some kind of porn star, and I can literally see the dirty fantasies flickering across his mind. I snap my fingers in front of his face. "Earth to planet Bay!"

Embarrassed because I'd caught him staring, he tears his gaze from my body and refills our glasses. "Ten kids disappeared in the last couple of weeks. Some of them were found, but they've"—he hesitates—"changed."

Gosh, getting him to spill the story is like getting blood out of a stone. "Changed how?" I try to sound causal, but my voice is higher than usual.

He scans through the room, and when he's certain no one is listening, he leans in. "They're possessed," he whispers.

What is it with hot guys and stupidity? Sure, there's the all-jocks-are-dumb-as-bread law, but Bay doesn't strike me as an arrogant asshole who only dates brainless cheerleaders. "Is that supposed to be some kind of crappy bartender joke?"

Bay's expression is dead serious. "I wish," he croaks. "But as I said, it's been all over the news."

Oh boy, he's serious about this possession shit.

"Son, can I get ma drink or what?" an elderly biker shouts from the other end of the counter.

Bay waves a hand in the air. "Be right there." He pulls a newspaper out from behind the counter and hands it to me. "Check this out if you don't believe me."

When Bay takes off to serve the grandpa version of Jax Teller from *Sons of Anarchy*, I skim through the cover story. Victims show extremely aggressive behavior, speak in languages they'd never learned, and claim to hear demons. Damn, this reads like an article in *Weird NJ*, a semi-annual magazine of the strange in New Jersey, not *The New York Times*.

I throw the paper aside and rub my temples. What the hell is going on? Children can't be possessed.

"Told you." Bay's deep voice startles me. "There's some weird shit going down in Bakersfield. Maybe you should stay in Texas."

"You don't sincerely believe this crap, do you?"

He pulls a barstool out and takes a seat. "I've seen the CNN coverage, angel. I guess I do."

I burst out laughing. "What, did they show footage from *The Exorcist*?"

Bay's jawline hardens, and the muscles in his arms tense. "This isn't funny."

I tilt my head to the side and sigh. "Actually, it is. These kids aren't possessed." Humanity's knowledge of possession is limited to flicks like *Evil Dead* and *The Exorcist*. Most of the stuff Hollywood invented, though, is a whole lot of bullshit and has nothing to do with reality.

Bay cocks a brow. "And you're a specialist in possession because?" A pale yellow aura engulfs him, hinting at the excitement, boiling beneath the calm façade.

I bat my thick lashes. "I'm Constantine. Exorcist, demonologist, and Master of the Dark Arts."

His deep laughter roars through the bar. "Damn, I gotta say, you look fucking awesome for a chain-smoking dude who's been to hell."

"Shut up," I say, smiling.

His intense eyes lock with mine. "Look, angel, my shift ends at eleven. You could give me a lesson in dark arts at my place."

"Sounds promising." I pull a twenty-dollar bill out of my lace bra and put it on the counter. "But I have to pass."

His eyes roam my body. "You're missing out, angel."

Peeking over Bay's shoulder, I see Grandpa Jax and his biker friends glaring. "Son," the old man hollers. "She ain't givin' it to ya. But I sure as hell will if ya don't start servin'."

Bay shakes his head and rolls his eyes. "Sorry," he mutters and heads over.

I grab my bag, stagger to the door, and wink at the guy with the shaved head and the gunmetal-blue eyes, knowing he was right. I am missing out.

****

"I can't believe you spent the night in the car," Alex bitches as we walk into the diner.

There's only so much a girl can endure at seven in

the morning, and Blake Shelton's "She Wouldn't Be Gone," the sound of sizzling hot oil, and the scent of fried bacon and scrambled eggs already works on my last nerve. "Why don't you just leave me the hell alone?"

Bathing in my misery, he grins. "What's wrong, Manda? Couldn't get laid last night?"

I really want to cut that stupid grin out of his face, but before I can get my hands on a knife, a middle-aged waitress with a pencil in her hair approaches us. "Welcome to Joe's Diner. Pick a seat, and I'll get you some coffee."

Following jerk-face to a table at the far end, I peek over the shoulder of a trucker and stop dead in my tracks. The man stares at the headline of today's paper. It reads: Another girl missing in Bakersfield.

"Manda?" Alex says. "What are you waiting for?"

A frown on my face, I stomp to a booth.

"Make it fast," he orders, shoving the menu at me.

Massaging my temples, I try to ease the stabbing pain behind my right eye, but it's pointless. Spending the night in front of my iPad has taken a toll on me. I read every article I could find about the missing kids. The MO is always the same. The kid goes missing from their bedroom, reappears after two weeks, and acts like a holy terror. In hindsight, I can't blame Bay for believing the whole possession thing. Watching the CNN footage was sort of scary.

I feel Alex's eyes on me. His expression is a mixture of worry and curiosity. "Wanna talk about it?"

He hasn't spoken to me since we hit the road, but now that I try to relax, he feels chatty? "About what?"

"Last night," he says casually.

"What about last night?" I grunt.

He cocks his head. "C'mon, you know what I mean. Since when does Amanda Bishop walk out of a bar alone?"

My gaze shoots up. "Did you spy on me, Alex?"

He rolls his shoulders back and grins. "Keep your friends close and your enemies closer."

I lock my hands on top of my head and close my eyes. What is wrong with him? Can't he at least give me a break until I've had my first cup of coffee? Drawing in a few deep breaths, I try to relax, but apparently, there's no rest for witches.

"Where the Wild Roses Grow" blares through the speakers of the diner. The melody makes me dizzy and nauseous. My heart pounds like crazy. Icy chills rush down my spine, and seconds later, I'm floating.

****

Black. That's what I saw when I opened my eyes. No Alex. No diner. Just utter darkness.

"Amanda," a faint voice gasped.

Hugging myself, I fought the bitter cold that wrapped around me like a thick pile of snow. "Who the fuck are you?" I shouted like a crazy person.

"We need your help."

Damn it, what in Christ's name was happening?

Spinning, I tried to get an idea of where the hell I was, but I could hardly see my own hand, let alone my surroundings. "What the hell do you want from me?"

Icy fingers circled my wrist. "You oughta help us."

An unexplainable wickedness crushed my corrupted heart. "I can't help you if you don't tell me who you are."

"You know me."

I trembled. "No, I don't."

"Turn around," the otherworldly voice ordered.

I'd rather run, but curiosity got the best of me. Jesus Christ, I couldn't believe what I saw. A bunch of girls, none older than ten, stuffed into dog kennels like animals. My attention was drawn by the apparition of a little girl, standing next to one of the kennels. Her white dress soaking wet and raven hair covered her face.

"Save them," she begged, pointing to the other girls.

I took a step toward her. "What is this place?"

"It's hell," she whispered, silent tears rolling down her cheeks.

I swallowed the lump in my throat and stumbled backward. But she advanced toward me, and her pale blue eyes locked with mine. "You can end this," she said as the skin fell off her face, and red flesh turned into white bones.

"Stop!" I screamed, horrified by what I saw.

She levitated toward me. Her skull twisted back and forth, jerked left, then right. The kid was like a skeleton puppet without strings. "Enfer les avaler,*" she said, pointing to the kennels.*

The ankh tattoo itched as I stared at the helpless kids behind their bars. "What's that supposed to mean?"

"Hell will swallow them," the kid explained, and bright white light flooded the room.

****

"Manda?" Alex snaps his fingers in my face. "Where the hell did you go?" he asks, wearing a worried expression.

Hell?

"Jesus, Amanda, talk to me. You look like you've just seen a ghost."

I think that's exactly what happened.

"Are you all right, hon?" The waitress stands next to me with the coffee pot in her hand. "Would you like a piece of sugar or a saltine?"

I ignore her and face Alex. "We need to talk."

Jerk-face cocks a brow. "So talk."

I look at the waitress, who instantly gets the hint. "Want me to come back later?"

I shake my head. "No." Skimming the menu, I point to the blueberry pancakes with syrup, fruit, and freshly pressed orange juice. "I'll have that."

"Bacon and eggs for me," Alex adds.

She nods, pours two coffees, and heads back to the counter.

When she's out of hearing, Alex bends over the table. "What's going on, Manda?"

Good question. I hoped he could answer it for me. "Why did you withhold the info about the missing kids?"

He frowns. "What kids?"

He works for the FBI, for Christ's sake! There's no way he didn't know about this. "The disappearing, reappearing, claiming-to-be-possessed-by-a-demon kids who are all over the freakin' news," I snarl through gritted teeth.

Alex folds his hand around the hot cup and stares at me as if I'm nuts. "I have no idea what you're talking about." His voice is even, and his aura shines a soft blue. Could he be telling the truth?

I pull the iPad out of my bag, open a browser, and shove it toward him. "Look for yourself."

Alex skims several articles as I tell him about the weird nightmare, and the even weirder vision, I just had. He listens patiently, and by the time our food arrives, I brought him up to speed.

"That's impossible," he says. "Children can't be possessed. Demons can only possess someone if the vessel agrees to it. Kids can't make that sort of decision."

I shove a forkful of the pancakes into my mouth and raise a brow. "Thanks for the supernatural lesson, Hawking."

He shoots me a look, puts the iPad on the table, and takes a sip of his cold coffee. "Do you think this has anything to do with Jesse?"

"Dunno. But he's a hunter, and being your brother, he wouldn't walk away from a case like that."

Alex runs a hand over his stubble and sighs. "You have a point," he groans. "But none of this makes any sense. Why would these kids claim to be possessed? Unless..." His eyes grow distant.

I put the fork down and wipe my mouth with a napkin. "Unless what?"

He shoves his full plate away. "Unless one of your witch sisters put a hex on them."

"I hate to break it to you, but this isn't *Hansel and Gretel*. We don't live in gingerbread houses, and we don't lock little girls in dog kennels."

He scowls at me, lips tight. "With your kind nothing is impossible."

I smile, because if I don't, I'll scratch the jerk's eyes out. "Why would the little girl come to me for help if a witch did this to her?"

A half-smile curves his lips. "I don't understand

why anyone would come to you for help, Manda. As far as I know, you only ever cared about yourself."

"It's what keeps me alive, Alex."

"No." He leans back. "It's what makes you lonely and selfish, Amanda."

Facing a wall of hatred and scorn, I rub my temples a little harder. "I don't wanna fight," I grumble.

He squints suspiciously. "Are you sick or something?"

My shoulders sink, and I avert my gaze. "No, Alex. I'm just tired of this shit. So how about a deal?"

He thrusts his fingers through his messy hair and frowns. "Why don't I like the sound of this?"

"Relax," I say, waving his comment off. "I just want us to stop fighting until we've found your brother."

Alex knits his brows. "You want a truce?" He sounds surprised.

I look him in the eye. "Yeah, just until we get to the bottom of this."

He gazes out the window. "I don't trust you."

"Your brother does," I counter.

He draws in a deep breath. "I know Jesse loves you, and for some unexplainable reason, you seem to care about him, too."

"So?"

His malachite eyes search my soul. "I guess we can call a truce."

A heavy weight lifts from my chest. "Good."

"I still don't trust you," he grumbles.

Glaring at his muddy blue aura, I nod. "I know, Alex."

Chapter 6

Final destination: Bakersfield.

Sounds melodramatic…but here's the thing: I hate California—too many pretty faces, and too much pretentious happiness—and I can't shake the bizarre feeling this trip will be my undoing. I'm not sure what worries me more, though, going against a bocor or spending too much time with Alex. Both could be fatal.

Drowning my sorrow with an iced latte at Starbucks, I wait till Alex books us a room at the Knights Inn across the street. It's less fucked up than other motels, and as long as I don't have to share the room with bedbugs, I'm okay with it.

I'm enjoying the warm sun on my tired face, eyes shut, when I sense testosterone and raging hormones. Awesome.

"You're very pretty," a weak voice croaks.

I open my eyes. A group of teenage boys, barely younger than me, check me out from head to toe. Jeez, can't a girl have a coffee without being hit on?

I'm about to pull my sunglasses down when a Zac Efron wannabe slaps Pimple Face. "You're such a pussy," he says with an evil grin.

The guys laugh their butts off, but Pimple Face's shoulders sink, and his aura changes into a depressing dark green. "Shut up, man. I had the balls to talk to her, didn't I?" he defends himself.

One look at the poor bastard makes me want to drag his ass to the nearest mall and get him a makeover. The boy is the king of Nerddom—plaid shirt, horn-rims, short-cropped hair, and don't even get me started on the blue suspenders. His so-called friends, on the other hand, live on the brighter side of life, and fifty bucks says they only hang with him because they need someone to do their homework.

"Loser," one of the morons coughs.

My gaze roams over the nerd. The boy has a lot of potential. He could be the next Mark Zuckerberg while his stupid friends will end up like Al Bundy.

"A girl like her would never hang with a loser like you." Zac Efron wannabe laughs, throwing a napkin at Pimple Face.

I should stay out of this, but I hate bullies. Grabbing my iced coffee, I get up, shake my hips Shakira-style, and head over to the nerd. "A girl like me," I say, running a finger over his pimpled face, "would love to hang with a guy like you."

He stares at me as if I'm some kind of alien. "Really?"

I give him a kiss on the cheek. "Really," I whisper in his ear.

"What the hell?" one of his moron friends mutters.

"Did she just kiss him?" another asks.

"Shut up," Zac Efron wannabe yells.

But nerd kid couldn't care less about their stupid comments. His aura beams the brightest, proudest orange, and I can feel what he feels—hope.

"Manda?" Alex shouts from across the street.

Shit, if he saw this, I'll never hear the end of it. Winking at nerd kid, I amble back to the Knights Inn.

A smile touches Alex's eyes as I walk up to him. "Not exactly your type," he says.

Rolling my eyes, I sigh. "What do you know about my type, Alex?"

He shrugs. "Enough to be certain he isn't on your radar."

He really thinks I'm that shallow, huh? "News flash, jerk-face," I snarl. "In a couple years, he'll be a rich dude with a Bentley in his garage. So tell me—how is that not my type?"

Alex frowns. "You're a lot of things, Amanda, but a gold digger isn't one of them." He studies me closely, and a smile touches his eyes. "Ain't nothing wrong with being nice, you know."

He thinks I did this out of the goodness of my heart? I liked him thinking I'm shallow better. "I don't do nice," I say. "Now shut up and give me the key to my room."

Alex hands it over. "You can take a shower. Then we'll hit the road."

Leaning against the wall, I cross my arms. "Did you track his phone to a certain address?"

He kicks a few stones. "That's the thing," he says, never meeting my gaze. "The battery of Jesse's phone must have died before I got an exact location."

My jaw drops. "So this search and rescue mission is more like a round of blind man's bluff?"

He purses his well-formed lips and says nothing.

I throw my hands over my head. "Oh, that's just great. How the hell are we supposed to find him if you don't even know his last whereabouts?"

Insecurity blackens his blue aura. "We'll hit the hotels, and start there."

He can’t be serious. Bakersfield is one of the largest cities in California. “Are you insane? There must be hundreds of hotels and motels. Do you have any idea how long it will take us to canvass them all?”

He clenches his jaw. “Do you have a better idea, Miss Know-it-all?”

I straighten my shoulders. “Sure.”

Jerk-face tilts his head to the side and arches a brow. “Well, what are you waiting for? Spill it.”

Isn’t it kind of obvious? Jesse came to see a bocor, so we should look for him. “What do you know about that voodoo priest?”

His husky voice trembles. “Not much. Just that he’s from around.”

“You gotta be fuckin’ kiddin’ me,” I growl.

Alex narrows his eyes at me. “Drop the bitch act, Manda.” Raw emotion hardens his god-like features. “Jesse took his notes with him. I guess he was afraid I’d come after him.”

What good is it to work for the FBI if he doesn’t know shit? I put a hand on my hip. “Some hunter you are.”

He scrubs his face, clearly tired of the argument. “You’re not helping.” His voice is laced with guilt and worry.

I’m not Alex’s biggest fan, but I hate to see him hurting. “Let’s talk to the parents of the abducted kids then,” I suggest.

He gives me an incredulous look, and when I don’t laugh, he shakes his head. “Great idea, genius. We don’t even know if Jesse’s disappearance is connected to that. Besides, what exactly are you going to tell them? Hey, I’m Agent Remington, and this is my witch friend. Could we ask your possessed kid if it knows a voodoo priest?"

"Douchebag," I say, nudging him in the ribs. "I'm trying to help here, in case you haven't noticed."

He throws his head back. "Look, I'm not trying to be an ass. But unless you come up with a better idea, we'll go with mine."

Alex's plan will never work, but when I see the sadness in his eyes, I don't have the heart to tell him. Jesse is his Achilles heel. Without him, his life isn't just empty, it's senseless. "Fine," I hiss. "Have it your way, but don't say I didn't warn you."

Trudging into my room, I shut the door behind me and drop my bags on the weirdly-colored carpet. I am so damn tired, and the ivory sheets are so fucking tempting. All I want is to lie down, close my eyes, and get some sleep. Instead, I stumble to the bathroom and strip. Life sucks.

My muscles relax under the hot water, but the sadness in Alex's eyes haunts me. The last time I saw him like that was the beginning of our end.

****

I slammed the mini-bar shut, frustrated with my sudden lack of self-control. What the hell was I thinking? I'd come to his room to end things, not to screw him without goddamn protection.

Hating myself for the lack of lady-balls, I'd opened the tab to get some water when his hoarse, sleepy voice startled me. "Manda, what are you doing? It's three in the morning."

The table bumped the backs of my thighs as I turned around. "Nothing. Go back to sleep," I muttered, hoping he'd leave it at that.

He searched my face. "Wanna talk about it?"

For the longest time, I just stared at him. His perfect abs, the mesmerizing face, the fatal eyes—fuck, the guy was perfection. But this—us—was wrong. He was a hunter. I was a witch. He was gentle, good, and caring. I was a selfish, evil witch resented by my own mother.

"Amanda?" He stepped forward until we were eye to eye. "What's going on?"

"Nothing," I barked. "Just go back to bed, all right?"

He moved forward until we were chest to chest. "Sure about that?" His hands trailed down my arms. "The wall is so much more fun," he said, kissing the edge of my lip.

My senses reeled. All I had to do was tell him we were over, but one touch, and I was a wet mess that hungered for more. "Alex," I moaned as he reached for the hem of my shirt. "Please."

Kissing the other side of my lip, he smiled. "Please touch me? Please leave me alone? Gotta be a bit more specific, Manda."

When I didn't reply, he pulled my shirt over my head and pushed me against the wall. Cupping my ass with rough hands, he trailed kisses down my neck.

I pressed my palms against his chest and wrapped my legs around his waist. Tension built in my belly as I felt his hard-on against my black lace panties. What in God's name was wrong with me? One second I wanted to get as far away from him as possible, and the next I wanted him buried inside me. "Alex," I choked out. "This is a bad idea."

He carried me to the table. When he set me down,

his eyes locked with mine. "With you, everything seems to be a bad idea." His gaze dropped to my lips, and before I could say anything, his mouth covered mine.

He kissed me so hard, my head bent back. Desire spread through my body like a blazing fire, and no matter how hard I tried to fight it, I needed him.

Running my hands through his thick hair, I pressed my legs against his rock-hard ass and pulled him closer. "Alex," I whispered against his lips. "I want you." My chest rose and fell with excitement and nervousness.

"Say that again," he ordered in a husky voice.

I pulled his boxers down. "I. Want. You."

The words broke the chains that restrained the beast inside him, and within seconds he was a wild, hot mess. Hauling me to the edge of the table, he shoved my panties down. His lips curled into a cocky grin. "I never thought I'd say this," he said, with hungry eyes. "But I think I want to keep you."

What? My heart cramped as the words replayed in my ears. Want. To. Keep. You. I wasn't a keeper; I was a fucking love-her-and-leave-her. Hadn't he gotten the message?

"Manda? What's the matter?" he asked when I stiffened.

Barely able to breath, I shoved him away. "I need to go."

His eyes went wide. "What?"

I jumped from the table, grabbed my shirt off the floor, and put it on.

"Amanda." He caught my wrist. "Talk to me. What the hell is going on?"

I'd played with fire, and now I had to live with the

scars. Spinning around, I drew in a deep breath. "We had a deal," I said, voice calm and steady.

He searched my face. "What the hell are you talking about?"

"This"—I pointed to us—"was supposed to be easy and fun. No strings attached. Those were your words, Alex."

He sighed. "We've screwed each other for two months, spent every freaking hour together, and had a pretty good time. Call me crazy, but I'd say that's a little more than mindless sex."

I shook my head. "This is crazy. You *are crazy."*

"Why the hell are you so scared of love, Amanda?"

"Love?" I laughed. "I'm selfish, arrogant, reckless, and irresponsible, remember? Love isn't in my vocabulary."

"No, Amanda." He took a step toward me. "You pretend to be all those things, but I've seen you. The real you."

I felt a nuclear explosion of anger in my gut. Who did he think he was, Dr. Phil? "I don't pretend. Ever."

"Yeah?" His eyes darkened as he closed the small gap still between us. "Then what the fuck were you doing just now?"

His proximity did crazy things to my heart, and I knew I had to get the hell outta there before I let him convince me we had a shot. "I don't do relationships, Alex. You know that."

He put two fingers under my chin and forced me to look at him. "What's the difference between what we had and a real relationship?"

I pulled back and swallowed the lump in my throat.

"What we had was a good time and pretty awesome sex. A relationship includes sharing problems and secrets, Alex."

"What's wrong with that?"

"Everything," I snapped. "I get it. You think you know me and all. But you really don't." I cupped his cheeks. "Trust me, Alex, you wouldn't like the real me." I gazed into a malachite ocean of sadness. "I'm sorry."

"So am I," he said and walked away.

****

I wrap a towel around my wet body, and wipe the steam off the mirror. There's a loud knock on the front door.

"It's open," I shout.

"Manda?"

"Be right there," I reply. Pulling my wet hair into a loose bun, I check myself out in the mirror. I have black bags under my eyes, and my skin is a little rougher than usual, but other than that, I look as stunning as ever.

"Manda, you coming or what?"

Wearing nothing but a towel, I yank the door open and give him a look. "Can't a girl take a shower?"

Alex's jaw drops as his gaze slides over my body. "What the hell, Amanda?"

A crooked smile tugs at my lips as I see the glowing red aura around him. "Shy doesn't suit you," I bitch as I walk to my bag.

"Jesus." He throws his hands in the air. "Just get dressed."

"Your wish is my command." I drop the towel, and Alex blushes like a teenager.

"Seriously, what the fuck is wrong with you? Don't

you have a moral compass? You know, like normal people?"

I grab a pink lace bra and panties from my bag and grin. "Hey, you were the one who said I should get dressed. I'm just following orders."

He could turn around or avert his attention, but his gaze is glued to my body, and his aura is drenched in lust and desire. It's sort of ironic. He hates my guts, but he still wants to screw me.

"Pass me the jeans?" I say.

He tosses them over and shakes his head. "You're unbelievable."

I shrug. "It's not like you haven't seen me in all my glory before."

His jaw hardens. "Doesn't mean I want to see your glory again," he snaps and stomps out of the room. "I'll wait in the car."

My inner bitch and I high-five.

Chapter 7

It's almost sundown when we barge into the Vagabond Inn, the last hotel on the visitbakersfield.com website. I'm starving, my feet ache, and Alex is on his worst behavior. Each time he heard the words, "Sorry, but there's no one here with that name," his mood got worse, and little by little he had turned into the not-so-incredible-version of the green monster, smashing down anyone standing between him and finding Jesse.

He stomps toward the hotel clerk like a man on a mission, but I grab his arm. "Alex."

"What?" he hisses, ogling the poor bastard behind the counter.

"Why don't you let me do the talkin'?" I try to sound casual, but there's an edge to my voice I can't even out.

Yanking his arm out of my grip, he frowns. "We don't have time for your sweet talking, Amanda." He stalks to the check-in desk, and I follow like a lost puppy.

Awesome. I must have left my dignity in the Salty Dog Tavern.

"Hello, my name is Miguel. How can I help you?" the cute, dark-haired desk clerk says. His adorable Hispanic accent puts a smile on my face.

"Hi," I say, leaning against the wooden counter. "We—"

"Are looking for this man." Alex slams a picture of Jesse on the counter. "Have you seen him?"

Miguel looks from the picture to Alex. His clueless aura confirms my worst fears. "I don't think so, sir."

Wrong answer, pal.

Alex's unconcealed anger charges the air. Fisting his hands, he meets Miguel's nervous eyes. "Check your computer. His name is Jesse Remington."

Miguel looks at me, and when I nod, his fingers fly over the keyboard. "I'm sorry, sir. There's no one here with that name," he says, eyes still on the screen.

Tapping his fingers against the counter, Alex watches the poor guy with eagle eyes. "Try Bucky Barns."

I bite my lower lip, choking back the laughter crawling up my throat.

Alex gives me the evil eye. "Just shut up, okay?"

I pretend to lock my lips with an invisible key.

"I'm afraid there's no Bucky Barns either." Miguel's Adam's apple trembles. The poor bastard wants to be anywhere but here right now.

Jerk-face's muscles stiffen. "What about Jules Winnfield?" he asks, leaning over the counter.

Miguel's eyes widen. "The *Pulp Fiction* character?"

There's a spark of madness in Alex's eyes as his fists connect with the counter. "Got a problem with that?"

Sweat runs down Miguel's forehead. Alex isn't just hot. He's tall, brawny, and his sheer presence is intimidating. "No, sir," he croaks, voice trembling.

"We don't have all day," jerk-face grumbles, pointing to the keyboard.

Skimming through the guest list, Miguel's dirty brown aura verifies my assumptions; no Jules Winnfield either. My gaze slides from Alex's fisted hands to his tense shoulders. I have to do something before he beats the poor guy up. Folding a hand over his arm, I look him in the eye. "He wasn't here."

Miguel nods. "She's right, sir. I'm sorry, but—"

Like a crazy person, Alex grabs the guy by the collar of his shirt and pulls him over the counter. "Sorry, my ass. Someone must have seen him. It's not like a man can vanish into thin air." Tension and anger settle over the check-in area like a ragged blanket. The end of the world must be nigh, 'cause I've never seen Alex lose his temper like this.

Seizing hold of his jacket, I yank. "Okay, who the hell are you, and what have you done to Alex?"

"Let. Go," he says, murder on his face.

I hold his gaze. "So you can beat the crap out of the poor guy?" I cock a brow. "Yeah, I don't think so."

Miguel's eyes go wide with fear. "I-I swear, the man you're looking f-for isn't here," he stammers.

"Alex." I take his face in my hands. "You gotta pull it together, man. We'll find him, I promise."

Alex relinquishes his grip on Miguel, and jerks free of my hands. "Don't act as if you care, Amanda."

From the corner of my eye, I see Miguel reaching for the phone. He's going to call security, or worse, the cops.

Spinning around, I flip my gorgeous hair over my shoulder and put on my best fake smile. "I'm sorry. He's got some daddy issues. Thanks for your help, though."

Miguel clenches the phone and nods. "Just get out,

please," he says, his voice impregnated with terror.

I haul Alex's stupid-ass butt outside.

"What the fuck is your problem?" he yells the second the door slams shut behind us.

I burst into laughter. "My problem? What the fuck is your problem, Alex? Do you think acting like Rambo will bring Jesse back?"

"But doing nothing will?" he counters, voice hard as steel.

Crossing my arms, I glare at him. "I told you this was a stupid idea."

A muscle in his jaw pops. "At least I had one." He thrusts his fingers through his hair and kicks the wall. "Fuck, can't you just do a spell or something?"

A spell? Now it's official; Alex has lost his marbles.

I roll my eyes. "You of all people should know spells are fuckin' dangerous." Drawing in a deep breath, I sigh. "But there might be something else I can do."

He casts me a sidelong glance. "Yeah, what's that? Killing a virgin to read her blood?"

I shake my head at his sarcastic comment and extend my hand. "I need pen and paper."

"Writin' a letter to Santa or what?"

One more word and I'll kick him in the nuts. "I'm going to ask the devil to drag you to hell. Pen. Now."

"This better be good," he grumbles, handing me a blunt pencil.

I jot a few things on a ten-dollar bill and frown. "Definitely better than doing jail-time for assaulting a desk clerk," I mouth as I pass him the shopping list.

"A sharp knife, red and black candles, bourbon,

and a Band-Aid?" A WTF look on his face, he waits for an explanation. "What the hell are you up to?"

I rub my temples to ease the pain that's building. "Just get the stuff, dude."

"Whatever," he grumbles, heading to the car.

We hit the next grocery store, and while Alex gets the stuff on the list, I rest my head against the black leather seat and gaze out the window. I could have gone with him, but after the stunt he just pulled with Miguel, I needed a break from jerk-face.

Despite the beautiful weather, and the fact that it's Friday, the streets are strangely deserted. No kids, no couples—just a raven across the street that has been watching me for a while now. I sense its uneasiness and see the fluffed up, shiny black feathers. *What are you trying to say, bird?*

Its head swings to a small white house on the other side of the street.

What in God's name? The Victorian is cloaked by a massive black fog. How did I not see this? Every house has an aura, but this one ain't ordinary. It's one helluva protective shield. During my twenty years as a witch, I have never seen anything quite like it.

I unbuckle my seatbelt and open the car door. The rational side of my brain tells me to stay the hell away, but there's a magnetic pull that lures me across the street.

The raven's eyes drift from the house back to me. The little creature seems as amazed as I am. A shield like that needs a lot of juice. Whoever lives here must be a descendant of freaking Merlin.

My little black friend jerks its head to the right, looks me in the eyes, and croaks.

What is it, buddy?

It hops toward the white fence that encircles the beautiful lawn and stops in front of a mandala drawn on the pavement with orange chalk.

Wait, isn't that a voodoo symbol?

"Can I help you?" A sweet voice startles me.

I look up. An elderly woman wearing a white Boohoo sundress and a fancy hat smiles at me from the porch. Holy Mother of God! I haven't seen such a brilliant purple aura since Grams died.

Walking toward me, she flashes a brilliant smile. "Can I help you, love?"

I know it's rude to stare, but I can't take my eyes off of her. "I…I…was just…" Why the hell am I stammering? "I was admiring your garden, ma'am," I say.

"And your little friend here"—she points at the raven—"is it admiring my garden, too?"

I shrug. "Yeah, apparently, the bird digs gorgeous gardens."

The woman throws thick gray hair over her shoulder and grins. "Would you like to come in? I just made some sweet tea."

Her aura has great appeal, but there's no freaking way I'm going in there. "Thanks, but I'm waiting for a friend."

She points across the street to where Alex leans against the passenger side of the Mustang, watching us from a safe distance. "He's more than welcome to join us. That is, if he leaves his guns in the car."

I think I like this woman, but I still won't cross her threshold. "Don't think that's a good idea."

She draws closer. "Your friend"—she tilts her chin

toward Alex—"won't find what he's looking for unless, he starts to trust."

Damn, she's good.

I smile. "He sorta has issues with that."

Her honey-colored eyes look right into my soul. "He isn't the only one."

I'm so not in the mood for a witchy therapy session. "I should be—"

Bending over the fence, she reaches for my hand and pulls me closer. "Did you see her?"

Bewildered, I glare. "What?"

"The little girl," she whispers. "Have you seen her yet?"

I pull back. "How do you—"

The old woman lets go and steps back. "Follow her, and you will find what you're looking for."

What is it with witches and speaking in riddles? "What's that supposed to mean?" I ask a little harsher than intended.

"You'll see," she assures me before striding back to the porch.

A fraction of a second later, my little black friend spreads its wings, and flies away. I'd do anything to trade places with the bird. Instead, I return to my black cage.

"What was that about?" Alex asks.

Unhinged, I stare at the black shield and shrug. "She's a witch." Thinking of the mandala, I'd say a voodoo priestess to be exact.

"Yeah, I figured. What did she say?" There it is, the hunter gene. I sensed it the moment I looked in his eyes after he "rescued" me from Mister Sinister. Some hunters stumble into this lifestyle. Not Alex and Jesse, though; they were born with the curse of sensing the supernatural in the blink of an eye, which makes it so much harder to believe Alex didn't know what I was.

A warm breeze blows a strand of hair across my face. "Something about following the little girl in my vision to find what we're looking for."

Alex laughs. "And you believe her?"

Do I?

One side of my mouth curls up. "I guess."

He pulls the keys out of his jeans and opens the passenger door for me. "Witches lie, Manda."

I blow out a long, annoyed breath. "Have you never read *Pride and Prejudice*?"

"Pride and what?"

I raise my brows at him. "Are you kiddin'? Jane Austen? Mr. Darcy?"

He shakes his head.

"Keira freakin' Knightley," I say, putting a hand on one hip.

"Ah, that Victorian crap where the chick falls in love with the guy after visiting his multimillion-dollar estate?"

Pushing past him, I climb into the car. "Gosh, you are such a romantic, Alex."

"No, Manda, I'm a realist," he mutters as he starts the engine and maneuvers the car out of the parking slot.

I scrub my hands over my face and focus on what's really important. "Did you get my stuff?"

He nods. "You're not going to stab me with that knife, are you?"

I arch a brow at him. "Not a serial killer, remember?"

A cocky-as-hell grin tugs at his lips. “So you say.”

Unbelievable. The guy is un-freaking-believable.

Chapter 8

I get rid of my uncomfortable shoes and fling myself on the squeaky bed. I'd give an arm and a leg to catch up on some sleep, but that's not on the table. The faster we find Jesse, the sooner I'll get rid of Alex for good, and that's what I want, right?

Opening the grocery bag, I check if Alex got me everything I need. Of course, Captain Responsible never disappoints: candles, knife, bourbon, Band-Aids, and on top of that, a few sandwiches.

I unwrap the sandwich and start filling my empty stomach when my phone rings and Bonnie's name flickers across the screen. Shit, between being abducted and dealing with jerk-face, I must have forgotten to tell my neurotic best friend I couldn't make it to New York. She's going to kick my ass.

Swallowing the last bite, I put her on speaker. "Hey, baby girl."

"Don't you fucking baby girl me. Where the hell are you, Amanda?" Saying she sounds pissed wouldn't do her anger justice.

Crushing the wrapper of the sandwich, I aim for the bin and miss. "Jeez, stop yelling, will you?"

Bonnie snarls like a Chihuahua. "Where are you?"

I pull my tank top over my head and stumble to my suitcase. "Bakersfield," I say matter-of-factly.

"Bakers what?"

A silly grin spreads across my face as I picture her benumbed expression. “Bakersfield,” I repeat.

She clears her throat. “What in God’s name are you doing in fricking Bakersfield? Fuck, Amanda! You’ve got a dorm room waiting for you, not to mention your super-hot, adorable, amazing best friend slash roommate who’s on the brink of a nervous breakdown.”

I shake my head. “Jesus freakin’ Christ, why do you always have to be so melodramatic, B?”

“Melodramatic?” she yells. “I have to share *our* dorm with a goddamn nun, and my so-called best friend didn’t even send me a text to say she’s not going to make it. So excuse me if I’m not in the mood to talk daisies and daffodils.”

I grab an old, oversized T-shirt and put it on. “One day soon you’re gonna have a heart attack.”

Bonnie sighs heavily. “Damn right, and it’ll be your fault.”

“Love you, too, baby girl.”

“Amanda,” she hisses. “Stop fooling around and tell me what the fuck is going on with you. I thought you wanted to start over.”

“I do,” I assure her as I step out of my skinny jeans.

“Then why the hell are you roaming through Bakersfield when you should be here at NYU with me?”

I drop down on the comfy bed and glare at the ceiling. I really don’t want to tell her the truth, but this is Bonnie. The girl knows me better than my own mother. She’d smell my bullshit from miles away.

“Earth to bitch-planet,” she snaps.

I throw my hands over my face, bracing myself for

what's about to happen. "It's Alex," I finally admit.

Silence.

"Bonnie?"

Not a single word.

"Jeez, B. Say something." Anything would be better than the silent treatment.

She draws in a long, pained breath. "Alexander 'I put a bullet through your brain' Remington?" There's the melodrama I was talking about.

"The one and only," I say, clenching my teeth.

"Oh. My. God. Is he hunting you?" Her voice is thick with worry. "I mean, I can come and get you. Bring my brothers if necessary."

Her brothers? I'd give my soul to see how that would play out. Two of the most powerful voodoo priests I know against the toughest witch hunter I ever met. Practically screams bloodbath.

"Calm down, B." I sit up and run a hand over my battered face. "It's not like that. He sorta…" I trail off.

"He what?"

The girl is a real pain sometimes. "He sorta needs my help," I groan.

Not a word.

"For the love of God, would you stop that silence thing you've got going on and fuckin' talk to me? Please?"

"What the hell do you want me to say?" she asks, astounded.

"Anything is better than nothing," I shoot back.

"All right," she barks. "How about, have you lost your goddamn mind? Do I have to remind you what he did?"

A girl doesn't forget when a guy tries to kill her,

but isn't she the one who always preaches that everyone deserves a second chance? "No, but—"

"But? Oh my God. Oh my fucking God. Oh my—"

"Relax." I cut her off before she gives poor God a freaking migraine. "Jesse is missing," I blurt.

"So?" She sounds like a goddamn fury. "Have him file a missing person report."

There's no arguing with her. Smartass always has all the answers. I decide to go with the truth and nothing but the truth. "Alex made me an offer." I wrap the blanket around my naked legs. "If I help him find his brother, he'll never bother me again. Besides, it's really not that big a deal. I'll be in New York ASAP."

"Not that big a deal?" she screams. "Do you even realize how ridiculous that sounds?"

Thank the Lord in heaven I put her on speaker. "Amanda, the guy tried to kill you, and he's—"

I stop her before she crosses a line where there's no turning back. "Don't you dare, Bonnie."

"But—"

"No buts. I know exactly what Alex is, and you should know better than to bring this up." Who sounds like a fury now?

Her short, shallow breaths echo through the speaker. "I'm just worried," she murmurs.

I know she is, but I'm a big girl. No babysitter needed. "I can take care of myself. Been doing it for a long time now."

"If you say so," she says, probably crossing her arms.

Bonnie never could let go of a fight, so changing the topic seems like the best thing to do. "Can you do me a favor?"

"No," she barks, which actually means yes.

"Your mom is still a big name in the voodoo scene, right?"

"Yeah," she says hesitantly. "Why?"

"Can you ask her if she knows a bocor in Bakersfield?"

"What's a bocor got to do with this?"

Another thing I'd rather not tell her, but beggars can't be choosers. Bonnie's mom knows everyone in the voodoo scene, and the way things are I could use all the help I can get. "Jesse wanted to meet one here. Now he's missing. You do the math."

That might have driven her over the edge. "Are you insane?" She sounds terrified. "Bocors are frickin' dangerous. You could get killed, Amanda!"

Drama queen is killing my last nerve. Yeah, she's my best friend. Correction, my only friend, but the girl suffers from ghost sickness. "Just ask her, okay?"

Bonnie is about to object when a loud bang on my door makes me jump. "Manda?" Alex's deep voice thunders through the room. "You awake?"

Exchanging one neurotic for another. Good times. "Listen," I say. "I gotta go. Love ya, baby girl."

She draws in a deep breath to argue, but I disconnect, and moments later, Alex bursts in.

"Jesus, what is wrong with you?" I bark as he strolls toward me like he owns the place. "Can't you wait till I open the door?'

His gaze glides over my bare legs. "Can't you wear decent clothes?"

Last time I checked, I could wear whatever the hell I wanted in my room. But I'm too damn tired to put up much of a fight. Getting on my feet, I grab my trainers and put them on. "Better?"

He nods, but his pink aura says otherwise. For a guy who loves the truth, he lies a lot lately.

I empty the grocery bag.

"New lover?" he asks, dusting the cobwebs off a beat-up old leather chair.

A butterfly knife in my hand, I turn around. "What?"

"On the phone," he says as he relaxes in the chair.

So he's not just a freaking liar, but also a stalker? Awesome.

Running my thumb over the blade of the knife, I sigh. "Not that it's any of your business, but I was talking to my roommate."

He cocks his head to the side. "You're really serious about this NYU shit, huh?"

Freeing the bourbon from its brown condom, I nod. "Yep."

He rests his legs on my bed and leans back. "What's your field of study?" he asks with a crooked smile.

I want to kick his legs off the bed and cut the silly grin out of his face. Instead, I take a deep breath and swallow all my resentment. "Why do you care, Alex?"

Hands up in defense, he arches a brow at me. "Relax. Just trying to have a conversation. You know, like normal human beings."

The way he highlights "human" makes my belly cramp. "Don't," I warn.

Alex rolls his shoulders back. "Hey, you're the one who asked for a truce," he says, as if he didn't just insult me.

I tighten my grip around the butterfly knife.

Payback is a bitch, a lesson he'll learn in a second. "Get up," I order, knife in one hand, silver bowl in the other.

His eyes go wide. "Hell no," he barks. "You're not going to use that knife on me."

I put a hand on my hip and give him a smile that says don't ever mess with the girl holding the freaking knife. "Do you want to find your brother or not?"

That's all the encouragement he needs. In a fraction of a second, Alex stands in front of me, his face only inches from mine. I feel his hot breath against my cheeks. "Now what?" he asks.

I refuse to meet his eyes, but his proximity turns my knees into jelly. "Give me your hand," I mutter, secretly cursing myself for my lack of self-control whenever he's near.

"Are you serious?" he asks; voice harder, eyes like flint.

I ignore the shivers that course down my spine. "Just trust me, okay?"

The only sound in the room is the hum of the fan and his raspy breath. "I once did," he eventually says. "Didn't end well for me."

Words stick in my throat, I freeze. What does he expect me to say? Sorry I didn't tell you I was a witch? Sorry I accepted that fucking ride when every fiber in my body told me to run? Sorry we met? None of that will change a damn thing. Pulling myself together, I gather enough courage to look him in the eye. "You came to me for help, Alex."

He runs his fingers over his stubble and extends his right hand. "Yeah, I guess I did." He shoots me a warning glance. "Just don't kill me, all right?"

Tracing the heart line on his palm with the blade,

my pulse quickens. I have to get this right. If I cut into the wrong line, I'll blow the best shot we have.

"What are you looking for?" he asks, brows knit.

"This," I say as I slice through the branch of Alex and Jesse's relationship. He jerks, but I hold him in place. "Damn it, Manda. That hurt."

I roll my eyes. "Don't be such a baby." Squeezing his flesh, I catch the crimson red drops with the silver bowl.

"You're not going to put a hex on me, are you?" His voice drops dangerously low.

My cheeks burn. "If putting a hex on you was that easy, I would have done it a long time ago." Once I have enough blood, I grab a towel from the bed and press it on the cut. "Hold that."

I was talking about the towel, not my gaze.

"Alex," I say. "Press the goddamn towel on the cut."

"Yeah, sorry," he murmurs.

His fingers brush over my hand, sending jolts of electricity through me. Being that close is dangerous, and judging from the look in his beautiful eyes, he feels the same way. *Focus, Amanda!*

On what, his prefect jawline? No, problem.

No. The wound.

Right, he's still bleeding. Breaking eye contact, I stick the Band-Aid on his palm. "Done."

"Now what?" he asks, never taking his eyes off me.

I'll rip your clothes off and talk dirty to you. Shit, I think it's time I cut back on *Fifty Shades of Grey*. Gathering my fucked-up chi, I point to the bourbon bottle on the bed. "Now we drink."

Alex squints. "And how will getting wasted help us

find my brother?"

Shouldn't witch hunters have some sort of magical background knowledge? Ah right, I almost forgot. The bitches slay first and ask questions later.

"Alcohol expands the consciousness and triggers the release of dopamine, a learning transmitter," I explain.

He sighs. "English, Amanda."

I throw the knife on the bed. "I'm going on a vision quest, and the bourbon is going to drown out my superego."

He peers at me. "Superego? Who the hell are you?"

His stupid comments are seriously starting to piss me off. Crossing my arms, I shake my head. "What? Just because I'm blonde, I can't be smart?"

He waves the comment off. "That's not what I meant."

"Then what did you mean?"

"I don't know." He scrubs his fingers through his hair. "I mean you're a witch, but you kinda sound like a scary mixture of Albert Einstein and Victor freaking Frankenstein." His voice is rough and deep, almost sexy.

A bitter smile tugs at my lips. "I see. So you didn't assume I was brainless because I'm blonde, but because I'm a witch, is that it?"

"Jesus, Amanda. Stop twisting my words. All I want to say is you make witchcraft sound like a goddamn science."

I take that as a compliment. "It sorta is," I say, grabbing the bourbon bottle. "Witches are like modern Galileo. Feared by ignorant hunters like you for our knowledge and wisdom."

Alex closes the gap between us. “Hunters fear witches, because they’re dangerous, backstabbing, manipulative, evil creatures.”

Why do I even bother? It doesn’t matter what I say. Doesn’t matter what I do. For Alex, I’ll always be the enemy. I unscrew the top on the bourbon and take a large sip to drown my anger. Who cares what he thinks of me? He’s just an ignorant moron.

Chapter 9

A lot of bourbon and a massive argument later, Alex left to get more booze. Good choice, considering I'd been a millisecond away from killing him. It's one thing to accuse me of cold-blooded murder, but claiming I'm an alcoholic made me go all crossbones on him. It's a freaking shame the fork only hit his leg, 'cause I was totally aiming for his goddamn head.

Enjoying my alone time, I connect my iPod to the speakers and turn up the volume to the max. The lyrics of the first song on my fuck-the-world playlist speak to my soul. Screw Alex. He only sees black and white, which is why he doesn't know shit. The world is full of gray zones like me, and unless he comes to terms with that, he'll never know what it's like to be me.

I dance through several songs, but when a sexy R&B voice asks me to "wiggle" I lose my shit and go crazy. The song sparks a blazing fire in the pit of my stomach, penetrates my non-existent heart, and works my body like rough, breathtaking sex. Twerking like there's no tomorrow, I let go of all the shit that's been bugging me for days. But just when my heartbeat is completely in sync with the rhythm, the music stops.

"What the fuck?" Alex barks.

Spinning around, drunken from the beat, I find him next to the speakers. Awesome, there goes all the fun.

Eyes narrowed, he glares at me in typical jerk-face

fashion. "What the hell are you doing?"

Completely out of breath, I grin. "I was just—"

"Trying to imitate a striper on crack?" he says, arms crossed. "Yeah, I can see that."

The desire to kill him is almost too strong to ignore. I point to the tequila bottle in his left hand. "Just give me the booze, you moron."

Alex tosses the bottle on the bed. "Sure you need more? From where I stand, you look shit-faced enough."

Two options. One: I pretend I didn't hear him. Two: I strangle him.

Going with option one, I stumble to the bed and grab the tequila. Jerk-face could have at least had the decency to get good old Jose, but I guess he figured I wasn't worth more than El Amos. Whatever. I unscrew the wooden cap and down a good bit of the cheap shit. "Want some?" He could definitely use some.

Tension tightens his frame, and he shakes his head. "You're having enough for both of us," he says in a low judgmental tone.

I shrug and take another sip. "Your loss, baby."

His lips move, and I'm sure he's giving one of his famous responsibility speeches, but I turn up the music and drown him out. If I needed someone to bitch about my lifestyle, I'd call my sister.

A few large gulps of tequila, and the sick beat of the music does what good old fella bourbon couldn't do—clouds my brain and makes the world a better place. It feels so damn liberating; I almost forget Alex is still in the room.

Sadly, he reminds me of his presence. "I think you've had enough," he says, fingers wrapped around my wrist.

Yanking my arm out of his grip, I stumble backward, almost knocking down the TV. "Not…enough to…to find your brother." My tongue and brain are officially living on two different planets.

Alex rolls his eyes and reaches for the tequila in my hand. "You're going to poison yourself, Amanda, and just for the record, I won't take you to the ER." The guy sounds like my mother, and that's anything but a compliment.

I'm not sure if it's the scathing look on his face, or the alcohol fucking with my brain, but all of a sudden I want to hurt him. Not physically. That wouldn't be painful enough. I'm talking real pain. The kind that shapes nightmares. I press a hand against my hip. "You would totally take me to the ER." A sour taste in my mouth, I take a step back. "And you know why?"

Alex draws up to his full height and with one swift move, closes the gap between us. "Enlighten me," he says calmly.

I slide my hand over his sharply defined chest. "Because you need me to save your little brother." I throw my head back and laugh. "Isn't that ironic? You screwed up, and now you need the help of the witch you hate so much to fix your failure. God, it has got to suck to be you."

An angry red aura swirls around him. "Give me that bottle, Manda." Lunging, he jerks the tequila out of my hand and places it on the table next to him.

I should probably shut up, but the need to provoke him and freaking El Amos cloud my senses. "What, can't handle the truth, honey?"

He pins me against the wall, a spark of madness

flickering across his eyes. "Tell me," he says as his hands land on the wall above each of my shoulders. "What is it with you and your bad-girl attitude? Daddy issues? Did he hate your guts, or did he not buy you that puppy you always wanted?" A wicked smile tugs at his lips; he manages to lean in even farther. "I bet your psychopathic behavior is more of a mommy issue, am I right? What did she do? Cancel the ballet classes or take away your credit cards?"

Son of a bitch! The heat of the tequila is nothing compared to the firestorm raging inside me. The bastard has no clue about me or my family. Besides, we can't all grow up with Sunday picnics and bedtime stories.

He puts two fingers under my chin. "Amanda Bishop, speechless? What's the matter, honey? Can't handle the truth?"

He's just trying to get to me, trying to prove his point, but I'll be damned if I give him that much power over me.

Swallowing the lump in my throat, I lean so close, my lips almost brush his. "It must be hard to accept for a hero like you, but some of us are simply born evil. And as far as I remember, you enjoyed my evil."

"That's right," he whispers. "Enjoyed. Past tense." Letting go of my hand, he steps back. "Let's be honest for a second. Take off the bitchy armor and the cocky attitude, and tell me what's left, Manda."

I trace his jaw with my index finger. "Firm boobs, nice ass, and an IQ higher than your Mustang's mileage."

The stupid look on his face is priceless. What did he expect? That I'd break down and cry? Sorry, I don't blink that easily.

Alex shakes his head. "You are so above yourself, even Lucifer would envy your pride." He points to the tequila. "Go ahead. The faster we get this over with, the better."

For once, we're on the same page.

When the tequila unleashes its vicious effects, my limbs are rigid and heavy as hell. I feel like I'm riding a fucking wave swinger, and the damn mattress engulfs me like quicksand. It's time for the ritual.

Pushing myself up from the bed, I gather my supplies and go to work. Dipping the knife into Alex's dried blood, I fight the dizziness blurring my peripheral vision.

Pull it together, girl.

I carve Jesse's name into the candle. I hate blood magic; it must have been invented long before AIDS killed thirty-five million people.

Alex watches me from a distance. "How are my blood and a candle going to help us?" he asks, breaking the silence.

"Look who's talking," I mock him.

He fists his hands around his wild hair and cocks a brow. "Can't you just answer the goddamn question, Manda?"

I could, but where would be the fun in that?

"Your blood is my connection to your brother, and the flame of the candle my anchor during the vision quest," I explain as I finish the last letter.

"Makes total sense," he murmurs.

I wave him over. "I need you to hold that candle for me. Can you do that?"

"Whatever you say."

The mattress sinks under Alex's weight, and when

I lift my lashes, I see the golden spots in his irises. Once upon a time, in another life, I drowned in those eyes. Now they only remind me that nothing lasts forever.

I pass him the candle, take one last sip of the tequila, and shudder. I'm so going to puke my guts out after this. "Okay," I say, wiping the booze off my lips. "Let's do this."

"Ready?" he asks, and when I nod, he reaches for the Zippo in his jacket and lights the candle.

Stabilizing my breath, I focus on the flame of the candle. Red, orange, yellow, blue, green, and black. The colors cloak the wick like a warm winter coat. The layers represent the colors of the aura, and to find Jesse I have to ride the red wave, pure passion and unconditional love.

Inhale.

Exhale.

After each breath, my body grows heavier and my mind more distant.

Jesse. I want to see Jesse.

But when I close my eyes, it's not Jesse I see.

****

Alex couldn't lie to her. Anna was a good girl. She deserved the truth, but how on earth could he explain he hunted witches and monsters for a living? The job didn't exactly come with a "how to explain your creepy-as-hell-life to women" handbook.

Sure, he could show her his FBI badge and claim he was a federal agent. But that was only half the truth, because even if Carter hadn't recruited him and Jesse for the PAU, he'd be out there hunting. It was his calling, his destiny, and he had long given up fighting it. Besides, knowing he'd killed a few evil bitches made him sleep better at night.

"Alex?" Anna snuggled against him, her eyes searching his. "Do you love me?"

The question caught him off-guard and left his mouth dry.

"Alex?" Her voice grew weaker.

He kept his eyes on the ceiling. The girl was a keeper, but love was for children and he'd grown up to be a man. "You mean a lot to me," he said after some time.

Anna wrapped the silk sheets around her petite body and sat up. "What's her name?"

The sadness in her eyes weighed heavy on him, but he was genuinely confused by her question. He hadn't slept with another girl since they had met three weeks ago. "What do you mean?"

She faced him with an artless smile. "The girl that broke your heart. The one you still love."

He opened his mouth, determined to assure Anna he wasn't in love with her anymore. He wanted to tell her how she had deceived him, played him, and at the tip of his tongue was the word "ruined."

Then it hit him like a lightning bolt. He had instantly thought of Amanda. The mesmerizing smile, the breathtaking emerald eyes, the faint scar on her hairline, the wavy blonde thatch. The witch had possessed his mind, and there was nothing he could do about it.

Anna's gaze dropped to her fingers; she dug into the blanket as if trying to hold onto her dignity. "She's lucky, you know?"

He cupped her cheeks and forced her to look at him. "It's not like that. I don't—"

She rested a fingertip on his lips. "Don't, Alex. Don't ruin what we had by lying to me."

He wasn't going to lie to her. He was nothing like the treacherous witch who had played him. Brushing a strand of hair out of her face, he looked into her eyes. "She's still under my skin, Anna, but I could never love a girl like her."

Anna touched his face, kissed his full lips, and smiled her purest smile. "We can only hate what we once loved. Only be hurt by those we care about, Alex."

****

Jerking my eyes open, I see Alex's terrified expression.

"What the hell just happened? You were shaking like crazy."

Unless Jesse had transformed into a hot brunette, I was at the wrong place, at the wrong time. Story of my life.

"Manda?" Alex's voice is gentle. "Are you all right?"

"I'm fan-fuckin'-tastic, Alex." Why wouldn't I be? It's not like I thought he wouldn't move on. Hell, I'm glad he did, and from what I saw, Anna seemed nice enough. Too nice for me, but tastes differ.

Wearing a worried expression, he folds a hand over my shoulder. "Seriously, you look like crap. Is it Jesse? Did you see him?"

His touch electrocutes my heart, and I instinctively brush his hand off. "No, I saw something else."

Alex draws back, his face pale, almost petrified. "What did you see?" The fear in his voice is enhanced by the gray of his aura. Jerk-face looks a lot like the criminals on TV caught red-handed. I'm talking *SVU* and *Major Crimes* here. "Amanda," he snaps. "What did you see?"

I study him for a moment, trying to understand what has him on edge, but I lose focus when his eyes lock with mine. "Anna," I say, averting my gaze. "I saw Anna."

Heaving a sigh of relief, his face lightens. "You saw Anna and nothing else?" He sounds excited, almost thrilled.

I don't know why seeing him and Anna after hot sex makes him so happy, and frankly, I don't really feel like asking. I point to the candle. "Hold it up, Alex."

Without resistance, he obeys, and I concentrate on the flame.

Jesse, where are you, man?

The flame burns brighter than before, its colors more sharply defined.

C'mon Jesse, help me out. Show me where you are.

Closing my eyes, I focus on my heartbeat. It's slow, but steady. Strong, but broken. Then a voice like rustling leaves calls my name. "Amanda."

"Who are you?" I whisper into the darkness.

The girl with the raven hair materializes in front of me. Her pale skin has a translucent glow, her lips are the color of blueberries, and her white dress is soaking wet.

"Follow her, and you'll find what you're looking for." The old woman's voice thunders in my ears as the little girl extends her hand.

Oh boy, I'm going to regret this. But I take her cold, tiny hand regardless.

****

Drops of water fell to the ground, echoing through

an utter darkness.

Drop.

Drop.

Drop.

As if the water counted the time for Jesse—seconds, minutes, maybe even hours had passed, but he couldn't say for sure. The fierce pain in his right temple had obscured his perception.

He knew he had to open his eyes, but no matter how hard he tried, his eyelids refused to move. What had he been thinking when he walked into this mess? Maybe he should have listened to Alex, but this wasn't just about them anymore. It was about the kids. They were his responsibility now, and he had to save them.

Warm liquid ran down his forehead into his eyes. The iron smell was unmistakable. He was bleeding. Damn, how the hell was he supposed to save those kids if he couldn't move?

"He's a hunter. We need to get rid of him."

Fear clutched Jesse's guts when he realized he wasn't alone. They, the bastards who had done this to those poor kids, were with him. In his state, he could never take them both down. Who was he trying to kid? He couldn't even take on one.

"I have a better idea." The French accent of the second man was so thick Jesse could barely understand him.

"Hey, what are you doing?" the other one asked.

Laughter echoed off the walls as Jesse was hit by thick powder thrown in his face. Inhaling the weird stuff, he almost coughed his lungs out. He wrestled for air, but soon felt dizzy. The powder wasn't just messing with his lungs. It crawled into his brain.

****

Barely able to breathe, I yank my eyes open. What I'd seen squeezes my guts so hard, I feel sick.

"What's the matter?" Alex asks.

I want to answer, but the muscles in my jaw won't move.

My expression must be horrifying, because Alex blows out the candle and takes my face in both hands. "Amanda?" He's genuinely concerned. I can see it in his eyes, his face, and his aura. "Manda, talk to me. What did you see?"

I coax my lips open, but the bitter tequila crawls up my gullet into my mouth.

"Shit, Manda! Say something."

Shoving him away, I run to the bathroom. Barely making it to the toilet, I vomit until my knees shake.

Chapter 10

I've gulped down a gallon of water, had the greasiest breakfast ever, taken two cold showers, and swallowed a whole pack of aspirin, yet I reek of tequila, and my brain has the consistency of pudding. The last time I felt this fucking miserable, I had partied with a hot Russian exchange student who taught me the words, "no more" and "vodka," are never used in the same sentence.

"I really don't think that this is a good idea," Alex mutters, twisting the Mustang around another sharp corner.

Poor guy looks as bad as I feel. Sometime between puking my guts out and lying half unconscious on the bathroom floor, I had managed to tell him what I saw. Goes without saying he didn't take the news well. For the longest time, he just sat there, unresponsive and desperate. I knew he needed something to hold onto, and that's when I came up with the idea to pay the old woman a visit. She was, after all, the one who told me to follow the girl with the raven hair.

"If anyone knows what's going on in this godforsaken town, it's her," I say, hoping my gut feeling won't disappoint.

"But—"

"She knew about the girl," I say, resting my head against the car seat. "There's a good chance she knows more."

Alex's hands are clenched around the steering wheel as if it is the only thing keeping him from falling apart. "I hope you're right," he groans, his aura a manifestation of fear and self-loathing.

Me too.

Buildings and street signs stream by in a blur. The cruel sunlight burns my eyes, forcing me to pull my sunglasses down. Between Freddy Krueger's claws scratching my skull, and ants celebrating a triumphal procession in my head, I feel like my mind is either going to shatter or melt. I must have said it a million times, but from now on, I'm going to steer clear of booze.

"What makes you think she's going to help us?" Alex asks as we pull up to the small Victorian house. "For all we know, she could be in on this."

She could be in on whatever the hell *this* is. But something tells me she's not, and if life has taught me one lesson, it's that I can always rely on my instincts. "Just trust me on this one, all right?"

He shifts the car into reverse, and backs into an open slot on the street. "Trust you, huh? I hear that a lot from you, lately."

I shift my head to the side. "We have no idea what we're up against," I say. "But if we want to get through this, we have to be able to rely on each other."

Killing the engine, he faces me. "Amanda?"

"Hm?"

Alex's gaze shifts from me to the pentagram hanging around the rearview mirror. "I'm sorry."

Great. Now my hearing is fucked up, too. "Come again?"

Hands still on the steering wheel, he clears his throat. “I said I was sorry.”

So my hearing is fine, but Alex is obviously losing his freaking mind. Why else would he apologize to me for—wait a minute, what the hell is he apologizing for?

“Sorry for what?” I ask.

Throwing his head back, he lets out a sharp breath. “For acting like a jerk when you were just trying to help.”

He really just said that, didn’t he? If he isn’t losing his mind, he’s definitely suicidal. “Look, if this is one of those sharing and caring moments, then—”

“It’s not,” he assures me. “But I’m man enough to admit when I make a mistake.”

I push my sunglasses up and sigh. “It’s okay. You made up for it when you held my hair back while I had a date with the toilet.”

“So we’re good?”

Our eyes lock. “Yeah, Alex. We’re good.”

I reach for the door handle, but he stops me. “There’s one more thing,” he mutters under his breath.

Looking over my shoulder, I roll my eyes. If he wants to hug it out, he’s got the wrong girl. “What, you need a written statement that I accept your apology?”

Alex frowns. “I need you to know I crossed a line when I called you an alcoholic.” He averts his gaze. “I know all about your dad, and it won’t happen again. I give you my word.”

I spin around, jaw dropping. “Wait, how do you know—”

“Jesse told me,” he says matter-of-factly.

Bastard! Is that the reward I get for trusting him? Maybe I should let him rot in whatever hell he’s in.

I ignore the seizures in my stomach and straighten. "My dad did the best he could for me, Alex. I don't blame him or my freakin' mother for who I am."

"Our parents shape us, Amanda."

A bitter taste crawls up my throat. "Maybe so. But we make the final cut, and this"—I point to myself—"is the life I chose." Then I yank the door open and get out.

Taking a deep breath, I fill my lungs with fresh air. It's a beautiful day. Birds chirp, a warm breeze blows through the lively street, and the faithful sun warms my dried out skin. Nevertheless, I can't shake the eerie feeling this is the quiet before the storm. Maybe Alex was right, and coming here wasn't such a great idea after all.

Alex jogs toward me. "Ready?"

"No guns," I remind him.

He pulls his shirt up, exposing his six pack. "Happy?"

Damn, he's in even better shape than he was.

"Wanna frisk me?" he asks, his voice smoky.

I so should. I mean, what if he's hiding a knife in his boxers?

Annoyed with my libido, I look away from his V-line. "Let's just go."

As we stroll down the street, I spot the old lady in her garden, watering her plants. "Be nice," I warn Alex when we approach the fence.

"Why, because she's one of your witch friends?"

"Technically, she's not a witch but a *mambo*." I flip my hair over my shoulder and smile. "And let's not forget she's the key to gettin' rid of you for good."

Alex sighs. "Very charming, Manda."

I shrug. "Charmin' is my middle name."

He bites on his lower lip. “I thought stab-worthy bitch was,” he says, a smile touching his eyes.

This is going to sound weird, but I sorta prefer the bitching to the caring and sharing. Probably makes me a masochist, but who cares?

Approaching the fence, I clear my throat to call to her, but she’s already walking toward us. “I’ve been expecting you,” she announces with that sing-song voice of hers.

“I hate witches,” Alex grumbles next to me.

I ignore him and focus on the old lady. Her pink dress dances around her legs, and her skin shimmers silky coral in the morning sun. It’s weird. Everything about her reminds me of Grams: her confident posture, graceful walk, but above all the mesmerizing purple aura wrapped around her like a satiny bed sheet.

An everlasting smile on her lips, she draws closer. “Would you like that sweet tea now?” she asks, leaning against the white picket fence.

“If you’re still offering,” I reply.

“I sure am,” she says. “Come on in.”

I pass through the gate, but when Alex tries to follow, the woman blocks his path. “I know what you are, son, and you’re more than welcome to join us, but only if you put that knife in your back pocket in that fancy car of yours,” she says calmly.

“Seriously, Alex?” I snap, pissed he lied to my face. Guess I should have frisked him after all.

His lips form a straight line. “Just a little precaution,” he insists, shrugging.

The old woman puts her hands on her hips. “I see where you’re coming from, son. But I assure you, no harm will come to you in my house.”

Watching David and Goliath show off in front of me, I can't help but laugh. The lady is at least fifty years older and ten inches shorter than Alex, yet she stands there fearless.

Although it's entertaining, I have to move this along or we'll be here till next Christmas. "Alex," I mutter annoyed.

Murder on his face, he meets my gaze. "What?"

"We don't have time for this shit."

A million thoughts must bolt through his head, because his aura changes color like a goddamn mood ring. Eventually, though, his shoulders sink. "All right, but I'll blame you if we get killed."

What doesn't jerk-face blame me for? "I'll take that risk," I say, lifting my chin at the car.

As he's heading back to the Mustang, I give the old lady my best smile. "I'm sorry. Trust issues, remember?" I don't normally apologize, but Alex is acting like a complete moron, and the fact the woman resembles my grams messes with my fucking head.

"Don't worry, love. He's a good guy, you know?"

Too good, that's the problem. "A little difficult to handle at times," I groan.

Patting my back, she smiles. "That's one thing you guys have in common."

I don't like the way she emphasizes "one thing," and I'm about to ask her why she's defending the guy who just violated her house rules, but Alex returns before I can. "Better?" he taunts her with a mischievous grin.

"Much," she says, pointing to the beautifully decorated porch. "I'll get some tea. Do make yourselves comfortable."

The instant we step on the porch, the wind chime above the door starts swinging. The randomly created melody reminds me of a soothing lullaby.

Alex, ever the hunter, scans the place as if it's a war zone, apparently, expecting to see a sniper hiding behind the snappy lawn gnomes.

I fling myself into a flower-power chair. "Relax, Alex."

Hands up in defense, he takes a seat in the white rocking chair next to me. "Better safe than sorry."

"You know what they call guys like you?"

"Hot? Irresistible? Mind-blowing?"

"Paranoid," I snarl.

Alex leans back and shakes his head. "You might want to work on those cocky retorts. They ain't what they used to be."

Before I get a chance to prove him wrong, the old woman returns with sweet tea, cookies, and donuts. Putting the tray down, she pours three glasses. "I hope you like it. I made it this morning," she says, handing Alex the first glass.

The look on his face is rib-tickling. You don't have to be a witch to know he wonders if the tea is spiked with poison. I know the woman sees it too, but instead of scolding him, she passes me a glass, and then takes a large sip. When she doesn't drop dead, Alex relaxes and downs half the glass at once.

Our host offers me a cookie. "Have one, love."

I shake my head. "I really appreciate your kindness, ma'am, and I hate to be the white rabbit here, but we really don't have time for a cozy tea party."

"Real smooth, Manda," Alex growls.

Whoa! He's acted like an asshole from the moment

we walked onto her property, and when I cut to the chase, he's bitching at me? What is it with him and his fucking mood swings?

I part my lips to snap at him, but the woman nips the argument in the bud. "It's all right, son." She puts the plate down and takes a seat across from me. "I know why you're here, and I will answer all your questions. But first I'd like to know your names if you don't mind."

Fair enough. "I'm Amanda Bishop, and this," I point to the jerk next to me, "is Alex Remington."

"Pleasure to meet you. I'm Hedwig."

Alex almost chokes on a cookie. "Like Potter's owl?"

She flashes him a brilliant smile. "Exactly."

My eyes go wide. "Wow, Alex. I never figured you for a Potterhead."

He shrugs. "Guess you don't know me as well as you thought."

I laugh. "Are you kiddin'? I can read you like an open book, and I mean that quite literally."

Hedwig's gaze drifts from Alex to me. "Yet, you haven't seen all the pages, love." A glimmer of gold surrounds her purple aura. "In fact, you skipped the most important ones."

What's that supposed to mean? Seriously, witches and their freaking riddles—they drive me nuts.

Alex's fingers dig into the hand rest, and he shifts uncomfortably. "If you guys are done with your witch crap, I'd like to go back to the real problem." He pulls Jesse's photo out of his jacket and holds it under Hedwig's nose. "Have you seen my brother?"

She ogles the pic. "I'm afraid I haven't." Soft blue

engulfs her. She's telling the truth.

Alex's jaw hardens. "I knew this would be a waste of time," he snarls, shooting daggers at me.

Not ready to give up yet, I face her. "You said we would find what we're looking for if I followed the girl, right?"

Nibbling on her cookie, she nods.

"Well, I was on a vision quest last night, and the girl took me to some kind of dungeon where," I point to Alex, "his brother lay bleeding and unconscious on the floor while a douchebag with a French accent threw some kind of green powder in his face."

The moment I mention green powder, Hedwig pales. "What else did you see?" she asks, voice shaky.

"Nothing," I confess. "Everything went fuzzy after that." I put the tea on the table. "Look, ma'am, I've seen the shield around your house, and I know enough of voodoo to figure you're one helluva mambo. So please help us."

Hedwig rises from her chair and leans against the wooden railing, facing the garden. "Most of us live in peace with the world. We don't harm anyone. But the ones born dark do horrific things."

Alex gets to his feet and stalks toward her. "What's that supposed to mean?"

Hedwig closes her eyes and draws in a deep breath. "Your brother was turned into what we call a *zonbi*."

Hell, I feared she was going to say that.

"A what?" Alex shouts like a lunatic.

My pulse jackhammers against my neck. "Zonbi is the creole word for zombie," I stammer, still hoping this is just a bad dream.

Silence.

Then Alex bursts out laughing. "This is a joke, right?" He walks toward me. "Amanda, tell me this is some weird witch joke," he says, pleading with me.

My gaze drops. I wish I could, but there's a reason why even my kind doesn't deal with bocors.

Alex kneels in front of me and puts his hands on my shoulders. "Amanda." His voice drops dangerously low. "Tell me she's kidding."

Looking up, I face the terror in his eyes. "I'm sorry, Alex. I can't."

Shaking his head like a maniac, he jumps up. "So what you're saying is my little brother has transformed into *Resident Evil*. Is that it?"

"No, son. Your brother does not consume human brains, nor is he undead."

"Oh, yeah, then what does he do? Star in an episode of *The Walking Dead*?" Alex hides behind his sarcasm, but his muddy blue aura tells a much darker and far more depressing story.

Hedwig shifts from one foot to the other. "The green powder is a drug. It gives the bocor control over your brother's mind."

When reality hits, Alex stumbles back to the rocking chair. "Can it be undone?"

Hedwig's eyes shoot to me. "I don't know. I don't practice with both hands."

Alex stares at me. "English please."

"She doesn't do black magic," I translate.

"But," Hedwig continues. "Every poison has a cure, and if someone can find it," she looks me in the eye, "it'll be you, love."

No pressure there. Winding a strand of hair around my finger, I frown. "Even if we find a cure, we still have no idea where he is."

A nervous brown aura spirals around her, and she starts fiddling with her dress. "If you find the kids, you will find his brother." The woman might be powerful, but all the witch-juice in the world can't conceal she's hiding something.

I'm about to ask her what that is, but Alex interrupts me. "And how do you suggest we do that? Find the kids, I mean."

"We could talk to the ones that came back. You do, after all, work for the FBI," I remind him.

"And risk exposing the PAU and hunters all over the States?" he barks. "Great idea, genius. You know there's a reason we don't work high-profile media cases."

Hedwig's eyes grow distant. "There might be another way," she says, catching our full attention. "One child was in particularly bad shape. Her parents had her committed to a mental asylum in Los Angeles."

"LA?" Alex and I say in unison.

She nods. "If I remember correctly, the news said something about the Freud Hospital."

Now that Alex has a lead, hope urges him to action. "All right." He jumps to his feet. "Let's go."

My eyes go wide. "To LA?"

"No," he snaps. "To New York."

Tired of his stupid comments, I frown. "Can I use your bathroom first, ma'am?"

Hedwig points to the door. "Sure, love. First door on the right."

"Thanks," I say as I head inside.

Walking out of the bathroom, I admire the interior of the house. It's just as cozy as the porch—flowery sofas, white drawers, wooden floor, and oh my God, are these wind chimes? On every freaking window? This is weird. Mambos practice their gifts by inviting spirits into their homes, lives, and bodies. Wind chimes do the exact opposite. They keep them out, the good ones and the bad ones.

Voodoo mandalas are drawn on the floor by the windows. The ones I recognize are warding off evil, and the others I have never seen before. Talk about paranoia.

Rubbing my wet hands on my jeans, I head back.

“You have to tell her, son,” I hear Hedwig whisper and stop dead in my tracks. I take a peek and find her sitting next to Alex.

Alex looks even more miserable than five minutes ago. “I can’t.”

“Tell me what?” I ask casually as I join them.

Eyes wide, Alex gets on his feet. “That I appreciate your help.” He looks at Hedwig. “There I said it. Happy?”

Judging by the way Hedwig dodges my gaze, I’d say that’s a whole lot of bull. Damn, where’s Edward Cullen when a girl needs him?

“We better get going.” Alex grabs my arm and hauls me down the steps, not even giving me a chance to say goodbye.

Chapter 11

Here I am in the city of angels and superstars, and all I can think of is Hellraiser's freaking puzzle box. That's pretty much what the Freud Hospital looks like. Located near LAX, the massive glass cube rises high into the azure sky, its façade reflecting a large degree of sadness and pain. Usually, I avoid places like this at any cost. Too many uncontrolled emotions always mess me up, one of the few downsides of being a witch. Some of us, including me, soak in other people's emotions like a human vacuum, and that can be irritating to say the least. But since this is our best shot at finding Jesse, I'll just have to grit my teeth.

"Are you sure they'll let us talk to the kid?" I ask as we cross the parking lot.

Fiddling with his black tie, Alex blows out a frustrated breath. "Carter, my supervisor at Quantico, notified them. They're expecting us." It's amazing. Jerk-face learned how to shoot a gun when he was nine, but knotting a tie is an unsolvable mystery to him.

I better put him out of his misery, or we'll never make it inside. Grabbing his arm, I pull him back. "Let me help you."

"Don't tell me you've attended a perfect housewitch seminar," he jokes, watching me work on an immaculate Windsor knot.

"My dad taught me how to do it," I confess.

Securing the tie under the collar of his white shirt, I fold the satin fabric down and smile. "There you go."

He catches me staring. "What?"

I avert my gaze. "Nothing. It's just you clean up nicely for a guy who sleeps in ripped jeans."

He points to my outfit. "Right back at ya."

After we left Hedwig, we'd taken a little detour to the motel to change into something that looked more federal agent and less juvenile delinquent. Alex has on his suit and tie, while I rock a pair of black skinny jeans, high-heels, and a blazer I bought for Gram's funeral and never intended to wear again. I raise a brow at him. "I look like a goddamn teacher, Alex."

"A hot teacher," he corrects me, a cocky grin on his lips.

Wow, was that a compliment? "Are you sick?"

Alex makes a face. "All I'm saying is that less stripper and more teacher suits you."

Yep, that sounds more like him. "You know," I say, one hand pressed against my hip. "You're pretty much the only guy I know who can compliment and insult a girl at the same time."

He bats his thick black lashes. "What can I say? I'm multitasking." The guy is so full of himself, he gives arrogance a new definition.

"You're a multitasking jerk," I say as we stroll toward the building.

Shaking my hips, I head straight to the reception desk, where a lanky guy in his early twenties plays *Call of Duty* on an iMac.

The moment he spots me, his eyes go wide. "H-hello," he stammers like a third-grader who has just come eye to eye with his senior crush. "How can I help you?" There's something in his hollow gaze that gives me the creeps.

You could stop staring for starters.

Alex slams his badge on the counter. "Special Agent Remington, and," he looks at me, uncertain how to introduce me, "Special Agent Bishop. We're here to see Isobelle Watson."

I grin. Special Agent? I kinda like the sound of that.

Creeper Dude frowns. "FBI, huh?"

His aura a confident orange, Alex straightens. "Yes, and we don't have all day, pal."

Creeper Dude grabs a universal keycard from his desk and points to the elevator. "Well, follow me, Special Agents." His voice is loaded with envy.

What happens next is the most awkward elevator ride of my life. Obsessed with my two ladies, Creeper Dude gives Peeping Tom a run for his money. Alex, always the protector, does his best to shield me from his weird glares, but the dude is still drooling all over me. I breathe a sigh of relief when we reach the second floor, and the doors finally slide open.

"It's the first room on the right," Creeper Dude, whom I believe to be the next Ted Bundy, explains as he unlocks a massive glass door. "Guess I should warn you though. The chick is a real nutcase."

"Thanks for the warning, but we'll take it from here," Alex says sharply.

Despite the guy's lack of intelligence, he keeps quiet and heads back to the only place where someone like him can make friends. Hell? No, the internet. Different word, same meaning.

When I'd heard the word asylum, I imagined a lot

of things. Albert Einstein wannabes with crazy hair, tell-tale-heart killers looking for evil eyes, and yellow-wallpaper chicks with diaries. But nothing prepared me for the horror inside room 213.

Straitjacket. Shackles. Drugs. And in the midst of it all, a little girl who whispers, "Mary had a little lamb, little lamb" on repeat.

"Jesus," Alex mutters under his breath. "That is—"

"Fucked up?" I offer, never taking my eyes off the kid.

Walking toward the ghostly girl, he nods. "Yeah, that sums it up."

Isobelle's long brown hair is scattered across a white pillow, and her otherworldly blue eyes are fixed on the ceiling. Like a woodland flute, her voice echoes in the sterile room, singing that same damn song over and over.

I swallow the initial shock and brush a strand of hair out of her face. "Sweetheart, can you hear me?"

Her cracked lips move. "*Je viens pour toi. Tais-toi! Tais-toi!*"

"What is she saying?" Alex asks.

Is he for real? The only sentence I know in French is *voulez-vous coucher avec moi.* "Do I look like Google translate?"

A flicker of annoyance crosses his face, and I know he's got something nasty to say, but he quickly shoves it to the back of his mind. "No, but you're the witch. Can't you mutter a translation spell or something?"

Where does the PAU get their witch-knowledge, *Charmed*?

Raising my eyebrows, I glare at him. "Sure, Alex. Let me just snap my fingers and I'll translate."

He narrows his eyes. "Seriously?"

"No." I rest a hand on the kid's forehead. "Isobelle, can you hear me?"

"*Tais-toi*! *Tais-toi*," she yells like a broken record.

"Hey!" Alex snaps his fingers in front of her face. "Look at me."

No reaction. Literally. She doesn't even blink.

Bending over her, jerk-face runs a finger over her cheek. "We need your help, sweetheart. Can you talk to us?"

She stiffens.

"Isobelle?" he tries again, louder.

This time she slowly turns her head and meets Alex's eyes. The air grows dense. In a blink of an eye, she parts her lips, and high-pitched screams escape the depths of her tortured soul.

Jesus, what the hell is she, the New Jersey Devil? I cover my ears, but the screams pierce my brain like a freaking hunting knife. Good job, Alex.

Stumbling backward, jerk-face stares at me helplessly. "Do something," I read from his lips.

"What am I supposed to do?" I shout.

He shrugs helplessly. "Dunno. But you better hurry before the medical staff shows up."

Isobelle tosses and turns like a maniac. But the straitjacket and shackles hold her down. More screams redden her scarred, pale face. I don't know how much longer she can keep this up, but I'm pretty sure the glass building is going to shatter into pieces soon.

I take her face in both hands and force her to look at me. "Shhh… It's all right, sweetheart."

She jerks her head back and forth, desperately trying to fight me off. But I immobilize her head with one hand and put my index finger on her third eye, massaging it gently.

"What are you doing?" Alex asks as Isobelle's screams fade.

"Something my grams used to do when I was a kid," I explain.

Alex comes closer. The moment Isobelle lays eyes on him she stiffens and quivers. "Step back," I order. Applying more pressure to her forehead, I try to get a reading on her, but her emotions are all over the place.

"Isobelle, listen to me." My voice is too deep to mimic Gram's, but I try my best to soothe her. "You gotta take a deep breath. Can you do that?"

Still struggling, she stares at me. "He's coming."

The fear in her voice sends shivers down my spine. "Who's coming?" I ask, drawing circles on her forehead.

A ray of black blazes from her third eye. "The demon," she says in a hushed tone.

When her irises disappear, and I gaze into the whites of her eyes, she looks one helluva lot like the antagonist of *The Ring*, and I always hated that movie.

"Isobelle?"

She doesn't react.

This is getting us nowhere. Time for Plan B, aka a little trip to Consciousland. I close my eyes and picture a ray of golden light breaking through the blackness. Pure energy runs from my fingers into her head, and when darkness is conquered by light I get a glimpse of—

****

The humming of the air conditioner pulsated through Isobelle's room. Pulling her blanket over her mouth, she lay in her bed, staring at a poster of Katniss Everdeen that hung on the wall. She wanted to be as brave as her, but the voice she had heard for days scared her. What if tonight was the night? What if the demon came and got her? Would someone help her? Her mommy and daddy slept in the room next to hers, but would they be here in time?

"Je viens pour tois. I'm coming for you, Isobelle," the voice in her head taunted again.

She kept her eyes on the Hello Kitty lamp and prayed tonight wasn't the night. She begged God to keep her safe, promised him she would be a good girl from then on. No more fighting with her brother. No more secret Vampire Diaries *sessions with her little sister. With each minute that passed, her eyes grew heavier, and the dark twisted fantasies lost their hold over her.*

Until.

She heard it again.

The voice.

But this time it sounded different. More real, closer. "She's pretty," it said.

Fear cramped Isobelle's stomach, and she blinked her eyes open. Two dark figures stood in her room. She tried to call for help, but someone pressed a hand over her mouth.

After dragging her out of bed, one phantom pointed to the window. "We have to hurry."

"Don't worry. They're fast asleep," a much older voice said.

Isobelle's eyes were wide open. Terror flushed her system as her gaze drifted from one shadowy figure to the other. Fight, she told herself. She started kicking, but only hit the air.

"This one's wild," the older man said cheerfully.

"Too wild," the one with the alien accent said as he covered her nose to block the air supply.

****

My heart beats like a fucking runaway train. The girl messes me up in ways I can't even explain. It's almost as if her emotions crush me like a thick, heavy pile of snow, and if I don't break the connection, I'll be buried under a deadly avalanche.

Yanking my eyes open, I pull away.

Isobelle is fast asleep. She must have exhausted herself screaming.

"What did you see?" Alex whispers, careful not to wake her.

I hide my trembling hands. "She was taken from her room." My voice is as shaky as the rest of me, and I feel like a total wimp. Clearing my throat, I try to pull myself together. "Same guys who have Jesse, Alex."

He steps closer. "Are you sure?"

"Positive. Same voices, same disturbing accent."

His eyes shoot up. "Did you see their faces?"

I shake my head and try not to sound like a pathetic little girl, but fail miserably. "It was too dark."

Alex reaches for my face. "Are you all right?"

His fingers have barely brushed my cheek when I pull back. "Peachy," I say, sounding less confident than intended. "If I dig deeper, I might be able to see where they held her," I murmur, fixated on Isobelle's battered body.

Pointing to my trembling hands, he says in a voice thick with worry, "Sure you're up for another round?"

I arch a brow at him. "I'm fine."

He doesn't buy it—I can see it in his eyes—but Alex knows better than to bug me further.

Closing my eyes, I bring my finger back to her third eye, and her energy instantly connects with mine.

****

Water dripped from the ceiling, echoing through an eerie darkness. Isobelle sat in the corner of the dog kennel. Head resting on her knees, she listened to the soft whimpers of the new kids that resonated through the damp air. They would beat the tears out of them, she thought. Her bruised face was proof of it.

Heavy footsteps approached her prison, and her heart skipped a beat. She prayed they took another kid today. It was a terrible wish, but she couldn't do it again. Not today.

The rusty gate of the dog kennel squeaked as the man with the scorpion tattoo on his wrist unlocked it. Isobelle kept her eyes downcast. On her first day, she had made the mistake of looking in Scorpion Man's face. Her punishment had been ten lashes with the whip.

"Get up," he ordered in that strange accent she'd grown to hate.

She didn't move. If he wanted her, he had to come and get her.

Bony fingers reached inside her new home, trying to grab her. "I said get out!"

"N-o." The word came out broken.

Scorpion Man wrapped cold fingers around her ankle. She wanted to fight him off, but she couldn't. She was too tired to resist. He dragged her out of the kennel, tearing her white nightgown in the process. It didn't hurt; pain was no longer something she felt.

Isobelle's heart hammered against her ribcage. "Please," she cried. "I just want to go home."

His cruel laughter floated through the dungeon. "You are home." Grabbing a fistful of her hair, he hauled her past the other kennels.

One of the new kids, a little girl with blonde hair, watched in horror. Isobelle knew the expression on her face; it was the same she'd had when she saw for the first time what they did to the others.

She'll get used to it, Isobelle thought. They all did.

"Sit down," Scorpion Man yelled, pushing her onto the filthy mattress in the center of the dungeon.

Isobelle hated the mattress; it was dirty and reeked of fish. Just like her.

"Switch the camera on," the older man said, stepping out of a dark corner, wearing the same creepy clown mask as always.

Scorpion Man walked to the camcorder pointed at the mattress. "Why rush? We have time."

"Save your breath and do it."

Scorpion Man shrugged and pushed a button. "Whatever you want."

The bright white light of the camera blinded Isobelle. She closed her eyes and hugged her knees.

"It's okay. We're going to have lots of fun," Clown Man said, running a hand through her hair.

"Don't," she begged as the beast pinned her on the mattress, suffocating her under his weight.

He grabbed her chin. "Look at me, Scarlet."

She shook her head and shut her eyes. My name is Isobelle, she thought. It's Isobelle.

"Open your goddamn eyes," he yelled, unbuckling his belt.

But she didn't.

She hummed an old song her mom used to sing to her. "Mary had a little lamb, little lamb." The scent of roses returned. So did the sharp pain.

It went on for hours, weeks, months, or maybe just minutes. It was impossible to say.

****

Tears burn through my closed eyes. I pull my hand away. Shaking like crazy, I gasp for air.

"Manda?" I feel Alex's hand on my shoulder, but instantly jerk away.

"Don't touch me," I warn.

"What's the matter?"

I'm going to kill them. That's what's the matter. I don't care if Alex puts a bullet through my brain or if kiss my new life goodbye. I will kill those bastards.

"Manda, are you…" he pauses. "Crying?"

"Allergies," I croak and make a run for the door.

Chapter 12

What the hell am I doing here? I could have been in New York by now, living a normal life as a fucked-up-always-drunk student. Instead, I'm glaring at mammoth waves crashing on Manhattan Beach's shore, watch wannabe Pamela Andersons play volleyball, and can hardly breathe because I'm being suffocated by what I saw and felt.

Inhaling the salt-impregnated air, I try to forget, but the dog kennels and Isobelle's eyes haunt me. What the fuck is wrong with these guys? Abducting little girls. Raping them on a daily basis. How can someone get off on this shit? And where the hell is God when all of this goes down? If I had his power, I'd bring forward the freaking apocalypse.

I gaze at the azure blue ocean and try to control the hurricane building up inside me, but the lethal storm is raging and out for blood. I'm no saint, but anyone who abuses magic like this deserves to die. My heartbeat thunders in my ears while I picture a million ways to rip those monsters' hearts out—blunt spoons, nasty chainsaws, sharp fingernails—it all sounds painfully tempting.

"Hey." Alex interrupts my twisted thoughts. "Look what I found." Taking a seat next to me, he hands me an iced coffee and holds a box of yummy cupcakes under my nose. "Apparently, these are the best in town.”

“Says who?” I ask, eyes on the sea foam.

Alex loosens his tie and flashes me a lopsided grin. “The lady who sold ’em.”

Arching a brow, I peek at the box. “Lemon?”

“And strawberry,” he adds as if it isn’t awkward he still remembers my favorite flavor. He takes a bite, and his eyes roll back in pleasure. “Damn, they’re awesome. You should have one,” he suggests, shoving the box toward me.

I draw in a deep breath and shake my head. “I’m good, Alex.” I know exactly what he’s trying to do, and while I appreciate his sweetness, I don’t need his pity. I shed a few tears, so? Doesn’t mean I’m one of those pathetic girls who need a guy to cheer them up.

He takes another bite and shrugs. “Your loss, my gain.”

My lips curl into a half-smile. “You don’t even like lemon,” I counter.

Bright pink swirls around him. I can literally see his embarrassment at being caught doing something nice for me. “Whatever,” he snaps. “If you won’t eat ’em, I will.”

“No, you won’t,” I say, grabbing a cupcake.

He studies me with a victorious smile. “Admit it. They’re good.”

“I’ve had better,” I lie, mouth full.

We finish the box off in silence, and although I know sooner rather than later, I will have to tell him what I saw, I’m glad he hasn’t fired any questions at me yet. It reminds me why I was drawn to him in the first place. Alex is, without a doubt, a self-righteous jerk whose world is black and white, but he also belongs to the rare species that gives you space and allows you to come clean on your own terms. For a girl like me, that means everything.

As the sun gently dips into the ocean, I dust the glittering sand off my jeans and face him. “We should head back.”

Drinking in the beautiful sunset, he sips his latte. “We’ll stay the night. Head back tomorrow.”

“What?” My voice trembles. “Why?”

Not taking his eyes off the water, he says, “It’s late and—”

“No.” I hold a hand up to stop him. “You don’t understand, Alex. We need to get back and find these kids and Jesse.”

The second I mention Jesse’s name, his aura darkens and his breath quickens. “Do you know where they’re being held?” he asks, trying to keep his voice even.

What kind of question is that? Would I still be sitting here if I did? “No, but—”

“Do you have a name or a description of the guys who have ’em?”

Thinking of the clown mask gives me the chills. “No, I don’t. But—”

“Then there’s nothing we can do today,” he says matter-of-factly.

My jaw drops. How the hell can he be so calm? Right, I almost forgot. Alex didn’t see what they did to Isobelle. What they’re still doing to the other kids. Ignorance really is bliss.

Alex looks up. “Listen,” he says, putting a hand on my thigh. “I want to find them too. God knows I do, but we have to be smart about this. I have a friend here who specializes in Santeria and Voodoo. He might be able to help us."

A friend, huh? In other words: another hunter.

Crossing my arms, I pout. "You're delusional if you think I'm going anywhere near another hunter."

He cocks a brow and laughs. "Are you serious?" he asks, and when I don't answer, he laughs even harder. "Oh God, you are. You can't sincerely believe I want to be seen with a witch. That's crazy, Manda."

Here we go. There's the Alex I've grown to hate. My pulse races. "Of course, we wouldn't want to hurt your reputation," I snarl through gritted teeth. "I'm curious, though. Are your hunter friends okay with the fact you were screwin' a witch?"

He cocks a brow. "I wasn't screwing a witch," he clarifies. "I screwed a girl who lied to me. There's a difference."

Wow. How the hell did we go from I-cheer-you-up-with-cupcakes to you-were-the- biggest-mistake-of-my-life in the blink of an eye?

I'm about to go ballistic on him when he makes a calming gesture. "All right, calm down, lil' avenger. I didn't mean to hurt you, but working with a witch is against everything a hunter believes. Jesus, I'd never hear the end of it if anyone knew."

Alex's apologies suck ass. "You're a douchebag, Alex, a first-class douchebag."

Knocking the sand off his trousers, he jumps up. "Yeah, you're right. But I'm a douchebag who bought you lemon cupcakes."

"No," I say as I get up. "You're a douchebag who thinks buying lemon cupcakes justifies being a douchebag."

Alex pulls a pair of sunglasses out of his jacket. "Chicken and egg, Manda."

Stomping away, I yell, "Egg and chicken, Alex."

****

Jerk-face booked us into the Hacienda Hotel. I totally dig the pool just around the corner, but I still think we should have gone back to Bakersfield. I know we don't have much to go on, but sitting in LA watching reruns of *Criminal Minds* while Alex is out and about with one of his hunter pals doesn't help either.

Growing increasingly twitchy, I dial Bonnie's number and put her on speaker. She answers on the third ring. "Ah, look who's calling. If that isn't Miss I-ditched-my-best-friend-for-a-hunter," she barks.

"Hello to you, too, Miss Grumpy."

"Oh, please." She pauses for dramatic effect. "Cut the crap, Amanda. You are the worst friend ever, leaving me all alone with that Catholic abomination who calls me a slut because I dated two guys in the last two weeks. I mean, how can I ever forgive you? Plus, I had to sleep with our prof to make sure you'll still have a place at NYU when you finally get your ass over here. All right, maybe I didn't sleep with him, but I totally flirted with him." If fast-talking were an Olympic discipline, Bonnie would win gold.

"Are you done bitching?" I ask after she's been quiet for longer than a second.

"For now," she says, snorting.

I heave a sigh of relief. "Good. May I speak now?" I take her groaning as a yes and continue. "What's goin' on with you, B? Since when do you care if someone calls you a slut?"

"I don't know," she moans. "That chick is killing me. I mean, just because her chastity belt interrupts the blood supply to her brain doesn't mean I have to take that shit from her."

I laugh. "Damn right, baby girl. You don't have to take shit from anyone, and I promise you, I'll kick that chick's Pope-fearing ass as soon as I get there."

I don't need to see her face to know she's smiling from ear to ear. "Promise?" she asks.

I cross my heart. "Scout's honor." No one messes with my friends.

"You're awesome."

"I know," I say, shrugging it off. "Feeling better now?"

"Tons." Then her voice grows more serious. "How's the Alex situation?"

Sound casual. "We get along." I sound more miserable than casual, but what can I do?

"Are you guys… I mean are you…you know…"

"Having sex?" I finish for her. "No, B. I don't make the same mistakes twice."

"Good," she says a little too fast. "I mean…you know…"

"Yeah, I know what you mean," I assure her. Not in the mood to talk about jerk-face, I change the topic to something far more important. "Hey, did you talk to your mom yet?"

I hear the impact of her hand as she smites her forehead. "Hell, I almost forgot."

"Forgot what?" I ask, curious.

"Mom said that—" A faint knock on the door interrupts her.

"Hold on, B. Room service just knocked." I fish in

my bag for change and head to the door.

"Your order," the waiter announces, holding a tray with soda, salad, and fries under my nose.

I grab my dinner and smile. "Keep the change," I say, handing him the money.

Slamming the door shut, I return to the bed and nibble on the fries. "Sorry, B. You were sayin'?"

"I can't believe you get to order room service while I'm stuck with the nun."

I shove a forkful of the salad in my mouth. "No. I mean, what were you goin' to say about your mom?"

"Right," she grumbles. "I asked my mom if she knew a bocor in Bakersfield, but according to her, the Bakersfield voodoo scene is dead."

The knot in my belly tightens. "Awesome," I mutter under my breath. How the hell are we supposed to find the bastard when even the best-connected mambo I know hasn't heard of him?

"There used to be two big covens, though," Bonnie continues. "But after that shit went down in the 80s, most of them left town."

I take a sip of my soda and wipe my lips with a napkin. "What shit?"

She clears her throat and switches to her TV anchor voice. "Apparently, a couple of kids claimed they were sexually abused during black masses. The town went crazy. I mean, literally. It turned into full-blown hysteria. The cops made some arrests, but they were all released after officials stated the kids had vivid imaginations, and none of it ever happened." She takes a breath. "However, the two covens decided it was better to move on. Couldn't risk a 20th century witch trial, I guess."

I almost drop my fork. "Are you serious?"

"Wouldn't lie about it," she assures me. "Besides, it's all over the internet. Just Google Kern County child abuse cases."

This is déjà vu all over. Child abuse, mass hysteria, and black magic. There's no way this isn't connected to the present situation. The question is how?

"Amanda, you still there?"

"Yeah." Reaching for the iPad, I abandon my food. "B, I gotta go, but I need one more favor."

"Sure. Anything."

Opening a browser, I brace myself for her reaction. "Find me an antidote for the zombie drug?"

Silence.

More Silence.

Laughter.

"Jeez, I think my hearing is off," Bonnie says, still laughing. "I could have sworn you just asked me to find an antidote for the zombie drug."

"I did," I mutter as I type Kern+County+Child Abuse+Cases into Google.

"Are you fucking shitting me?" she yells. "Please tell me you won't mess with a bocor and his fucking zombie?"

I bite my lower lip. "Of course not."

"Then why do you need a cure?"

"Because I'm going against a bocor who turned Alex's brother into a zombie, and kidnaps and rapes little girls," I say.

"Oh my God!" she shouts. "Did the hydrogen peroxide percolate through your brain? There's no antidote. No cure. And even if there was, it would only be known to those who practice with both hands."

"Every poison has an antidote," I say, browsing the 44,100 search results.

"This is Alex's doing, isn't it? I'm so going to kill him."

"This isn't about him, B." Okay, maybe it is. But I'm not in the mood to be preached at by her. "Just call Melinda and tell her to check Gram's grimoire. There must be something that can help us." I pause and clear my throat. "But don't tell her I'm the one asking, okay?"

"For the love of God, Amanda. Don't you think it's time to grow up and face your sister?"

I'm even less in the mood to hear her thoughts on me and my sister. "Just do as I said," I order and cut the line.

Gaze glued to the screen of the iPad, I skim through a link that reads Kern County—Witch Hunt or Satanic Child Abuse? Thirty defendants convicted of child sex abuse and related charges from 1984 through 1986. Convictions were later overturned. Eleven children told police they had been forced to kill younger children and witnessed such killings. Children accused their parents of sexual abuse and witchcraft. More victims had come forward. Police and District Attorney kept them in protective custody. Parents denied allegations, claiming State of California is on a witch hunt. Satanic slayings and human sacrifices were investigated by police. Police dug up land to search for sacrificed victims. Nephew of accused rapist couple accused uncle and aunt of slaying animals in Black Masses. Victims later recanted their testimony.

The shit reads like a bad horror screenplay. I'm about to hit YouTube to watch a documentary about the gruesome stuff when my phone vibrates. A text from Alex.

"Where r u?"

I reply, "My room. Where else would I be?"

He types, "Meet me at the bar in 10. Don't be late!"

I throw the phone in my bag, shut the iPad, and eye my barely touched dinner. Guess eating is overrated.

Chapter 13

Meet me in ten, he said. Don't be late, he wrote. Well, guess what? I'm on my third soda, but Alex is nowhere in sight. I abhor tardiness, but since sharing Isobelle's story isn't exactly on my bucket list, I consider not strangling him. Though, I might change my mind if he doesn't show up soon.

Twiddling with my straw, I watch a foreign couple through the large mirror behind the bar. Judging from the way they look at each other, I give them ten minutes before they screw each other in a restroom. Man, I hate lovebirds.

The blonde, mega-boobs waitress approaches me with a smile that's faker than Coco Austin's butt. "Tough day?" she asks, pointing to the three empty soda cans in front of me.

California girls, don't you just love 'em? Who doesn't love their depressing happy-go-lucky attitude?

Having a hard time not staring at her silicone-pimped cleavage, I shrug. "What can I say? The city of sun and fun has turned me into a sodaholic."

Throwing her head back, she grunts like Miss Piggy. "That's funny."

I have a nasty reply on the tip of my tongue, but hunter-heroic shows up in time to save her. "Sorry," he says. "The traffic in this town is—"

"From outer space?" I groan, eyes on Miss Piggy.

The chick drools over Alex as if he's Hollywood's new boy toy. He isn't even sitting yet when the blonde vamp bends over the counter and shoves her boobs in his face. "You look like an Elijah Craig kinda guy, am I right?"

I'd like to believe she treats every customer with so much care, but the hotel doesn't strike me as a brothel.

Alex's eyes slide over her plastic-surgeon-sculpted body, his aura almost instantly changing into a brilliant red. "Sounds good," he says with a boyish grin, totally digging her.

It doesn't come as a surprise to me he has the hots for her. It is, after all, common knowledge among guys that lust has no dignity. I'm still a little disappointed, though. Somehow, I always thought Alex liked his chicks a bit more classy.

Hips shaking, boobs bouncing, she grabs the expensive bourbon from the shelf behind her and pours him a shot. "Let me know if you need anything else. I make the best Sex on the Beach in town."

Excuse me, I think I need to throw up.

Alex's gaze jumps from her cleavage to her ass. "I bet you do," he says, voice like pure sex.

"Check please!" the foreigner yells as his chick disappears inside the restroom.

I look at my watch. Nine minutes. Damn, I'm good.

Miss Piggy smiles a brilliant, unnatural smile and winks at Alex. "Be right back."

"Seriously?" I snap when he's still ogling her ass. "Are you suffering from sex deprivation, or do you like them mentally retarded and compliant?"

Alex slowly tilts his head to the side. "Jealous?" he

asks, lips curled into a devilish grin.

I cover my mouth with both hands. "Oh. My. God. You've got me there." I point to my perfect, natural body. "How could I keep up with a brainless, silicone-implanted Miss Piggy, right?"

He sips the bourbon. "Spare me your sarcasm, Manda."

Arching a brow, I glare at Miss Piggy, who's serving a customer on the other side of the horseshoe-shaped bar. "Will do," I snarl. "Only if you spare me the pathetic flirting though."

You sure you're not jealous?

Ignoring the voice in my head, I take a sip of soda and turn my attention to what's really important: the kids and Jesse. "Any luck with your hunter pal?"

Alex studies me closely. "He didn't have a zombie cure, if that's what you're asking. But…" He pauses and takes another sip. I hate when people stop midsentence to dramatize what they're about to say.

"But?"

Alex's lips curl into one helluva smile. "I have a name," he announces proudly. "According to my source, Jesse was looking for a guy who goes by the name of Baron Samedi."

I almost choke on my drink. "What? Are you sure?"

His smile fades. "Yeah. Why? Do you know him?'

Do I know him? Is he kidding?

"I thought your hunter pal was a voodoo specialist?"

Alex's features harden. "Just answer the damn question, Manda."

A frustrated breath escapes me. "Baron Samedi is

the god of the dead. There's no way our bocor goes by that name unless—"

Glass in his hand, Alex straightens. "Unless what?"

"Unless our bocor sold his soul to Samedi."

Alex's voice drops low. "Would you stop talking in riddles and tell me what the hell makes you think our bocor sold his soul to that Samedi guy?"

I give him the what-kind-of-a-hunter-are-you look and sigh. "Voodooists invite loa—"

"Loa?" A mist of confusion clouds his eyes.

"Loa are gods," I explain, and when he nods, I continue. "Anyway, voodooists invite loa into their bodies and offer them gifts so they fulfill their prayers. Each deity has a specific power. So if you're crazy about a girl who doesn't give you the time of day, you call upon Oshun, the love goddess, offering her honey, a comb, or money."

Alex taps his fingers against the counter. "Cut to the chase, Manda."

I shoot him a look. "Samedi is the loa of the dead and the only one who can be bribed into harming people. Let's say you want to castrate your cheating boyfriend. All you have to do is offer him a cigar, rum, and twenty-one peppers, and the deal is done. But if you keep calling him to do your bidding, his price increases. To call yourself Samedi and use his full potential, he will ask for your soul."

"Great," he moans. "So what you're saying is my brother and these kids are hostages of an ancient god and his puppet?"

"Not exactly," I say. "Samedi isn't really a god. He's a rogue reaper who found a loophole that gave him what he always wanted."

"And what would that be?" Alex asks, jaw clenched.

"Worshippers," I reply and take a sip of soda.

"Are you fucking kidding me?" he yells, drawing way too much attention to us. "Couldn't the dude build himself a church or temple like normal sociopaths?"

I glance around. "Keep your voice down," I say, pointing to a couple of eavesdropping customers.

"I don't want to keep my fucking voice down," he shouts, slamming a fist on the counter. "What I do want, however, is for you to tell me how we kill the bastard. Is there a spell or some other witch-mojo to take the freak out?"

I know he's mad, but he needs to calm the fuck down. People are already staring, and with everything that's happening, it isn't smart discussing magic in public. "You can't kill a reaper," I whisper. "It would upset the natural order."

Ogling me as if I'm crazy, he cocks a brow. "The natural order? The *thing* is a killer, Amanda."

I massage my temples. "Yeah, smartass. Killing kinda comes with the job description of a reaper. Our real problem is the bocor. The loa doesn't give a shit about your brother or these kids. He just does what the bocor asks him to do."

"Fuck." Alex reaches for the bourbon and downs the rest in one swallow. "What the hell was Jesse thinking, messing with a voodoo jerk who's best buddies with a freaking reaper? The boy must have lost his fucking mind." He looks me in the eye. "I mean, that's insane, isn't it?"

"Actually, it's ingenious," I admit.

"What?" If looks could kill, I'd be in witch heaven

by now.

Scared he might suffer a stroke, I wave Miss Piggy over and point to Alex's empty glass. "Refill."

Playing with a strand of her hair, she fills the glass. "Anything else?" she asks, flashing Alex a sexy smile.

Jerk-face ignores her, and I almost feel sorry for Miss California. "We're good," I assure her, and once she stomps away like a pouting child, I face Alex. "Jesse is looking for a way to save his friend from hell right?"

Hands around the short glass, he frowns. "Tell me something I don't know. Like why the fuck you think he's a genius for getting himself turned into a zombie?"

Aren't badass hunters supposed to have some brains? "It's real simple. Samedi is a reaper, and what do reapers do?"

"Kill?" he says.

I play with a strand of my hair. "Yeah, smartass. But they also deliver the souls to their rightful places. Heaven, hell, purgatory."

Frustration rolls over Alex's face. "So?"

"If Jesse could cut a deal with the bocor, he would have ordered Samedi to spare Jesse's friend's life, and hell couldn't get the guy's soul."

Alex's aura is a mixture of guilt and fear. Staring at his scarred knuckles, he downs the second shot. "Dammit, Manda. Do you listen to yourself?" He slams the glass on the counter. "You sound like this is a game of Monopoly. Strike a deal with the bitch of a narcissistic reaper. Get a hell-free card. And pay with what? Your soul?"

"Relax," I say, laying a hand on his shoulder. "Jesse is a zombie."

Alex's bitter laughter roars through the bar. "You sound like that's a good thing."

I shrug tense shoulders. "It sorta is. Zombies can't make deals. They are under the influence of the bocor and have no freewill. Everyone knows deals like that are void."

Alex squints. "Is that supposed to make me feel better?"

Hell, yeah! Zombies I might be able to handle. Deals with Satan, psychotic bocors, or sociopathic reapers, not so much.

I nod. "At least he still owns his soul."

Alex lets out a sharp breath and traces the bags under his eyes. "Manda?"

"Hm?"

"Do me a favor," he says with a half-smile. "Don't ever try to cheer people up. 'Cause damn, you have a gift for making things worse."

That should be an easy promise to keep. "Done."

Since it's all about sharing, I should probably let him in on what I saw earlier. "Alex, there's something else." I try to sound casual, but my voice is shaky as hell.

"Spill it."

Trying to keep it together, I tell him everything, from what I saw connected to Isobelle to the info I gathered from Bonnie. He listens patiently, but every time I mention the dog kennels or child abuse, he curls his hands into fists and clenches his jaw. After I've told him every disgusting detail, he stays quiet. I can't blame him. It's hard to wrap your head around this shit without losing it.

"Alex, are you okay?" I ask, as his eyes grow more

and more distant.

"Sure." Flashing me a half-hearted smile, he gets up. "I'll be right back," he says, and heads to the restroom.

Staring at my empty soda can, I suppress my inner hurricane once again and focus all my energy on Alex. He's far from okay. His brother is a brainless slave, serving a child-abusing bocor who happens to be under a reaper's protection. Could it be worse?

As a matter of fact, it could. What if the bocor forces Jesse to take part in the abuse?

"Hey." Miss Piggy snaps her fingers in my face.

Where did she come from?

"What?" I'm not in the mood to talk Kardashians or other pointless bullshit.

She throws her extensions over her shoulder and leans in. "Is he your boyfriend?" she asks, heat flooding her cheeks.

With narrowed eyes, I glare at her. "Who?"

Miss Piggy presses a hand against her heart, ogling me suspiciously. "Are you serious?" She points to the restrooms. "The woman-eater you're with."

I need a moment to adjust my brain from child-abusing bocors to I-want-to-screw-your-friend.

She straightens, her dull aura radiating bright red. "I mean, oh my gosh," she moans, fanning herself with a menu. "He's so…so…"

Out of your league?

"Unbelievably hot," she squeaks like a stupid cheerleader. "I bet he's good."

The red aura. The blushing. Jeez, I know exactly to what she's referring, but I'm not going there. "Only one way to find out," I say, trying to play cool. But anyone with a brain would hear the annoyance in my voice.

Proving she doesn't have one, she flashes me an excited smile. "So you two aren't…"

"Nope."

"Is he single?"

Do I look like his personal hookup assistant? "I guess."

"You don't mind if I…"

"Honey," I say, "you can do him all night long. I don't give a shit."

"You're awesome," she says cheerily before turning to a dude with an empty beer glass.

Strange, I don't feel so awesome right now.

"What was that about?" Alex asks, eyes glued to Miss Piggy's peach ass.

I shrug off the incident. "Just girl stuff." When he doesn't take his eyes off her booty, I realize he really wants to try her Sex on the Beach. I pull a few bucks out of my bag and force a smile. "I think I'll call it a night."

Alex knits his brows. "It's quarter past nine."

Putting the money on the counter, I nod. "Guess I'm gettin' old."

"Wait," he says, grabbing my wrist. "I'll go with you to your room."

Missy Piggy watches us. She secretly pleads with me to fulfill her dirty dream. He'd forget all about her if I allowed him to come along. I also know he wants her, and why should I screw this up for him? After all the drama, he deserves a little fun.

"You should stay," I suggest, pointing to Miss Piggy.

Alex instantly gets the message. His gaze darts

from her to me and back again.

Damn, who thought he would actually consider screwing her?

Before he comes up with a lame excuse why he can't bed Miss Piggy, or worse, why he should, I pull my wrist free and leave.

Chapter 14

I'm tired, but every time I close my eyes, I'm plagued by images of Alex and Miss Piggy. Staring at the light of the crescent moon that slices through the chiffon curtains, I come to the conclusion there's something seriously wrong with me. Jesse is a zombie. Little girls are being abducted and raped. Yet all I seem to be able to think of is which Kama Sutra position Alex and Miss Piggy are working on.

Closing my eyes, I toss.

He screws her.

And turn.

He screws her not.

I glare at the ceiling.

He screws her.

I pull the goddamn blanket over my head.

He screws her not.

Man, who am I kidding? Being near Alex is killing me. It's a lesson I've already learned. Back then, when he didn't know what I was, he found a way to tear down all the walls I'd carefully built around my heart. Falling for him was like breathing. A natural necessity. I just couldn't help it. Not that I didn't try. Believe me I did. But there was something about him that got under my skin. Pretty stupid, considering our mutual hate is practically predestined. He's a hunter. I'm a witch. Skinheads don't fall in love with Latinas. Nazis don't date Jews. And witches don't screw hunters—it's simple like that. In theory. But the heart is stubborn and reckless. Always wants what it can't have, and never considers consequences.

God, I sound like one of these pathetic *Twilight* chicks. Hello, brain to libido! The guy tried to kill you twice.

Hell, I need a smoke. I've managed to steer clear of the toxic shit for the last eighteen months, but there's only so much a girl can take without throwing all her new life resolutions out the window.

Shoving the blanket away, I sit up. It's quarter to ten. If I'm lucky, I'll find a gas station somewhere close by. Pulling my up hair in a messy bun, I slip into my jeans. A loud knock on my door makes me jump.

"Manda?" Alex's deep voice roars from the hall. "It's me. Open up."

What did I ever do to you, Universe? I know we will all pay for our sins sooner or later, but I'm afraid I'm running out of currency here.

Stalking to the door, I wrap my fingers around the doorknob. "Go away. I'm sleeping." I'm not in the mood for bedtime stories or after-glow auras.

His rich laughter rings in my ears. "No, you're not."

"Yes, I am."

"I know you're leaning against the door, Manda. Just let me in."

"How do you—"

"I can see your shadow," he says matter-of-factly. I almost forgot why the freaking FBI enlisted him in the first place.

"I'm tired. I'll see you tomorrow." Sounds stupid,

but it's the best I can come up with.

"Fuck, Manda. Stop fooling around."

Alex is way too stubborn to just go away, so I put on my poker face and open the door a tiny crack. "What do you want?"

"Can I come in?"

I lean against the door and arch a brow. "Why?"

Sticking to his jerk act, he ignores my question and pushes past me. Stumbling backward, I shoot daggers at him. "What the fuck, Alex?"

His gaze travels all over me. "I was going to ask you the same thing," he says with a crooked smile. "What the fuck, Manda? Why the hell did you disappear? And don't even try that 'I'm getting old' shit on me."

Is he for real? Giving him the evil eye, I'm a little surprised when his aura beams an insecure dark green rather than the expected lusty red.

"Manda?"

"What?" I hiss, one hand on my hip, the other still clenched around the doorknob.

His malachite eyes pierce right through my soul, and I feel naked and exposed. "Jesus, Manda. For once in your life, be honest with me and tell the truth." His voice is soft, but demanding.

The truth. I don't even know what that is anymore. I guess that's the price you pay when you tell lies for a living. At some point, the truth fades into oblivion.

I clutch the doorknob tighter, ready to tell him to get the fuck out. He reaches behind me, slamming the door shut. My heart leaps in my chest, and I swallow hard. "Are you fuckin' crazy?"

He stalks toward me. "Why did you go?"

Fed up with seeing his god-like face, I frown. "I was tired. Still am."

"Bullshit," he says, forcing me against the wall. "Why don't you just admit it?" Alex is so close I smell the bourbon on his breath.

My heart races like a Shelby Mustang, but I won't avert my gaze. Can't show weakness. "Admit what, Alex?"

"That you're jealous," he whispers, his lips brushing my ear.

I laugh, not because any of this is funny, but because I'm the witch, yet he's the one with the sixth sense. Holding onto the little self-control I still have, I force my spine into a straight position. The muscles in his chest rub against my shirt, and my heart throws a tantrum. "You wish," I say hoarsely.

Hands land on the wall on either side of my head. Our faces only inches apart, the hair on my skin crawls.

Run!

My gaze goes from Alex to the door, but he knows what I'm up to and shakes his head. "No way. You won't run again."

"Again?" I snap. "When did I ever run from you, Alex?"

He pushes his fingers through my belt loop and pulls me closer. "You were running the second I laid eyes on you."

Whoa, what is this? The freaking *Twilight Zone*? Half an hour ago, he was drooling all over Miss Piggy, and now he has me pushed against a wall, hellbent on getting a jealousy confession out of me? Not happening.

His rough fingertips draw circles on the skin above

my waistband, and breathing becomes a privilege I no longer attain. I try to step back, bring some space and air between our heating bodies. I feel like a rat in a trap. "What do you want from me?" My voice sounds like sandpaper.

An awkward silence fills the room, and his fierce eyes find mine. He doesn't have to answer my question, because his cherry aura speaks for itself. We've been here before, and it didn't end well.

****

The bar was packed, but Alex didn't give a shit. He stood there, hand around my wrist, eyes searching my soul. "What is wrong with you, Amanda? Is this all just one big game for you?"

I arched a brow and grinned. "Dunno what you're talkin' about." That was a lie, but hey, no one could blame me for not going down the Buffy and Angel road.

He pushed me against the wall. "I said you could ride with us, but I won't put up with your shit any longer." He fisted his hand around his hair. "Why don't you do us both a favor and say what you really want?"

"And what would that be?" I asked.

His features hardened, but his eyes were soft. "Me."

Who the hell did he think he was? There was nothing about him I wanted, not his worn out, ripped clothes, not his ridiculously awesome abs, and certainly not his freaking amazing eyes.

"Get lost, Alex."

"In you?" he asked, arching a brow.

When had he become so cocky?

I had to pull myself together. Alex wasn't just your

ordinary bad boy. He was fatal. I averted my gaze and took the longest breath ever. "I don't want your heroism, your smartass attitude, or your I'll-risk-my-life-for-every-human-being-on-earth crap."

"Good." His rugged fingertips dug into my ankh tattoo. "'Cause I don't want your selfishness, your stab-worthiness, or your attitude." He brushed hair out of my face. "No strings attached," he said, his hot breath tingling on my alert skin. "That's what we can both agree on."

I needed some air. Some space. A brain. I had never lost control, but there was something about Alex that made me want to fall.

Pressing my hand against his chest, I felt his heart racing. "This is a bad idea," I heard myself mutter as his lips connected with mine and the world around us came to a stop.

****

Tracing a finger over his hard chest, I try to shake the memory off, but I still feel his mouth on mine. Alex might look like a god, but he kisses like Satan himself. No guy had been able to live up to him, and no matter how much I hate to admit it, he ruined me. In every possible way.

His ridiculously full lips are dangerously close. "The question is: what do you want, Manda?"

What do I want? I want to run my hands through his hair, rip his shirt off, feel his sweat. I want him to get lost inside of me. Push faster, harder. I want one more night.

That's fucking insane.

Biting my lower lip, I let my gaze drift from his striking face to his rock-hard abs. Sanity is overrated!

I'm about to wrap my hands around his neck when the scent of incense crawls into my nose.

I stiffen. "Do you smell that?"

"What?" he asks, his lips brushing mine.

I shove him away. "Incense," I say as the Kylie Minogue song "Where the Wild Roses Grow" starts playing in my head. "Something isn't right." I feel it in my bones.

Alex wears a worried expression and steps back. "What is it, Manda?"

"I don't know, but—"

The ringing of his phone cuts me off.

Startled, Alex pulls the cell out of his jacket and pushes the accept button. "Yeah?" he croaks, followed by a long silence. "When?" he asks, face pale. "We're on our way." Disconnecting, he stares at me, transfixed.

"What happened?"

His gaze drops. "It's Isobelle."

No, don't say it. Please, don't.

"She's dead."

Chapter 15

"I don't give a shit about PAU policy, Carter," Alex barks into his phone. "I have a dead kid on my hands, at least a dozen are being held as sex slaves, and my brother is a freaking zombie… Yes, zombie… No, we don't need to alarm the government." Pacing the creepy hallway of the morgue, he curls his hands into fists. "Dude, I don't have time for this shit. Get me the fucking names of every pedophile and anyone ever accused of child abuse in Bakersfield. ASAP."

Dead kid. The words send chills down my spine. An hour ago, my biggest problem had been my insatiable desire to screw Alex. Now I'm standing in a freaking morgue, waiting to see the body of a ten-year-old girl

"Do I have to remind you of Bridgewater?" Alex sounds tired and looks miserable. "Good. And Carter, hurry up."

I lean against the wall and glare at the fluorescent light. Isobelle is gone. Just like that. I try to wrap my head around it, but every cell in my body bristles at the thought. I ain't stupid. When I signed up for the Rescue Jesse Mission, I expected drama, even a little danger. But never in my wildest dreams had I anticipated ending up in a morgue to examine the body of a girl who had been through more shit than any grown-up could relate to.

Shoving the phone in his pocket, Alex walks toward me. "You okay?" he says, leaning against the wall next to me.

"I'm fuckin' awesome," I mutter as weighty footsteps echo down the hallway.

A guy in green hospital scrubs approaches us. He's about fifty and has bags under his eyes the size of moon craters. "Agents Remington and Bishop?"

Alex nods. "Yes."

"I'm Dr. DaSilva," he says. "You're here for Isobelle Watson, I assume?"

I flinch at the sound of her name, but Alex keeps his cool. "That's right. Have you determined the cause of death yet?"

The doctor pulls one side of his mouth up. "My best guess right now is an internal hemorrhage, but we will be certain after the autopsy."

After the autopsy?

Pushing off the wall, I stagger toward them. "All due respect, sir, but we don't have time for this. We need answers now."

Alex gives me a look, and Dr. DaSilva frowns. "It's been a busy night, Agent. We had a gang shooting downtown."

Gang shooting sounds bad, but a dead ten-year-old outweighs just about anything. "And we have several missing kids," I shoot back.

Dr. DaSilva blows out a frustrated breath. "I understand, but I'm on my own. And as you can see," he holds his hands up, "I've only got two of these."

So he doesn't want to help us, huh? Well, I guess I just have to help myself then. "Can we see Isobelle now?" I try to sound calm, but there's an edge in my voice I can't even out. The doctor's gaze travels over my face. "Sure, but I need to see your ID first."

Alex shoves his badge under the man's nose. "Have the parents been informed?" he asks while Dr. DaSilva thoroughly examines his ID.

A dark, fearful blue swirls around the doctor. "Yes, they're on their way." The defeat in his voice is loud and clear. He must have done this a million times—talking to parents who had lost their child—but his expression tells me he'll never get used to it.

Dr. DaSilva pulls his gaze from the badge. "Wait here," he grumbles, walking to a massive sliding door at the end of the hallway.

Alex leans in. "I know that look, Manda. What are you up to?"

I swear, sometimes it's scary how well the boy knows me. I pull my bun tighter and straighten my jacket. "I'm going to find out what happened to Isobelle."

He crosses his arms and studies me closely. "And how are you going to do that?"

I manage a half-smile. "What good is it to be a witch if you can't summon the dead?"

His jaw drops. "You're fucking crazy," he says, eyeballing me as if I've just murdered his puppy. "This is a morgue. You can't just summon a dead girl."

I shrug. "Watch me."

Ignoring his grimace, I check my bag for the things I need. Eyeliner? Check. Pen and paper? Check. Two quarters? Check. A lighter? Shit. "Alex?"

He looks up.

"Do you have a lighter?"

He pulls a black Zippo out of his pocket. "Do I

want to know why you need this?" he asks before he hands it over.

"Probably not."

"Agents." Dr. DaSilva waves us over. "You can see her now."

I draw in a deep breath. "You need to buy me some time," I say as we head toward the massive sliding door. "Can you do that?"

Alex knits his brows. It's obvious he doesn't like my plan, but he nods. "I'll try my best," he promises, and then we walk through the door into the morgue.

Dr. DaSilva stands next to me. "Right there," he says, pointing to the autopsy table at the far end of the room.

Damn, the man wasn't kidding when he said he'd had a busy night. Holding my index finger under my nose to block out the smell of death and decomposition, I gawk at a dozen black vinyl bags. This sucks. One minute you're planning your future, and the next you find yourself stuffed into a body bag.

"Ready?" the doctor asks, hand on the zipper of Isobelle's bag.

Alex's fingers brush my hand, and I get a glimpse of his messed up emotions. Anger, disbelief, shock—he feels it all. "Go ahead," he says, hiding his emotions under a façade of confidence.

The metallic sound of the zipper gives me the chills, and all of a sudden, Alex's words ring in my ears. "Take off the bitchy armor and the cocky attitude and tell me what's left?" Right now, the answer to that question is weak knees and cardiac arrest.

The doc parts the plastic, and I stiffen at the gruesome sight. Isobelle's long hair is glued to her scalp. Her skin is translucent, and the dried blood around her mouth and nose makes her look like a bloodthirsty vampire.

Breathe, Amanda. I try to, but my throat is blocked. Sick to my stomach, I stumble back and bump into a scale stand that hosts a freaking heart.

"Would you like to wait outside?" Dr. DaSilva asks.

Alex looks at me with a worried expression. That's a new freaking record. Yesterday, I cried in front of him, and now I can't handle a corpse? If I keep this up, he might actually think I have a soul.

"I'm good," I say, straightening.

The doc shrugs, clearly not buying it. "If you say so."

Meeting Alex's gaze, I point to the door. "Get him out," I mouth.

He pats the doc's shoulder. "Dr. DaSilva, would you show me Isobelle's personal belongings while Agent Bishop takes a look at the body?" The FBI voice really suits him.

Uncomfortable with the idea of leaving me alone with Isobelle's corpse, Dr. DaSilva twists his mouth. "Sure," he says reluctantly. "Follow me."

Alex peeks over his shoulder and gives me a warning glance. "You better hurry," I read from his lips before the door slides shut behind them.

Since I have no idea how much time I have, I pull pen and paper out of my bag and write down the spell. They are tricky, dangerous little bitches. One misplaced word, and instead of summoning the dead, you end up raising them. Keeping my trembling hand steady, I jot down the last sentence and skim through it. Looks good.

Yeah, but what if it doesn't work? Gram's spells never failed. Remember Sissy? My lips curl into a smile. How could I ever forget that white ball of fur? She wasn't just the smartest cat to ever walk this earth; she had also been one of the best things that ever happened to me. The kitten and I shared everything, including mutual dislike for my mother. Every time Desperate Housewitch went on a rampage, Sissy threatened to scratch her eyes out. Unfortunately, her overprotective streak had also been her downfall. After biting my mother in the heel because she had accused me of being the source of all evil, Mom chased her out of the yard, right under the wheel of our neighbor's car. I couldn't picture life without her, and when I found the summoning spell in Gram's grimoire, I figured it would bring her back for good, *Pet Cemetery* style. Guess I should have paid more attention to the words. What a stupid and naïve eight-year-old I was.

Spell between my lips, I pull the eyeliner out of my bag and draw pentagrams on Isobelle's stiff palms. The black char smears on her leather-like skin. Gross.

My hands grow sweaty. There are a million things that can go wrong, but I read the spell anyway. "I call upon the ancient gods: Moira, who cuts the thread, Hecate, who cheats death, and Isis, savior and guardian of all dead. Allow me to speak to this spirit from the other side, so I may see what took her life."

Closing my eyes, I visualize Isobelle in the asylum. Her clouded eyes, her heavy breath, her glass-shattering screams. "I call upon the ancient gods; Moira, who cuts the thread, Hecate, who cheats death, and Isis, savior and guardian of all dead. Allow me to speak to this spirit from the other side, so I may see what took her life."

Focusing all my energy, I rest my hand on Isobelle's chest and repeat the spell one last time before I hold the paper in the flame of the lighter.

Something's not right, though. The paper scarcely burns, and it takes several attempts until the spell finally goes up in flames. Every kid knows the outcome of a spell can be measured by the speed in which it burns, but I can't give up now. Pulling the ferryman's reward out of my bag, I put the quarters on Isobelle's forehead and wait.

The clock ticks the minutes away, but there's no sign of her spirit. I watch her dishonored body and wait, but the kid is as dead as she can be, and her soul is nowhere to be seen. I run my hand over her forehead. "Isobelle," I whisper. "I need your help."

Nothing.

What did I expect, an answer?

Maybe.

Now what?

I repeat the spell louder.

It's hopeless.

Faster.

Nada. *Niente*. Nothing.

Harsher.

Ah, fuck it. This isn't going to work.

The monster in my head is right. This is a lost cause. Grabbing Isobelle's rigid hand, I'm wiping off the eyeliner when a chilly breeze sweeps my hair.

"Isobelle?" My gaze drifts through the room, but there's no sign of her spirit.

Am I that desperate I've started imagining things?

I shrug the incident off and brush my thumb over a pentagram when an electric humming charges the air and the fluorescent light flickers.

"Amanda." I jump at the sound of the metallic voice.

Spinning, I scan the room. "Isobelle, is that you?"

The autopsy saw on the table next to me trembles. "You did this to me," the inhuman voice shrieks as the air grows colder, and my breath becomes visible.

"What are you talking about?" I ask shakily.

"You'll see," the voice replies as a violent wind blows through me.

First, there's an eerie silence. Then high-pitched screams and painfully bright flashes of light. The world spins, or I do. The earth trembles, or maybe my legs do. It's impossible to say. Stumbling backward, I knock into the autopsy table. Whatever the fuck this is, it's worse than a bad acid trip.

****

Between the crescent moon and the sparkling stars, Isobelle looked angelic. She had slept through most of the day, and to her surprise, without another nightmare. She didn't know why she felt better, but she was certain it was connected to the woman and the man who came to see her today. The woman's fingers had worked magic on her forehead, she was sure about that.

Isobelle's tired eyes found the moon, and she made a wish. Maybe, she thought, maybe things will get better now. Holding onto her newfound hope, she closed her eyes.

"I warned you." Isobelle opened her eyes. "Don't tell anyone, I said. Don't ever try to remember, I told you." The demon's accent turned her blood to ice.

"No. No. No," she cried, terrified. "Leave me alone."

A shadow stepped out of the corner. "You are a risk, petite monstre, *and risks need to be eliminated."*

Isobelle braced herself for Scorpion Man's wrath, but as the shadow came closer, she realized this wasn't Scorpion Man. The shadow wasn't a man at all.

"It's time," the creature with the top hat whispered, reaching for her hand. It was a gentle touch, quick and insignificant. But what it did to her was brutal and meaningful. Her chest cramped. Her throat tightened. Warm liquid welled out of her nose. And the figure just stood there, watching her gasp for air, laughing as blood bubbled out of her mouth.

Isobelle eyes grew wild with fear when she realized she was choking on the very thing that gave her life.

****

The pressure on my chest is unbearable. "Is this my fault?" I whimper as Alex and Dr. DaSilva return. Did Isobelle die because I tried to get a glimpse of what had happened to her?

"Amanda?" A horrified expression on his face, Alex runs toward me.

"Agent Bishop," Dr. DaSilva screams. "What happened?"

What the hell are they talking about?

I try to gulp, but my throat is blocked. Drops of crimson fall to the floor, and when I run my hand over my nose, I see what has them so scared.

My blood.

I can't breathe.

I can't see.

And, eventually, I don't feel.

Chapter 16

Between dazzling light that sears my retinas and utter darkness that leaves me blind and restless, my head reels. I totter backward, bumping into something hard. There's no pain, though. Not even a little sensation. Just my mind telling me my hip knocked into cold steel.

What the fuck just happened? Alex? Dr. DaSilva? They were here with me. Now they're not. I look around. My heart gallops like a racing horse, but my body is rigid and numb.

"Alex?" My voice echoes through the electrified air, as the clock above the sliding door blinks into existence. The watch hands move way too slowly. Shivers roll down my spine. "Dr. DaSilva?" I croak.

White noise pulsates in my ears. From the corner of my eye, I see shadows dancing through the fey room. "Alex, where the fuck are you?" I don't mean to sound hysterical, but I do.

The static sound decomposes into terrifying voices. "Who are you?"

"Can you help us?"

"I need to pick up my daughter."

"Where are we?"

"D is going to kill me."

They all speak at once.

That's it! I'm outta here. Pressing my hands against

my ears, I head for the door. Out of nowhere, white mist appears. What the—

Like a mad swarm of bees, it rushes toward me, knocking the standing scale over and sending the organ on it flying.

“Where do you think you’re going?” a bloodcurdling voice thunders.

I look from the mist to the heart. If this is a nightmare, I should write this shit down and send it to Stephen King. If not, well, then I’m totally screwed. “Who the fuck are you?” I shout, heart leaping inside my chest.

The autopsy saw on the metal table springs to life, and shrill laughter penetrates the dull air. Carried by an invisible hand, the lethal saw flies at me, stopping only inches from my neck. “I,” the white mist says, “am the spirit you called.”

Awesome. Just awesome. A crazy-ass, Goethe-quoting spirit points a saw at my neck. Shadows lurk in every corner, and Alex is freaking gone. Could this day get any better?

Actually, it could. Look around. Don’t you know what this place is?

The morgue?

Really? Then where the hell is Alex? Think, Amanda.

I hold my breath and scan the room. Distinctive echoes, ghostly lightning, and clocks that count seconds as minutes. Ring a bell?

No way. This is crazy.

Crazier than white mist that holds you at saw-point?

“Shut the fuck up,” I order the voice in my head.

This can't be happening. I mean, there's no freaking way I'm in—

Limbo? Hate to break the bad news, but that's exactly where you are.

But you have to be—

Dead? Congratulations, Amanda. You've just won a ticket to Disney World. Too bad you won't need it anymore.

I know spells can backfire, but this is madness. I'm twenty for Christ's sake. There's no way I'm dead.

Fear corrupts my voice. "What the fuck did you do to me?"

The air sizzles as the mist takes on human form, and not just any human form but Isobelle's. Her otherwise blue eyes are charcoal, and she looks furious. "This is your fault," she screams, bringing the saw closer to my neck. "You should have left me alone."

My chest tightens. There are a lot of things I should feel guilty about, but trying to save Jesse sure as hell ain't one of them. "I'm sorry for what happened to you," I say, eyes on the spinning blade. "But this isn't my fault, Isobelle."

"I'm all alone," she says, a fire blazing in her eyes. Literally. Her eyes burn. "I just wanted to go home. Now, I'll never go home again."

"Home?" A shadow steps out of a corner. "I need to go home, too," it whispers, taking on the form of a woman in her early thirties. Putting a hand on the gaping hole in her chest, she cries. "My daughter is waiting for me."

"My wife will kill me if I'm late for my surprise party," a guy mutters as he approaches Isobelle and me. Half his face is blown away, the rest of his head barely attached to his spine.

Disgusting. I should take a snapshot of him and send it to the NRA, adding a note that reads, "This is what guns can do."

"Shut up! All of you," a rough voice warns. "Ain't nobody going, but me. D is going to shoot ma ass if I don't deliver the package." The jerk is covered with gang tattoos, and despite the multiple gunshot wounds to his stomach, he keeps up his bad-boy attitude.

The gateway of hell, I could handle. But being stuck in Limbo with Casper the unfriendly psycho and some messed up spirits who don't even know they're pushing up daisies—not so much.

I focus on Isobelle. "I know you're angry, and trust me you have every right—"

"Damn right," she says. "None of this would have happened if you had left me alone."

I get it. The kid is pissed off. Who wouldn't unleash the inner beast if life had screwed you like this? But enough is enough. Eyes on the saw, I grab Isobelle's wrist. "Put that thing down," I order, my voice brimming with the confidence of the dead. I mean what can she do? Chop my ghostly head off?

Isobelle's ghost jaw drops. "You don't get to tell me what to do," she pouts.

Evil spirit or not, I see nothing but a wild child. "You wish, young lady." I bend her hand, forcing her to drop the saw. "I've summoned your sorry ass, and I'm sure as hell able to send you back. So stop acting like a holy terror. Do I make myself clear?"

Even in the afterlife, I'm nothing but a liar. Dead witch trapped in Limbo. There's no way my spells work here, but she doesn't know that.

The fire in her eyes turns into cold terror. "No," she cries, stumbling back. "Please don't send me to that place. It's so," her voice grows weaker, "so cold there."

Cold?

"Isobelle." I put a finger under her chin. "Look at me." And when she does, I continue. "Tell me where you've been."

She averts her gaze. "I don't know."

Every soul passes through a different Limbo. Fields with daisies and daffodils, a Nirvana concert, a freaking morgue, or simply the place where they took their last breath. Grams used to say it all came down to making the transition easier. But cold and lonely doesn't sound easier to me. "Can you describe the place?" I ask.

Isobelle's gaze drops to her bare feet. "Everything there is colorless," she says, breath quickening. "Kind of gray, but the worst gray I have ever seen. And—" She cuts herself off and looks around as if she's afraid someone might eavesdrop. "Although I'm alone, I hear…"

"What, Isobelle? What do you hear?"

Isobelle's shoulders sink. "Groaning. Laughing. Terrifying screams. And sometimes," her voice breaks, "sometimes, I hear my brother and sister. They want me to come out and play. But I'm too scared."

I step back. Gray. Cold. Laughing. Groaning. This isn't possible. Isobelle couldn't be—but the summoning spell took ages to work.

Fuck it, they didn't. They wouldn't. They hold them in dog kennels, rape them, and kill them. But would they really trap the soul of a ten-year-old in—

"Purgatory," I snarl through gritted teeth as reality

hits me like a bolt of lightning. Those fucking assholes trapped her soul in freaking Purgatory. Supernatural creatures like demons and evil witches are trapped there once they meet their end, but it sure ain't a playground for the souls of little kids.

"Isobelle." It comes out harsher than intended.

She looks up, hope flickering in those big eyes. "Can you get me out of there?"

I honestly don't know. But what I do know is she must have seen something that could blow their covers. Why else would they kill her and trap her soul in the realm of monsters? "If you want to get out of that place, you need to show me what you saw when they held you captive," I explain.

"But—"

I shake my head, unable to handle objections. "Remember the other kids?" I ask. When she nods, I continue, "They will do the same to them if you don't help me." I hold out my palm. "Give me your hand."

Her black eyes ogle me. "I don't trust you."

I laugh. "Story of my life, honey. But right now I'm your only shot at getting outta there." I point my chin at my hand. "So what's it gonna be, love?"

Weighing her options, she tenses. "What if he finds out?"

There are a million things a bocor could do to a spirit, but if I want her to trust me, I have to do what I do best. I have to lie. "You're dead, Isobelle. What else can he do to you?"

She curls her toes and sighs. "What do you want me to do?"

"Take my hand and focus on the one thing you were supposed to forget."

She looks confused. "What? How…"

I smile, or at least I try to. "Just trust me, okay?"

She nods and reaches for my hand. The second her fingers brush my palm, my head starts spinning.

****

Isobelle's hands were clenched around the cold iron bars. Her face soaked with tears; she tried to find a way out. But the steel was too solid, and no matter how hard she pushed and pulled, the bars didn't move. Katniss would find a way out, she thought. But she was neither as brave nor as clever as her heroine.

Hugging herself, she focused on the creepy chanting that floated through her prison. Although the words were alien to her, they still raised the hair on her arms.

"Francois, are you down here?" a male voice echoed off the damp walls.

Isobelle pressed her face against the iron. If the man saw her, he would surely free her, or at least tell the police.

Footsteps resonated through the dungeon, and seconds later expensive leather shoes stopped in front of her kennel. "Francois?" the man in the black suit hissed. "Where are you?"

The chanting died. "I'm right here, my friend." Scorpion Man's bare chest came into view. A weird symbol composed of lines, arrows, and circles covered most of his torso.

Isobelle glared at the creepy tattoo and wondered what it meant.

"Do you have it?" the other man asked impatiently.

"Absolument,*" Scorpion Man said, handing over a*

CD.

The man shoved the CD into a black leather bag that had the words Love Kids And Support PCAC embroidered on it. "Is that all?" He didn't sound happy.

"Oui, but," Francois cleared his throat, "we will have more. Bientot.*"*

"You better," the other one snarled, heading toward the exit.

Panic rushed through Isobelle. She couldn't let him go. He was her only hope of getting out. "Help." Her voice was weak, and she knew she had to grow some balls and raise it. "Please, help me!"

But he kept walking, never looking back.

****

So the bastard's real name is Francois, and the symbol on his chest happens to be the same one Hedwig had drawn on the floor. Call me crazy, but I don't believe in coincidence. My head swims with information. The symbol. Francois. PCAC. God, I feel like I'm missing something.

Isobelle tugs at my jacket. "Amanda," she whispers. "Don't send me back to that place." The black of her irises changes to a light brown and eventually to blue. "Please," she begs.

I don't think she deserves my pity after killing me, but no matter how hard I try, I just can't be mad at her. "We'll figure something out," I promise and mean it.

"Enough!" Tattoo Guy gets in my face. "I don't give a fuck about this stupid brat. Get me outta here now."

Is he for real? I don't mean to grin, but his stupidity doesn't give me much of a choice. "Get you outta here? Dude, you're dead."

The other spirits move closer. Shock transfixes their faces, or in half-face's case, what's left of it.

Tattoo Guy wraps his bony fingers around my neck. "Liar!" he yells, chocking the death out of me. "I'm not dead. But I will be if I don't deliver D's package."

"You stupid fuck," I croak as his fingers dig into my neck. "Your goddamn package is probably the reason all of you are here in the first place."

A flash of memory flickers across his face, and his grip loosens. "The shooting," he mutters. "I was on my way to D when they started shooting from the car." He lets go of me and runs a hand over the tattooed tear beneath his right eye. "Julio," he screams. "Fucking bastard shot me."

I raise my brows. "Do I look like I give a shit?" Isobelle is trapped in Purgatory, and I'm a dead witch. I couldn't care less about a fucktard who's responsible for the death of innocent people.

His eyes darken. I hate when spirits do that. "Get me outta here." He sounds so inhuman, even Isobelle steps back.

Jeez, where are the ghostbusters when you need them?

"And how am I supposed to do that, genius?" I cross my arms. "In case you haven't noticed, I'm just as dead as the rest of you."

The expression on Tattoo Guy's face changes into something incredibly dark. "You," he shouts, approaching me like a freaking beast. "Will." His fingers penetrate the skin on my chest and push toward my heart. "Help me."

Excruciating pain forces me to my knees. If I had known death would be this unpleasant, I'd have come up with an everlasting life spell by now.

Wait a second. I'm dead. I shouldn't even feel pain.

Isobelle's eyes widen as I flicker in and out of existence. "Amanda," she cries, but her voice sounds less like her and more like Alex.

"Amanda!" Wait that's Alex's voice.

What the fuck is happening?

Tattoo Guy continues to glare at me, but the morgue blurs. Shadows turn into light. Colors swirl around me like shooting stars, and the charged air electrocutes me.

"Amanda, open your fucking eyes." Alex sounds more desperate than ever.

"Step back."

Is that Dr. DaSilva?

Another burning sensation jolts through me, and I gasp for air.

Am I breathing? I draw more air in. Oh my God, I'm actually breathing.

"We have a heartbeat." Dr. DaSilva's voice thunders in my ears.

"Manda? Open your goddamn eyes!"

I'm dead. Didn't he get the message?

"Manda?" Alex's warm hand rests against my cheek. "If you can hear me, please." He trails off. "You can't die."

Now he cares? I focus all my willpower on my eyelids, but they weigh a fucking ton.

"Agent Bishop." Dr. DaSilva gently slaps my cheek. "Can you hear me?"

"Alex?" My throat is dry, my voice barely a whisper.

"I'm here." His hot breath beats against my cold face.

I blink my eyes open. "What happened?"

Eyes locked with mine, he rests a hand on my forehead. "You almost died."

"Actually," the doc says, his eyes drifting to the clock above the sliding door. "You did die." He wipes the sweat off his forehead. "Three minutes, Agent Bishop. That's a pretty long time without a heartbeat."

I push myself up on my elbows and look around. "You reanimated me on an autopsy table?"

Dr. DaSilva frowns. "It's not like we had much of a choice." A smile tugs at his lips. "Besides, who doesn't want to be resurrected on the autopsy table?"

Covering my bare chest, I make a face.

"Easy," Alex says as I sit up. He looks me over. "You scared the living shit outta me, Manda." He takes off his jacket and wraps it around my shoulders. "Don't you ever do that again, you hear me?"

Wiping the dried blood off my mouth and nose, I shrug. "Please, Alex. As if you care if I live or die."

His eyes darken. "Is that all you have to say?"

I shake my head and face the amazed doc. "The gang shooting downtown," I mutter.

"Yes?"

"Tell the cops to look for a guy named Julio."

"How do you know—"

"Just do it," I hiss as my feet connect with the floor.

Alex puts an arm around my waist to steady me. "Where do you think you're going?"

"The paramedics should be here any second," Dr. DaSilva announces.

I fake a smile. "I don't need the paramedics."

"Agent Bishop," he says, groaning. "Do I have to remind you your heart stopped beating?"

I hug the fabric of Alex's jacket closer to my chest and let my gaze drift over the body bags. "No, Dr. DaSilva. You don't."

"Amanda," Alex whispers. "What are you doing?"

I linger on Isobelle's lifeless body. "Whatever I have to."

Chapter 17

"How are you holding up?" Alex asks, unlocking my room at the Hacienda Hotel. We could be halfway back to Bakersfield by now, but the only way he let me dodge the paramedics was promising we'd stay here the rest of the night.

"Would you stop it already?" I get that he's worried, but he must have asked me that question a million times in the last hour, and frankly, I'm beginning to lose my patience. "I'm fine, Alex. Really." And that's the truth for a change. My spell backfired, I got a glimpse of Limbo, and Dr. DaSilva brought me back. No biggie.

Hand clenched around the doorknob, his gaze roams my face. "You don't look so good, Manda. Maybe you should have listened to the doc."

Great idea. "And spent the next few weeks in the hospital for no other reason than being labeled a medical freak? Yeah, I don't think so." Pushing past him, I switch the light on and stagger into the bathroom.

Alex leans against the doorframe. "What if your little trip to the otherworld generated permanent damage? Or worse, what if the bleeding comes back?" For a guy who claims he can shoot me in an instant, he wears a pretty depressing gray aura at the prospect of my final exit.

I press both hands against the sink and stare at my

fucked up reflection. Alex is right; I look more dead than alive. There's still evidence of the blood that cascaded from my nose and mouth.

"Amanda."

I face him.

"Did you even listen to me? You could die. Again." His gravelly voice sounds determined.

After a shitty day like this, I don't have the nerves to handle his overprotective, always-the-hero streak. Tilting my head to the side, I meet his intense gaze. "This wasn't your fault, Alex, so stop actin' as if you fuckin' killed me."

A faint pink infuses his aura, signaling I'm on the right path. "Sure it was," he says, looking worried. "You almost died because I forced you into this."

I laugh. "You don't get it, do you? I'm here because fate wanted me here." His lips part, but I keep going. "And I almost died because Isobelle blames me for her death, and you know what?" My voice breaks, but I regain control quickly. "She has a point. I should have known the bocor would sense me. I should have protected her. Instead, I took off because I was too weak to handle her emotions."

"Manda, this—"

"Don't." I hold up my hand, stopping him before he can finish what we both know will be a lie. "I'm a big girl. I can handle the truth, Alex." Turning on the faucet in the sink, I glare at the mirror. "Now, if you don't mind, I'd like some alone time."

He's reluctant, but knows better than to push me. "I'll be outside." He closes the door behind him.

Washing the guilt and blood off my face, I return to what's really important: freeing the kids, saving Jesse, and getting Isobelle out of Purgatory.

First thing's first.

Isobelle is safe for now. I haven't reversed the spell, which means her spirit is still in Limbo. Of course, Alex doesn't know that. Letting a vengeful spirit roam around won't exactly sit well with a hunter. But until I figure out how her soul can move to a child-approved afterlife, Limbo is where she's going to stay.

Jesse and the kids are a different story. Despite the visions, I still have no clue where to look for them. Since there's no such thing as a location spell, and I pretty much suck at dowsing, I'm seriously running out of magical options.

I dry my wet skin with a towel, glare at my trashed appearance, and think of the vision I had before Dr. DaSilva pulled me back. PCAC… PCAC… Why the fuck does that sound so familiar? When I thought the bocor had killed Isobelle because he was afraid she could blow their covers, I figured she had a location. That was wishful thinking, though. All she saw was a guy in a black suit with PCAC embroidered on his bag and the sigil on the bocor's chest. I'm trying real hard to see the bigger picture, but can't shake the feeling a piece of the puzzle is still missing.

I throw the towel in the sink and yank the door open. "Alex?"

A picture of misery, he's sitting on my bed. "Yeah?"

"Have you ever come across PCAC?"

The are-you-serious look on his face, he arches a brow. "Is that supposed to be a joke?"

"Do I look like I'm jokin'?"

Running a hand over his stubble, he pulls a face.

"Harpers Ferry? Mayor? Ring a bell?"

Oh. My. Gosh. Jamie. I smack my forehead. How the hell could I have forgotten that? Rushing toward the bed, I grab my iPad from the nightstand and double-click the home button.

"What's going on?" Alex asks, voice thick with worry as he stares at my trembling hands.

"Not sure yet." But if I can trust the thrilling sensation that roars through my guts, I would say I'm onto something. "Siri, Google Harpers Ferry Mayor Death."

"Searching Google for Harpers Ferry Mayor Death." What can I say? Siri is a girl's best friend, especially when her hands are way too shaky to type.

Alex, now behind me, peeks over my shoulder. "Would you please tell me why you're looking up the death?"

I ignore the question and follow a link that leads me to the same *Harpers Times* article Alex held under my nose a couple of days ago. Like a freaking machine, I scan the words. "Damn, I knew it!"

"What?" Alex's face is a canvas of confusion.

"Look at this," I say, pointing to the article.

His gaze flies over the words. "The popular mayor and founder of the Prevent Crimes Against Children (PCAC) Foundation, James McKenzie, 41, died earlier this week at his idyllic Harpers Ferry home." Still at sixes and sevens, he looks up. "Why am I reading this again?"

I turn the iPad around. "Was bleeding from mouth and nose," I quote. "Doesn't that sound familiar?"

A wave of annoyance floods the room. "What are you getting at?"

Hugging myself, I shake my head. "Isobelle was killed because she saw a guy in the dungeon who had PCAC embroidered on his bag. PCAC happens to be the organization founded by a pedophile, who happened to die in the exact same unnatural way as Isobelle. This isn't coincidence, Alex. It's a freakin' pattern."

"Or," he sighs as his hand fists around his wild hair. "You used the same spell on the mayor as the bocor did on Isobelle. And the PCAC thing is just happenstance."

Even when the facts are laid out in front of him, he'd rather blame me than consider the option I'm not a cold-blooded assassin. Hell, why am I even surprised? To Alex, I'll always be the evil witch-bitch.

My blood boils. "I didn't kill the freakin' mayor."

"Look, Manda." His gaze drops to the floor, and he draws a deep, long breath. "I want to believe you, God knows I do, but wherever you go, death follows." Unable to look me in the eye, he shakes his head. "Our deal stands. Help me find my brother, and I will let you walk. Even if you did kill the guy."

I jump the first four stages of grief and fall right into crazy-ass rage. "What is wrong with you, Alex?" I advance toward him like a psychopath. "Does your hate for me run so deep it corrupts every sense of reality?"

My quick heartbeat and the raw anger that bolts through me makes the world around me swim. Feeling nauseous, I stumble back, tripping over my own feet. "Whoa!" Alex shouts, grabbing my elbows and catching me just before I fall. "What the fuck, Amanda?"

I try to pull away, but his grip is too firm. "Don't you fuckin' what-the-fuck me."

Cupping my elbows, he leads me to the bed. “Sit.”

“I don’t want to—”

“Now,” he orders, forcing me down.

I feel miserable. My vision is blurred, my head hurts, and my heart celebrates Carnival in Rio. Maybe I should have seen a doctor after all.

I use the back of my hand to wipe the cold sweat off my forehead as Alex sits next to me. “All right.” His eyes lock with mine. “Let’s say I believe you.” I give him a look, but he ignores it and continues, unimpressed. “Then what you’re saying is PCAC is a cover up for a child pornography ring. That right?”

I haven’t really thought that far, but it sounds pretty damn reasonable. “Makes sense, doesn’t it?”

His aura radiates suspicion. The faint traces of blue in it, though, suggest he’s trying to keep an open mind. “There’s just one huge flaw in your theory.”

Leaning back on my elbows, I try to get my stubborn heart under control. “Which is?” I ask, focusing on my breath.

Alex’s physical and mental exhaustion weakens his voice. “Why would the bocor kill the founder of the organization?”

That I might know. I straighten and pull the rubber band out of my hair. “A day before the mayor died, his wife and daughter showed up at one of my readings. The second the kid walked in, I knew what the bastard had done to her.”

Alex raises a brow. “And?”

I bite the edge of my lower lip. “She threw ten thousand dollars in my face and asked me to kill her husband.”

“I knew it.” Disappointment tugs at his heart, and I

can tell he's back on the "she's a killer" track.

"No," I say, meeting his gaze. "You really don't. I threw her out, but you should have seen the look on the girl's face. I was her last hope. And I don't know…" I break off.

"You couldn't turn your back on her?" he asks more softly than before.

"The bastard had been raping her since she was six, and he would have never stopped."

Running a hand over his three-day beard, he frowns. "So you killed him?"

Averting my gaze, I shake my head. "No, but in retrospect, I think I am the reason he bit the dust."

Squinting, he studies me. "Explain."

I close my eyes and let the memories of that day wash over me.

****

Mother of the Year stood in the corner. "Please, isn't that enough?" she said, her voice trembling.

"What?" I barked, my index finger still pressed to Jamie's forehead. "Does the fact you've never attempted to save your little girl suddenly nag at you?"

Jamie had to re-live four years of abuse. It's not like that could have been done in a minute. I had to rewind her subconscious like an old VHS cassette and outsmart the natural defense mechanism in her brain at the same time.

"I-I…" she stammered, but I silenced her with my death glare.

Every inch of my soul wanted that ruthless bitch out of there. But Jamie needed an anchor. Someone she trusted. Even if that person didn't deserve her trust.

The kid's assaulted body shivered under my hand,

and I knew she was ready to dive deeper into her subconscious. Ready to face the night when this son of a bitch had conquered her body and soul.

"Listen to my voice, Jamie. Turn to your left, and you will see another door. It's right there in your room." I waited for the images to unfold in her mind's eye and then continued. "Now open the door. You're doing great. Ten steps will take you to a beautiful room. Follow them."

She did as I said and was back at the night that had changed her life forever. The night her father took away her faith in the world. "Don't, Daddy. Please, you're hurting me." She was sweating, crying, kicking. It was pure torture.

I wasn't the praying type, but then and there, I begged God to guide her through this, to save her from losing her mind. I knew it was a possibility. Messing with the subconscious was dangerous, and if I took it too far, she'd end up in a fucking loony bin.

"Jamie," I whispered in her ear as she fought through the worst night of her life. "I need you to listen to me, honey." The memory had her imprisoned, and she barely registered my voice. I closed my eyes and focused all my energy on her. "Jamie?"

Her shoulders twitched, and I knew she was listening.

"It doesn't matter what he says, honey. He's not allowed to touch you." I kept repeating the same damn thing until she relaxed a bit.

Good, I was getting through. "I want you to remember that feeling, Jamie. His hands on your skin. His breath on your face."

"No," she cried. "I don't want to." Although I had

sent her into a deep trance, part of her consciousness was still there. It desperately tried to protect her from the memories that could shatter her mind into pieces.

I drew a sharp breath. "Yes, you will, and whenever he comes too close, or as much as sets a foot in your room, this exact feeling will resurface. And you will remember my words."

Tears streamed down her cheeks. "I don't want to remember. I want to forget."

Here came the hardest part. "You can never forget, Jamie." I applied more pressure to her forehead. "But you can fight, and that's exactly what you're going to do when that feeling comes back. Do you hear me? You will pick up the phone, dial 911, and tell the operator what he did to you." Channeling her emotions drained me of all energy, but I cleared my throat and kept going. "Do you understand, Jamie?"

She didn't respond, but I felt her relaxing.

"And if there's no phone," I said, "you will scream for help as loud as you can."

"But the neighbors," Mother of the Year said.

If looks could kill, the woman would have died the worst death ever. "Shut up," I yelled. "Or I swear I will change my mind and kill you and your bastard of a husband. You hear me?"

Hugging herself, she stepped back and nodded.

I hated causing Jamie pain, but building a trigger in her mind was the only way to keep her safe. Her heartbeat slowed. "That's it, honey. Hold onto the fear, the pain, the anger. It'll help you defeat the monster."

I knew I had succeeded when she said, "He's a monster. Daddy is a monster."

****

For the first time since Alex learned I'm a witch, he doesn't look at me like I'm the devil reincarnated. "You think the bocor eliminated the mayor because whatever mojo you did on that kid would have sooner or later exposed him as a pedophile and put the organization under the scrutiny of the Feds?"

"It makes total sense, doesn't it?"

The synapses in Alex's brain work overtime. "Let's say you're right. What's in it for the bocor? I mean, you said it yourself. He never touched the kids."

"I don't know," I answer honestly. "But I'm pretty sure Hedwig has the answer to that question."

"Sweet-tea-offering-named-like-Potter's-owl Hedwig? Why's that?" If I didn't know better, I'd say Mr. I Hate Witches doesn't like the thought that the old woman could be involved.

"Call it a hunch," I say, pulling pen and paper out of my bag. "Your FBI pal is working on a list, right?"

Alex knits his brows. "Yeah, why?"

"Do you think he can narrow it down if we give him a profile?"

"Probably," he says. "But I've already told him what we know."

I'm not so sure about that. "Let's go through it again."

Wiping his palms on his jeans, he studies me with a weird look on his face as I jot down Bocor on one side of the paper and Clown Man on the other. "You really didn't kill the mayor?"

I shake my head.

His malachite eyes remind me of nightfall in a forest. "I'm sorry," he admits after a long pause. "I just—"

"You think I'm Satan's bride." I fake a smile. "And you were right, Alex. For a split second, I considered her offer."

"But you didn't do it."

I bite my lip. "I didn't. But we both know I'll never be the girl you so desperately want me to be."

He shifts closer, holding my gaze. "I'm not so sure about that, Manda."

My heart thunders in my ear, and I swallow hard. "Let's just focus," I suggest, pointing to the paper in my lap.

The sun is rising when I put the pen down and stretch my limp muscles. Alex slept through most of the night, and even though a little help would have been appreciated, I didn't have the heart to wake him.

His perfect body is spread over the length of the bed. I shake him a little. "Rise and shine, sleepyhead." Taking a last look at my notes, I wait for him to open his eyes.

Bocor

Francois

French speaking—French? Definitely born in a French-speaking country!

Scorpion tattoo on his hand.

Symbol on his chest—Hedwig?

Connection to PCAC—member of the foundation?

Goes by the name Baron Samedi.

Clown Man

Older

Pedophile—registered sex offender? Maybe accused during the Kern County child abuse cases?

Picks the kids—Local! Must know them or stalk them previous to their abductions.

Connected to the girl with the raven hair—is she Scarlet? Who is Scarlet? First victim?

Smell of roses—connection to the Kylie Minogue song—has a rose garden? Works with flowers? Florist?

The list is far from perfect, but it's all we've got.

"Have you been up all night?" Alex asks, his voice thick with sleep.

"Yep." I get up and throw the piece of paper on his chest. "It's time to call your FBI pal."

Chapter 18

Inhaling the scent of looming rain that wafts through the open windows of the Mustang, I dial Bonnie's number again.

"Did it ever occur to you she might not pick up on purpose?" Alex says, backing the black beast into a parking slot in front of Hedwig's house. Pulling a couple of *Fast and the Furious* stunts, he had managed to get us to Bakersfield within a little over an hour.

Ignoring his smartass comment, I press the phone against my ear, but like the other nineteen times, I go straight to voicemail. "Hot dudes with incredible sexual-healing skills and nice abs, leave a message. Racists, nuns, and bigots, go fuck yourself."

Un-freaking-believable. Twenty-four hours.

Freaking twenty-four hours, and still no word from her. Seriously, how long could it take for her to pick up a phone and call my not-so-beloved sister?

"Bonnie," I yell into the speaker. "Where the fuck are you? I swear to God, I'll put a no-sex hex on your ass if you don't call me ASAP."

One arm resting on the steering wheel and a cocky grin on his face, Alex ogles me. "There's no such thing."

Bugged, I throw the phone in my bag and look him in the eye. "Wanna bet your manhood on that?"

The stupid grin on his face diminishes. "And you

wonder why I hate witches," he grumbles, reaching for the door handle.

What can I say? We're a capricious species, and for a guy who's been buying the same brand of underwear since he was five, there's nothing worse than unpredictability.

Heavy clouds darken the sky as I step out of the car and stretch my saggy muscles. Lack of sleep and death have turned them into disgorged gum. "I so need a massage."

Cocking a brow, Alex leans against his car. "What, no spell for that?"

I roll my shoulders back and smile. "Why should I use magic if I have you?"

Pushing off the car, he shakes his head. "In your dreams, Manda."

The dreams in which feature Alex are less massage and more banging me against the wall or wrapping my legs around his poetic body while he screws my brains out. He doesn't need to know that, though.

Staggering toward the white fence, I almost expect Hedwig to come running, but she doesn't. Her beautiful garden is strangely deserted, and the wind chime that hangs from the ceiling in front of her door plays a crazy melody.

"What's the matter?" Alex asks.

A burning sensation spreads through my ankh tattoo as I open the garden gate. "I told you about the protective shield around Hedwig's house, remember?"

He nods.

"At the moment, it looks less like a shield and more like the fishnet pantyhose you hate so much."

He winces. Probably because the memory of that

fatal Halloween night one and a half years ago flickers across his mind's eye: us drinking, me wearing fishnet pantyhose, and him getting into a brawl. What a fun night that was.

"Maybe the spell wears off," he says, unable to look at me.

"Dunno, Alex." I glare at my itching wrist. "This house was the magical version of Fort Knox. Something tells me Hedwig ain't careless when it comes to protection."

One side of his mouth curves up. "Who's paranoid now?"

"Ha, ha, ha. Very funny."

Alex shrugs. "What goes around, comes around, Manda. You're the one who taught me that."

Being beaten at your own game kinda sucks. "Keep making fun of me," I say as we reach the door. "But I'm tellin' you, I have a bad feeling about this."

I'm ready to ring the bell, but Alex nudges me in the ribs. "Hey."

"What?"

"Go easy on her, okay?"

He wants me to play nice with a witch? I stare at him. "*Invasion of the Body Snatchers* or *The Exorcist*?"

He squints. "What?"

I tuck a strand of my rebellious hair behind an ear and cross my arms. "For you to be nice to one of my kind, you must either be possessed or taken over by aliens. So which is it?"

Alex's brows go up. "Just ring the bell," he orders, annoyed.

And that's what I do. Several times.

"Seems like no one is home," Alex says. "Maybe

we should come back later."

Or she's pretending not to be home because she knows what's coming for her. Fisting my hands, I bang on the door. "Hedwig!"

Nothing.

"I know you're home," I shout. "Open the door!"

But she doesn't.

Alex scans the area. "Keep your voice down," he warns.

Voice down, my ass. I hammer against the door like a lunatic. "Hedwig, open the goddamn door!"

"Can I help you?" I flinch at the sound of the high-pitched voice of Hedwig's neighbor. Miss I-wear-Valentino-shoes-and-a-Victoria-Beckham-dress-and-act-like-the-queen-of-Bakersfield leans over the white fence, looking at us suspiciously.

"Sorry about the noise, ma'am." Alex's lips curl into a mesmerizing smile. "We're looking for Hedwig, but she won't answer the door, and my friend is a little worried." Alex can be very charming. That is, if he's talking to someone other than me.

Playing with her thick, brown, fishbone braid, she eyeballs him from head to toe. Thank God, he's still wearing a suit. "I'm afraid I haven't seen her today, but I'm sure she's fine." The smile on her face is faker than the fakest thing in Faketown.

Enough small talk. I glare at Alex. "Open the door."

The lips of the hoity-toity neighbor with her nose in the air form a shocked *O*. "You can't just trespass," she says, hand pressed against a hip.

"Watch me," I snarl, voice razor-sharp.

Miss Perfect's jaw drops open, and she stumbles

backward.

Alex approaches her carefully. "I'm sorry. My friend here," he says, shooting me a sidelong glance, "is very impulsive."

"Impulsive," she mocks, arms crossed. "I think rude would be more appropriate."

That's it. I've had about enough of her attitude. "Aren't there any cookies you should be baking?" I snap.

"Manda." Alex pinches my arm. "Drop the bitch act."

Miss Perfect raises her brows. "You should go now," she orders, sounding more confident than she looks.

"And you should mind your own fuckin' business," I say matter-of-factly.

Alex grabs my elbow and pulls me closer. "Drop it, Amanda."

I pull out of his grip and glare at him. "Just open the goddamn door, Alex."

Miss perfect slowly retreats to her porch. "I think I'm going to call the cops."

"Wait." Alex walks toward her, hands in the air. "I know she's acting like a crazy person, but Hedwig had some heart issues lately. For all we know, she could be lying on the bedroom floor." His soothing tone, along with the perfectly sane explanation for my behavior, makes an impact.

The lines around Miss Perfect's eyes deepen. She seems almost concerned. "Oh my goodness." She cups her chin. "I had no idea. She never said anything."

Alex draws in a deep breath. "Why don't you call the cops while we try to find a way into the house?" he suggests.

My jaw drops, and I'm about to ask him if he's lost the last bits of his fucking mind, when nose-job-from-next-door nods. "Of course."

The second she's gone, Alex seizes hold of my arm, pulling me toward the door. "What's wrong with you?" he hisses.

"With me?" I laugh, throwing my head back. "What's wrong with you, Alex? You're the one who told her to call the cops when all you had to do was pull out your badge."

He shakes his head. "Don't turn this on me because you couldn't keep your stab-worthy, provoking mouth shut," he says, voice low. "We agreed to keep a low profile, and she didn't strike me as the kinda woman who keeps quiet when the FBI shows."

He has a point. My fucking temper almost screwed this up, but women like her instantly flip my bitch switch. So much attitude, yet spineless, just like my sister. I drop my arms. "If you're done preaching, how about picking the fuckin' lock, Alex?"

"You watch way too many movies," he says, turning the doorknob to the left. Of course, the door swings open.

Pushing past him like a woman on a mission, I stomp into the living room. "Hedwig?"

A full cup of tea rests on the ebony coffee table in front of the couch, and an episode of *Ghost Adventures* flickers across the old-fashioned monstrosity of a TV. But the woman is nowhere to be seen.

Alex's gaze drifts around the room. "Weird," he murmurs, his aura suspicious.

"What's weird?"

He reaches for the Beretta in his waistband. “Stay put. I’m going to take a look around.”

I’m all set to give him a lecture about emancipation and the fact that I can very well take care of myself, but he’s out of the room before I even get a chance to say, “Kiss my ass.”

I examine the room. Nothing seems out of the ordinary until I realize the wind chimes are gone and the symbols have been smeared.

Within seconds the temperature in the room drops, and the wooden floorboards behind me creak. “Amanda,” an icy waft of air whispers.

Stomach seizing, I slowly turn around. “Who the hell are you?”

What happens next is obscure, and I watch in utter horror. “Where the Wild Roses Grow” bursts through the speakers of the unplugged 50s radio. Walls crack. Glass shatters. Roses scatter on the floor.

“Amanda?” Alex’s voice is distant.

An antique cabinet next to the door shakes. A drawer flies through the room like a freaking fighter jet, and a photo frame lands in front of my feet.

“Amanda, what’s going on?” Alex’s voice is closer now.

I want to answer. Really, I do. But my eyes are glued to the photo on the floor, my jaw is somewhere down around my knees, and my voice took a vacation. What in God’s name? I blink several times, but the girl from my vision continues to smile at me. The one Hedwig had been so certain would lead us to Jesse. Standing in front of a lake house in a polka-dotted bathing suit, she has one arm around Hedwig and the other on the shoulder of a man with hollow blue eyes and grayish hair.

I pick up the photo and rub my eyes. Yep, I'm one hundred percent sure. This is the girl with the raven hair. My skin crawls, and the hair on my neck stands. Why didn't Hedwig say she knew the girl?

"What the hell happened in here?" Alex hollers, gun still drawn, looking over the mess. "Amanda, what the fuck did you do?"

My lips move, but not a single word comes out.

His warm hand squeezes my shoulder. "Manda, talk to me."

"She knew her," I croak.

"What? Who?"

"The girl from my visions. The one with the raven hair," I say, passing him the photo. "Hedwig knew her."

The instant Alex touches the wooden frame, a howling wind blows through the room. A fraction of a second later, gray smoke appears next to the antique cabinet.

He swallows hard. "Damn, is that…"

"A ghost? I'm afraid so."

Alex scans the room for a weapon. "Get the iron bar," he orders, pointing to the fireplace.

My last run-in with a child-spirit didn't exactly end well for me, but there's something about her that tells me she's not here to hurt us. I rub my sweaty palms on my jeans. "Relax, she's not vengeful," I assure him, walking toward the apparition.

"Follow me," she whispers.

And I do.

Alex is next to me in no time. "Christ, what the hell do you think you're doing, Manda?"

"Following my gut," I reply.

"Down there," the spirit says as the knob of the basement door turns and the door sweeps open.

I look down the stairs, but it's pitch black. Chills travel down my spine. Something's wrong. I smell trouble.

"You're fucking crazy," Alex yelps. "Couple of hours ago, you were almost killed by a spirit, and now..." He trails off.

And now I'm about to follow one into a basement that is darker than night itself. Yeah, I am nuts for real, but I'm okay with that. "You can stay here if you want," I say before I head down the stairs.

The hunter wouldn't be heroic if he didn't follow.

The steps wail under my weight, and my heart beats faster than Usain Bolt's while running the hundred meters. I would never admit it, not even under torture, but I'm glad Alex is right behind me. I feel safer with him there. Warmer.

Hell, it's so damn dark I can't see my hand in front of my face. Digging in my bag for my phone, I take another step and trip over a large object. My knees and hands connect with the floor. A sharp pain jolts through me.

"Manda?" Alex shouts. "Are you okay?"

Getting back on my feet, I wipe wet palms on my jacket.

"Amanda, say something." His voice roars through the basement.

"I'm good," I assure him. "Stumbled over something." The question is what?

The metallic clicking of the Beretta's safety lock being removed echoes off the walls. "Don't move," he commands. "I'm gonna find the light switch before you break your goddamn neck."

"Wouldn't that be the answer to all your prayers?" I snap, running a hand over the ripped fabric around my knee.

"Oh c'mon, isn't the you-almost-killed-me card getting old?"

My lips curl into a smile. "Nope. Never," I say as the lights come on.

Standing on the other side of the basement, Alex looks at me. I literally see the life draining from his face. He strides toward me. His aura is a mixture of shock and fear. "Amanda, don't freak, but I think you're bleeding."

I'm what?

Alex examines my bloody palms. "Are you hurt?" Worry thickens his voice. "Manda, did you hurt yourself?'

I don't know. Did I? My hands, my jeans, my shoes, they're crimson red. But there's no wound, no pain. Just lots of blood.

What the…

I spin around. A large pool of blood tickles into the floor by the stairs. Something that looks a lot like linguine ai frutti di mare is scattered all over the cement, and in the midst of it all is Hedwig. With a fucking hole in her head.

Running toward the bloated body, Alex curses under his breath.

It's a good thing I haven't eaten anything, because what I see turns my stomach upside down. Hands folded in a praying position, eyes glazed and lips stitched together with black thread, the old woman is decomposing on the floor. A scene right out of a fucking *Saw* movie.

I know Alex's hand is on my shoulder, but I'm too numb to feel it. "Wh-what happened here?" I stammer.

Kneeling next to me, Alex points at the wall. "Looks like someone was trying to send you a message."

I slowly lift my gaze and read *Stay Out Of This, Witch, Or You Will Be Next!* Of course, the artist used blood. If it weren't Hedwig's, I'd probably laugh at the cliché.

Dumbstruck, I look from Hedwig to the message. This is a nightmare. Stuff like this only happens in movies or books. Not in real life.

"What's that?" Alex asks, pointing to a shiny, silver chain wrapped around the old woman's praying hands.

I swallow the urge to puke. "Dunno."

Hedwig's bones crunch like cornflakes when he pulls it out of her grip, stiffened by rigor mortis. "Fuck," he whispers, holding a silver ankh pendant between his thumb and index finger.

My heart pumps faster than ever. I know this necklace. Worse, I know who it belongs to.

****

Mister Sinister's nose bled, and he moaned in pain. He had his back pressed against a brick wall, but his crazy eyes were fixated on me. "I'll kill you, bitch. I'll fucking kill you." The guy was the equivalent of a human parrot. "You're dead," he said. "Both of you."

He meant what he said, but I didn't... No, I couldn't waste my time on him. Hell, I had bigger fish to fry. The witch hunter with the mesmerizing eyes still stood in front of me, his gaze traveling over my body.

"Why the hell are you walking all by yourself in the middle of the night?" he asked, voice hoarse and sexy as hell.

I didn't reply. I was too busy forging a plan to get as far away from him as possible without being burned at the stake.

"Sweetheart," he hissed. "Do you hear me?"

Loud and clear.

"Alex?" Another voice floated through the starless night. "Dude, where the hell are you? I've got us a room with Pay-per-view TV and the Asian babes are on."

Alex, or hunter, or whatever his name was, turned around. "I'm here."

Out of the shadows stepped a taller, but slightly younger version of the hunter. Drinking in his appearance, I had no doubt these two were related and possibly gods in disguise. Same hair color. Identical sharp face structures. Bodies to freaking die for.

"Whoa," the younger one said with a boyish grin as he came closer. "Why didn't you tell me you had a date with Miss America? I would have gladly given you the key to our room."

"I don't do threesomes," Alex said, pointing to the asshole on the ground.

"I'm going to kill y'all," Mister Sinister said, wiping blood off his nose.

The younger guy, whose aura also revealed fifty shades of hunter, cocked a brow at Mister Sinister and laughed. "Buddy, knowing my brother, you're lucky you're still breathing."

Alex was still worried. "Seriously, are you all right? Did he hurt you?"

The question snapped me out of my pathetic delirium. I forced my spine upright and crossed my arms. "I was fine until you stuck your nose in business that doesn't concern you." The bitch switch had turned, and I was just getting started. "Who do you think you are? Captain freakin' America?"

The younger hunter stepped closer, the moon casting light on his chocolate-colored eyes. "Damn," he said. "Where did you find this one? I like her already."

"Found her in time to save her from this jerk," Alex replied with a cocky-as-hell grin.

Lava flooded my system, and I got right into his god-like face. "You saved me?" My laughter echoed off the brick walls. "Look, I know you have this whole knight in shining armor fantasy going in your head, but I'm not a damsel in distress, and I sure as hell don't dig your Prince Charmin' shit."

"I take it back," Chocolate-eyes said. "I don't like her. I fucking love her." He flashed me a brilliant smile. "I'm Jesse, and this," he pointed at hunter-heroic, "is my brother, Alex."

"Amanda," I muttered, still not sure why I hadn't run yet.

Jesse put an arm around me as if we were old hunting buddies. "How about I buy you a drink, and you keep dissing my brother?"

Alex shook his head. "I bet she's got somewhere to be."

I should have walked away. I should have told him his brother was right, but I didn't. Challenging my inner bitch never ended well. "Actually." I faced the jerk with the most beautiful eyes I had ever seen. "She *would be delighted to join you."*

"Awesome," Jesse said, directing me out of the alley.

Not sure if it was his open-minded baby-blue aura, the fact that he liked me for being a bitch to his brother, or the silver ankh pendant hanging around his neck, but I kinda liked this dude.

****

Sirens blare like hellhounds, and I push the memory away. Jumping to my feet, I grab Alex by the shirt. "We gotta go."

He didn't move. "He killed her," he says, not taking his eyes off the silver necklace that swings between his thumb and index finger. "Jesse killed her."

"You don't know that," I say softly as the shrill sound grows louder.

Empty eyed, he looks up. "Yes. Yes, I do."

Chapter 19

Paramedics, officers, and crime scene investigators—the cozy Victorian crawls with people. “Man, this shit is getting weirder by the second. First the abductions, and now this.” Even without looking, I know the rookie cop behind me is pointing to the smeared voodoo symbols. “Ever thought we might be dealing with a satanic cult?”

“Dude, didn’t you pay attention at our last seminar? Satanic killer cults don’t exist,” his partner explains proudly.

“Yeah, well, how about you tell that to the woman downstairs whose brain is sprinkling the walls?”

Officer Know-It-All sighs. “Killer cults are a myth. Satanic serial killers, however, are very real.” A hundred bucks says he got that from a *Criminal Minds* episode.

“Don’t know, man,” the other one whispers. “Call me crazy, but I doubt it’s a coincidence that *X-Files* over there found the body.”

X-Files, or in other words, Alex, stands across the room next to Detective Good-Looking. “It’s too late to run,” he says. “Don’t worry, I got this covered,” he assures me. Guess what? While I’m stuck under the scrutiny of a grumpy detective who watches too many *Homicide Hunter* episodes, Alex is having a nice little chat with the dude’s partner. Way to go, Alex.

"Miss Bishop, are you still with me?" Intense charcoal eyes stare at me.

Shifting my attention from the two rookie cops behind me to the older detective in front of me, I let out a frustrated breath. "I'm right here."

"Good." His raspy voice has the same effect as fingernails on a chalkboard. "Then please answer my question."

Question. Right. What was it again? Have you ever seen a unicorn? No. Would you date Bart Simpson? No. Ah, now I know. It's the same damn question he's asked me about a million times. "No," I say, moaning. "There was nothing out of the ordinary. Hedwig didn't open the door, and when we walked in to check on her, we found this." I point to the fucked up room.

Alex and I had agreed to stick to the initial story, and while we had most officers convinced we'd walked into this mess for no other reason than being responsible citizens who cared for their elders, the aura of Detective Grumpy told me he didn't buy the story.

"Right," he muttered. "Tell me again how you know Hedwig Beauchamp?"

I saw the protective shield around her house and knew she was a witch.

I let my head fall against the back of the soft flowered sofa. "She is—" Clearing my throat, I correct my mistake. "She *was* a friend of my grandmother's."

Tapping his thick fingers against Hedwig's ebony table, he arches a brow. "I see. And you're grandmother's name was," he stares at the notebook in his lap, "Caroline Bishop?"

"Yes."

Shifting to the edge of his armchair, he pulls one

side of his mouth up. "How come Hedwig never mentioned her?"

Feeling like the main suspect in a stupid crime show, I realize two things: A) Detective Grumpy is like a pit bull, and B) he takes this case personally because he probably knew Hedwig. Awesome. Next time Alex asks me to trust him, I'll run.

"They hadn't seen each other in ages, but since I was in town, I thought I would drop by to tell her Grams died four years ago," I explain.

"Hmm," he mumbles, jotting down each and every word. "One more question, Miss Bishop."

That's what he said two hours ago.

"Why did you go into the basement? You could have waited for the cops."

Oh, you know, the spirit of the little girl who led me down the stairs probably figured I was more capable of solving this crime than you.

Rubbing my temples, I swallow the annoyance that's pricking at me. "The basement door was ajar, and since my friend over there," I point to Alex who's now looking at me, "is an FBI agent, I asked him to check it out."

"And that's when you fell into her blood?"

Oh, for the love of God. Unable to hold back my anger, I jump up. "No! I shot her and thought it would be fun to wear her blood as a trophy. Isn't that what you want to hear? Seriously, this is ridiculous. The whole interview is a waste of time. I mean, shouldn't you be out there looking for her killer?"

A deadly silence creeps over the room. Everyone freezes, and all eyes are on me. It only takes a second until Alex is next to me. A calming hand on my shoulder, he faces Detective Grumpy. "Is everything, okay?"

"No," I say, pointing to the d-bag. "I've answered all his goddamn questions, and he still thinks I'm some kind of Natural Born Killer."

Alex frowns. "Calm down, Manda. The man's just doing his job."

His job? He's supposed to be out there looking for a freaking serial killer and a bunch of abducted kids. "I doubt that."

Detective Grumpy rises from the armchair, pulls a handkerchief out of his pocket, and wipes his mouth. "You know the drill, Agent Remington. I have to ask these questions."

"I know," Alex says, hands in his pockets. But when his eyes find mine, he understands if he doesn't get this douche off my back, I'll lose it, and that could get us into real trouble. Stepping toward the man, he points to the door. "Can I talk to you, Detective Titcher?"

The muddy brown aura around the guy tells me he'd rather eat the glass shards on the floor than leave me without supervision.

"In private," Alex adds when he senses his hesitation.

Detective Good-looking steps between d-bag and me. "It's all right, Rick. I've got this."

A frown on his face, Titcher follows Alex to the front door, leaving me with his partner. "I'm sorry for your loss, Miss Bishop." Now that's more like it. His words are sincere, his aura says compassionate, and his looks tell me he's the kinda cop who uses his handcuffs in his free time. Bring it on, baby.

I shrug. "Thanks, but I didn't know her that well."

"Still. It's hard to stumble—" He cuts himself off and glares at my blood-soaked clothes. "I mean…it must be terrifying to walk into such a horrific scene."

He has no idea how horrific that scene truly was. Between finding Hedwig and snapping Alex out of his trance-like state, we had two minutes until the cops showed, and while Alex hid Jesse's pendant, I'd wiped off the message on the wall. Or at least I tried to make it un-readable.

"I've seen worse," I whisper, thinking of Isobelle. The second he squints, I realize my mistake and mutter a lame excuse. "On TV."

"I understand." Sitting on the sofa, he pats the empty spot next to him. "Why don't you take a seat?"

Glaring at him, I shake my head. "Thanks, but your partner kept me sitting long enough."

A faint smile on his lips, his gaze drifts to the door. "He's—"

"A douchebag?"

"I was gonna say old-school, but I guess douchebag does the job."

I run a hand over my tired face and find myself smiling at the handsome detective with the pale gray eyes. "Did he know Hedwig?"

He nods. "They go way back. He was the leading detective on Scarlet's case."

"Scarlet?" My eyes go wide with curiosity. Without wanting to, I take a seat next to him.

"Scarlet Griffin. She was the grandchild of Hedwig's ex-husband, Walter," he explains, a wave of emotions flickering across his eyes. "Real sad story. Kid drowned in Lake Isabella, and her father, John, vanished the same day. Guess it was too much for Hedwig and Walter's relationship. They got a divorce and from what I heard, never spoke again." He averts his gaze. "It's what losing a kid does. Fucks up the best of us."

My head reels. Scarlet was Hedwig's step-grandchild? What the fuck is going on here? "And why was there an investigation?" I ask, knowing there's more to the story than a missing person's case and a drowned child.

"Well," he says, running a hand over his short-cropped cop hair. "I wasn't around in 1983, but from what I've heard, people thought Scarlet's death wasn't an accident. Back then the county was hunting demons. You know, satanic child abusers, Freddy Kruegers, that sort of crap."

"The Kern County child abuse cases?"

"Yep, the infamous twentieth-century witch hunt. Goes without saying what people thought when John disappeared after Scarlet's body was found floating in the lake. Everyone, including Walter, was convinced he had killed her to cover up his doings."

This is starting to get interesting. "What about this Walter guy? Wasn't he a suspect?" If there's one thing I've learned watching all those true crime stories, it's that the ones closest to the victim are always on top of the suspect list.

Lowering his voice, he shakes his head. "Walter is a good friend of Detective Titcher. He was the one who told Titcher he had caught John," he struggles with the next words, "doing some sick stuff to the girl."

You gotta be kiddin' me! Didn't these guys ever read the "How-to-solve-a-crime" handbook? Damn, they're cops. They should know blaming others to get their necks out of the noose is second nature with criminals. "Does he still live in Bakersfield?"

"Walter Griffin?" he asks with a genuine smile.

I nod.

Getting to his feet, he points to the roses scattered all over the floor. "He owns a flower shop nearby."

I think of the list I'd made for Carter. Florist. Check. Knows Scarlet, aka the girl with the raven hair. Check. Local. Check. This Walter dude fits the profile perfectly. He has to be Clown Man.

"Are you okay?"

I don't know. My head pounds, and my ass is vibrating.

"Miss Bishop?" Concern fills his voice.

"Yeah, I'm good," I murmur as I pull my phone out of my back pocket. Bonnie. Great. *Now* she's calling?

"It's okay," the detective assures me. "You can take the call, just," his gaze drifts to the door where Alex and d-bag cop are having a heated discussion, "don't go too far. We need to take your prints."

Prints?

As if he'd heard my thoughts, he bends his head to the side and smiles. "Don't worry. It's a common process. We need to eliminate yours to get the un-sub's."

Un-sub…Jesse…shit! What if he had killed Hedwig? Would Alex be able to cover this up? Having buddies at the FBI might help, but what if they refuse to cover up a murder? Would Jesse end up in jail for a crime he committed as a brainless zombie?

"Miss Bishop." Detective Good-looking's gaze

roams my face. “Are you sure you’re all right? Maybe the paramedics should have a look at you.”

I force a smile. “I’m good. Just have a real bad headache.” Or in other words, a real fucked up day. “Excuse me,” I say, holding up my vibrating phone. When he nods, I head straight to the kitchen.

Leaning against the marble countertop, I push the green button and press the phone against my ear. “I reckon you got my message.”

“Yes.” She sighs. “And before you go all witch-bitch on my ass, you should know your sister was less than helpful. She, and I quote, ‘Refuses to be a part of your self-destructive, selfish, suicide mission.’ Took me ages to talk some sense into her. Stubborn runs in the DNA, I guess.”

“Just tell me if you found—” I cut myself off and scan the room to make sure no one is nearby. “A cure.”

“I did,” she says, voice low. “But you should know there’s a catch. Your grandmother never tried the recipe.”

Peeking through the kitchen door, I see two coroners carry Hedwig out of the basement in a body bag. “Spill it, B. What do I need?”

“Whoa, what’s with you? Did Alex rub you the wrong way?”

I clench my jaw. “Bonnie.” There’s an unspoken threat in my tone, and she hears it.

“Physostigmine,” she eventually says. “You need to inject the zombie with it.”

“And that’s it?” My doubt is loud and clear.

“Yeah, according to your gram’s grimoire, bocors use devil’s breath to make their victims compliant. The physostigmine should reverse the effect of the drug. But as I said, it's just a theory."

Chipping the remaining nail polish off my nail, I draw a deep breath. "Guess it's time to put her theory to the test, hm?"

"Amanda." Bonnie's voice changes into a tired mumble. "I hate to say this, but I think Melinda has a point. What if the cure doesn't work? What if something happens to you? Think about L—"

"Leave him out of this."

"But—"

"I gotta go," I snap as the wooden floorboards creak under Alex and Titcher's weight. Ending the call, I rest my hip against the cool marble and wait for them with a fake smile on my lips.

"Important call?" the douchebag asks.

Facing him, I shrug. "Just my roommate," I answer honestly, figuring fewer lies are better with Titcher.

"I see," he grumbles. "Well, your friend will take you to the station. As soon as we get your official statement and your prints, you're free to go."

Awesome. The translation of that is an eternity of questions and disgusting police coffee. Exactly how I want to spend the rest of the day.

"C'mon." Alex puts an arm around my shoulders, directing me out of the room. "The sooner we get there, the faster we're done."

We're almost out of the house when Titcher's raspy voice stops us. "Miss Bishop?"

I spin around, ready to scratch his eyes out. There's something about this guy that turns my stomach upside down. "Yes?"

"You can't leave Bakersfield. Understood?"

I understand I want to stick your head in your ass,

douchebag. “Stay in Bakersfield. Don’t go to the university. Fuck up your life. Got it, Detective Witcher.”

“It’s Titcher,” he corrects me.

I smite my forehead. “Sorry, Detective Bitcher.”

Alex pulls me out of the house. “Are you crazy? He already thinks you’ve got something to do with Hedwig’s death.”

Yanking my arm out of his grip, I straighten. “Seriously, do I wear an invisible assassin tattoo on my forehead?”

“Must be your charm, Manda.”

“Jerk,” I snap, heading toward the gate.

“Wait.” He wraps his fingers around my wrist. “Put this on.” Taking off his jacket, he points to my blood-soaked clothes. “Because right now you look like a serial killer.”

I’m not the kinda chick that digs gentleman-like behavior, but walking through a crowd of curious bystanders with Hedwig’s blood all over me isn’t exactly on my bucket list. Choking out a lame, “Thanks,” I hug the fabric against my shivering skin and hurry to the car.

I use the ride to the police station to fill Alex in on what I’ve learned so far: the cure, Scarlet, and Walter Griffin, and Hedwig’s connection to them. I tell him everything, and he listens patiently.

Everything?

Okay, maybe I forgot to mention a tiny detail, but Alex is worried enough as it is. Telling him the cure isn’t a sure thing wouldn’t do him any good. So, yeah, I tell him everything he needs to know.

Chapter 20

Fingerprinted, interrogated by a guy who could easily reprise Bruce Willis's *Die Hard* role, and on the brink of a mental breakdown, I'm more than happy when we finally pull into the parking lot at the motel. I would have totally put a hex on Titcher's ass, but spending time in this hellhole, aka interrogation room, gave me enough time to come up with a plan. Get the physostigmine. Torture good old Walter into telling the truth. Kill the bocor, and save Jesse and the kids. Easy peasy.

"I've got Walter Griffin's address," I say, eyes glued to the iPad in my lap.

Alex doesn't even look at me. Jerk-face hasn't said a word since we got out of the station, and his self-blame is starting to mess with me.

"Earth to Mister I-Suffer-in-Silence."

No response.

"Hey!" I face him. "Did you hear me?"

"What?" He's annoyed.

"Walter Griffin. I have his address."

"Okay," he says.

Worried, I study him for a moment. "I'll take a shower, get rid of the blood, and then we need to," raising my voice, I highlight the next words, "break into a pharmacy."

Killing the engine, he looks out of the window to

the fading sun. "Okay."

"Alex." I put a finger under his chin, turning his face toward me. "I just told you we have to break into a pharmacy. Commit a felony. And all you have to say is 'okay'? What's going on?"

A weak smile on his lips, he averts his gaze. "Nothing. I'm just tired."

Depressed? Yeah. Frustrated? Definitely. Guilt-ridden? Absolutely. Tired? Not so much. "We have the cure, Alex. We can fix Jesse."

Yanking the door open, he nods. "I'll see you in a bit."

Awesome. I don't know what's worse, going against a bocor who killed two people and threatened to whack me next, or having to deal with a hopeless Alex.

He'll come around.

Hell, I hope so.

Staggering into my room, I strip down and step under the comforting, hot water. Rubbing the blood off my skin should feel good, but I can't seem to enjoy it. A few things just don't make sense. For starters, Hedwig's aura was brilliant purple. Nothing about her said she was part of a child pornography ring. Plus, if Walter really is Clown Man, and my gut says he is, then why would Hedwig divorce him if she had been a part of that shit? On the contrary, Hedwig lied to us. She could have ended this horror, prevented Isobelle's death. But she didn't. The woman also tried to keep spirits out of her house. Spirits like the one of Scarlet. Why would she do that unless she feared vengeance? Damn, what am I missing here?

Once the water runs clear, I wrap a towel around my exhausted body and step out of the shower. Glass cracks under my foot, and a sharp pain shoots through my leg. I look down. Blood drips on the broken picture frame lying on top of Alex's jacket, which I forgot to return.

What the fuck? I slide down the wall and take a seat on the floor. Pulling the glass out of my foot, I realize it's the photo from Hedwig's house. How the hell had that gotten here? Alex must have had it in his jacket. Pressing the towel on the bleeding cut, I pick it up.

Head pounds.

Heart races.

Hands shake.

And the bathroom fades into blankness.

****

"Scarlet?" John's voice echoed through the hallway. "Baby, where are you?" His throat was sore from calling her name, and he couldn't understand why she didn't reply. He also couldn't understand why his father had taken her to the lake house that late. If it weren't for Hedwig, he wouldn't even know where his little girl was.

Opening the door to his old room, he almost expected to find her asleep in the bed, but there was no sign of her. Where were they? He was grateful his father took care of her, especially since he worked long hours, and his boss didn't have a heart for single fathers. But he would have to talk to him about taking her on late-night trips.

"Dad?" He went to his parent's old bedroom. "Scarlet?" he called, bursting through the door.

The blood froze in his veins as the horror unfolded in front of his eyes. His little girl, his princess, lay on his father's bed, naked and bruised.

He rushed toward her and dropped down on his knees. Her raven hair barely covered her chest. "Scarlet, what...what happened?" he stammered, already knowing the answer.

She remained quiet.

"Scarlet, look at me," he begged.

But she couldn't. "I'm so sorry, Daddy," she whispered, tears streaming down her pale cheeks.

Seeing her like this killed him. How had this happened? And why had he not seen the terror in his angel's eyes? God, what kind of a father was he?

John brushed the hair out of her face and gently moved her head toward him. "Listen to me, baby girl. This is over. No one is ever going to hurt you again, I promise."

John's blue eyes were reassuring, but promises were meant to be broken. Hope was meant to be shattered. And when the baseball bat cracked her father's skull, she knew no one could save her. "Sorry you had to see this," her grandfather said, beating the last breath out of her father.

****

The lake house. That must be it. That's where they keep the kids.

Hobbling to the bed, I step into a pair of boyfriend jeans, pull an old T-shirt over my head, and rush to Alex's room.

I bang against the door like a crazy person, but it stays locked. "Alex!"

He doesn't answer. What the hell, dude?

Dialing his phone, I'm about to leave a nasty message on his voicemail when the hotel clerk's distant shout catches my attention. “Try the bar!”

I spin around and face the man whose office overlooks the entire motel. “What?” My hearing must be off.

“The bar,” he repeats. “He was headed there.”

I’m going to fuckin’ kill him!

Chapter 21

The clerk is either blind or drunk because there's no way Mr. Righteous and Responsible is hitting a bar while his brother goes all zombie assassin and a bunch of kids fear for their lives. Right? Wrong.

Bursting through the solid door of The Reckless Heart, I find him next to a brunette bombshell with a half-empty bottle of whiskey in his hand. Son of a bitch! What the hell is he thinking? Judging by the way he pulls the chick toward him, I'd say he isn't thinking at all. I cuss under my breath, ignore the pulsating pain that torments my foot, and push through the crowd, using elbows when necessary. One thing's for sure: I'm going to beat the fucking crap out of him. I mean, I get it. He had a rough day. But what about me? I almost died a couple of hours ago, was treated like a freaking murderer, and to cap it off, I'm stuck in this godforsaken town. So, if anyone has a reason to get drunk and screw around, it would be me.

"Manda," he says when he spots me, that cocky as hell grin on his stupid face. "So good to see ya, baby."

"Don't you fuckin' baby me," I hiss through gritted teeth. "What the hell are you doin', Alex?" I look from him to Miss I-love-to-nibble-on-your-ears.

"What's it look like?"

"Like you're getting your fuckin' ears pierced by that slut," I say.

"Hey," the future porn star shouts. "You can't let her talk to me like that."

I make a face unable to disguise the disgust washing over me. That's the kinda girl he digs when he's wasted? The sort who has a guy fight her battles for her?

Alex pats her back, but his eyes are on me. "Ah, don't mind her, honey. Manda is juuust…" His stupid grin intensifies. "Jealoussss."

I curl my hands into fists. *Relax, you can't kill him here. Too many witnesses.* I take a step toward the chick, because the next words are only meant for her. "He's right," I whisper. "I am a very, very jealous person." A psychotic smile on my lips that would send Michael Myers running, I step back.

"Oh my gosh!" Her gaze drifts to my bare feet. "Don't tell me you dated a freak like her."

Alex shrugs. "What can I say? I was young and needed sex."

I'm standing in the middle of a bar without shoes, but that doesn't give her permission to call me a freak. Done playing nice, I get into the chick's face. "You look like a smart girl. How about you go and lick someone else's ear before I show you what a freak I really am?"

Her jaw drops. "You're crazy." She faces Alex, eyes clouded with fear. "She's fricking crazy."

Alex sips his whiskey and laughs. "Relax, she ain't gonna hurt you."

I smile. "Sure 'bout that?"

She grabs her bag from the table, throws her hair over her shoulder, and shakes her head. "Whatever. I'm out."

Watching her stomp out of the bar, Alex raises a brow. “So.” He takes another sip straight from the bottle. “Since you scared the shit outta my one-night stand, you could at least have the decency to have a drink with me.”

I can’t believe I’m saying this, but I already miss the old Alex. Taking a seat next to him, I rest my elbows on my knees. “All right, spill it. What’s the matter with you?”

He waves the question off. “Nothing. I’m just having a lil’ fun. Aren’t you always telling me I should loosen up?”

I might have said something like that, but I hadn’t meant for him to drown his last brain cells in whiskey while the lives of innocent people are at stake. “Look, I know you’re upset, but I think I found Jesse.”

“So?” He gulps down the booze as if it’s water.

So? Jesus fucking Christ, when did I become the responsible party in our screwed up partnership? Jumping up, I grab his shirt. “Let’s get the hell outta here, Alex. We have a zombie to cure and kids to save.”

Fire ignites in his eyes. “You can stop pretending, Manda.” He puts his hands on my hips and pulls me closer. “You don’t care about Jesse, these kids, or me. And you know what?” He grins. “It’s all right. You don’t have to. God.” He looks me over. “I wish I could be a little more like you. Reckless. Selfish. Careless. Life must be so much easier for you.” It’s a miracle he doesn’t fall from his chair, trembling and all that.

“You’re right, Alex. Life is easier that way, but it’s also lonelier.” I tug at his shirt. “Now, are we done with your self-pity? ’Cause last time I checked, you had a brother to save.”

He rests his forehead against my belly and sighs. "I hate you, Amanda. I hate everything about you, but," his warm fingers burn through my tank top, "I also miss you." He looks up. "I miss us." His aura shows a hundred shades of truth, and my heart jumps a little.

It's kind of hard not to believe him when he looks at me like I'm the only girl in the world. But he's in a hopeless place, looking for distraction, and I'm not willing to be that. I draw in a deep breath. "You're wasted, man." I try to pull him to his feet, but the son of a bitch is heavy. "C'mon, I'll take you to my room, and we'll sober you up."

"Your room, hm?" Cocky as hell grin is back. "Manda, Manda…you trying to seduce me?"

The vein in my left temple pounds like crazy. I bend down. The scent of whiskey lingers between us like an invisible line. "Two options, Alex: Either you get up, move your ass to my room, and we sober you up—"

"Lame," he croaks.

I silence him with a look. "Or you keep up this attitude, I drag your goddamn ass to my room, and beat the crap out of you until you come to your senses." I smile. "So, what's it gonna be, jerk-face?"

Hands still on my hips, he pulls himself up. "Option three." He's so close his lips brush my cheek. I have a hard time controlling the reaction his proximity has on me, and I ain't talking fireworks or butterflies. Hell, I'm talking hard nipples and a painful throbbing between my legs.

"Alex!" My voice has a deadly ring to it. "I'm not gonna say this again. Move."

"Don't you wanna know what option three is?"

"No."

I try to put his arm around my neck, but he pushes me away, knocking the chair over in the process. His sadistic laughter echoes off the walls and most heads in the bar turn to us.

"You're the biggest mistake of my life." His eyes grow darker, colder. "Fuck!" He scrubs his face. "We wouldn't even be here if I'd just walked away that night." He takes a deep breath and looks in my eyes. "This is your fault, not mine. Yours."

I don't see how any of this is my fault, but I do know I'm done with his reckless behavior. Oh. My. God. Did I really just say I'm done with his reckless behavior?

Jeez, worry about the sudden outburst of responsibility later.

Grabbing his arm, I turn it violently behind his back. "I don't break that easily, dude, but I can promise you," I push his arm a little higher, "your arm will if you don't walk out of this shithole. Now."

The whole bar is enjoying the show when the grumpy bartender shouts, "Hey!" He points to a "Start A Brawl And I Shoot Your Ass" sign hanging above the shelves and says, "That isn't just decoration, sweetheart."

I am officially in the town of crazies. I push Alex toward the door, fairly certain he could still take me down, even as drunk as he is, but luckily he doesn't try. "We're leaving," I snap at the bartender, shoving the door open and directing Alex out.

"Will you walk if I let go?" I ask as we step into the chilly night. When he nods, I steady him and try to bring his sorry ass to my room. Good times.

He barely makes it to my bed before collapsing on the mattress. “All this time,” I say, pouring him a glass of water, “I thought you were the most responsible person I had ever met, and now that we could use a little responsible, you turn into the reckless version of Tony Stark, minus the good looks, charm, and millions in your account, of course.”

Spread out on my bed, he laughs. “Damn, girl, you sound like my mother.”

Careful not to put too much pressure on my wounded foot, I walk toward jerk-face and hand him the glass. “Why, does your mom have the hots for Iron Man?”

He makes a face and pushes himself up on his elbows. “That’s gross.”

“Yeah, well, hate to break it to you, but moms have a sex life too, ya know.” I point to the glass. “Drink up,”

“Water?” He laughs. “C’mon, Manda. You just put some real disgusting pictures in my head, so how about you get me a bottle of tequila?”

“Not going to happen.”

He doesn’t look happy, but downs the water anyway. “Now can I get tequila?” he asks, holding up the empty glass.

I get him a refill. “Nope, but you will get more water, buddy.”

“You’re such a bitch,” he grumbles.

I hand him the glass. “We’re back to spitting insults, hm? What is this, Alex’s nine circles of booze hell?”

He pulls me toward him, and suddenly I find myself in his lap, straddling him. “No, but since going to hell is inevitable," he says, his lips brushing the spot between my two ladies. "I might as well enjoy the ride."

I keep telling myself he's drunk. Doesn't change the fact that I want to unzip his freaking jeans, though. "You're out of your mind if you think I'm screwin' you, Alex."

"Am I?" He runs his thumbs over my bra, turning my nipples into rocks. "Then why does your heart beat like the overheated engine of my Mustang?"

"It does not," I insist.

He pushes up, and his hard-on presses against my sweet spot. "Yeah. Yeah, it does."

I dig my nails into his shoulders. "Alex," I moan, trying to get off him. "Stop it, please." It's supposed to sound like a goddamn order, but comes out as desperate begging.

His hands glued to my ass, he tugs me against his chest. "I know you want me." He kisses down my neck. "You always want me. Just admit it," he says, pulling my shirt up.

I close my eyes. Hips rocking back and forth, I enjoy the feeling of the fabric rubbing against my heat. I do want him. Fuck, I need him, but he's like a drug, makes you high and leaves you dry and boneless. "Alex, please…stop."

"Just one night." His husky voice makes my toes curl. "For the sake of old times. What do you say?"

What do I say? Hell, with his lips on my neck, I'm not sure if I'm still able to speak. My heart races and every cell in my body craves his touch. What about tomorrow, though? As soon as he's in his right mind, he'll regret this.

I know, but if I've learned anything from my trip to Limbo, it's that tomorrow might never come. I might as well enjoy today.

"Let me get lost inside you." His hand fists around a strand of my hair, hauling my head toward his lips. "Ruin you, like you've ruined me."

Like you've ruined me? The words reset my brain. "Stop, Alex!" I get off him, knees weak. "Just stop."

"Oh, c'mon," he says, pushing his fingers through my belt loops and pulling me toward him. "Since when does Amanda Bishop pass up a chance to get lucky?"

"Fuck you, Alex."

"I'd rather screw you," he says, shoving my already low jeans farther down and exposing the massive horizontal scar at my pubic hairline. "What the—" His eyes go wide. "H-how did this happen?" he stammers, concerned.

Shit. Could this day get any worse? I yank out of his grip and adjust my clothes. "As if you care." I draw a deep breath. "Just call your FBI pal and find out if Walter has a lake house. I want to get this over with. ASAP."

****

I can't believe I almost screwed Alex. What the hell is wrong with me? Sex depravation? Schizophrenic episode? Limbo aftershocks? Probably all of it. I should have banged that hot bartender in Texas. What was his name again? It started with a B. Bart? Ben? Bay! Right. Hot, mesmerizing Bay. Nice smile. Awesome abs. He could have gotten the need out of my system. It's not like Alex is the only guy who can turn me on.

I tighten my grip on the steering wheel and my knuckles pale. Focusing on the street signs, I try to think of something other than the throbbing sensation between my legs.

"Slow down, Manda," Alex says. Leaning against the cool window, he looks like he wants to bash his head against a wall.

"There's a bottle of water and a pack of aspirin in my bag. Be my guest."

He massages his temples. "What's with the water thing? Most people cure a hangover with coffee."

Turning left, I shrug. "I'm not most people."

Swallowing a dozen aspirin, he nods. "Clearly."

Choosing to ignore the undertone in his voice, I pull into the parking lot of the pharmacy. "I hope you still know how to pick a lock, Alex."

"I can't believe we're breaking into a freaking pharmacy," he mutters. "I mean, are you even sure this ominous cure works?"

Killing the engine, I draw a deep breath. "No risk, no fun."

"Great," Alex grumbles. "We're committing a felony based on 'no risk, no fun.' Could it get any worse?" He's definitely sober.

I smile. "It can always get worse, Alex."

Having a hard time lifting his head, he shifts in his seat. "On a scale from one to ten, ten being most likely, how sure are you Jesse and the kids are being held at this lake house you saw?"

Sometime between being real mad at him for treating me like a slut and feeling sorry for him because he felt sick, I had managed to tell him about my vision. I expected him to be happy we finally had a lead on his brother, but all I received was a suspicious glare.

Pulling the key from the ignition, I frown. "Nine

and a half. This Walter guy was obsessed with his granddaughter, and since all the other girls seem to be substitutes for her, it kinda makes sense he'd bring them to the place where it all started, right?"

"I guess," he mutters.

"Besides, I have never had a random vision."

He bends toward me. "How does that vision crap work? I mean, do all witches have 'em? And why don't you use 'em to win the lottery or something like that?"

I glare at the green neon sign above the pharmacy. "No," I say. "Not all witches have visions. Most of us have pretty good intuition, but visions are one of the unique gifts. And about the lottery, well, I can't see my own future. Can't even read my own cards. Never could. Sucks, but it's just the way it is."

"Unique gifts?"

"Yeah, some of us can manipulate people, others can read auras. The list is endless, and—" I cut myself off, wondering why the hell I'm telling a hunter what witches are capable of.

"And?" he says.

"And I'm pretty sure I shouldn't tell you all that stuff. You *are*, after all, a hunter." I open the door. "C'mon," I say as my feet connect with the asphalt. "Witch lesson is over."

"Manda?"

I peek over my shoulder. "Hm?"

"About what I said." He runs a hand over his face. "I didn't really mean it. Fucking whiskey screwed with my head."

I laugh. "Oh please, Alex. Blaming the booze? That's so not like you."

"It's not just that. I was angry. Wanted to hurt

someone." He averts his gaze. "I wanted to hurt you."

"As I said, I don't break that easily." I get out and head to the backdoor of the pharmacy.

The crescent moon slices through the buildings, casting a silver light on the dark alley while Alex picks the lock in no time. I smile. "Nice."

He yanks the door open. "Just hurry."

Pushing past him, I walk straight to the backroom door, which is locked too. "Your talent is needed."

Alex goes straight to work. "You do know pharmacies have silent alarms, right?"

Once the door opens, I push past him. "Yeah, not unheard of. Guess we better be quick then, hm?"

"Hey," he says, following me. "How come I've never heard of devil's breath?"

"Flashlight?" I mumble as we reach the large cabinets. He switches it on and points it at the drawers. "Devil's breath is better known as scopolamine or the zombie drug," I explain. Looking for the letter P, I scan the cabinets for physostigmine. There it is. Rushing toward the drawer, I open it.

"And you know this because?"

"I'm a fuckin' genius," I say, grabbing the flashlight out of his hand. Shit, there are a dozen drugs that start with P. Panex. Panheparin. Pardryl. Pavacot. God, who names this stuff? I go through the rest and finally find it. Hello, cure. Shoving the packet into my jacket, I shut the drawer. "Got it."

"Awesome. Let's get the hell outta here."

Won't argue with that. Alex pulls me toward the back door when I realize I forgot a crucial part. "Wait," I say, going back.

"What are you doing?" he hisses.

Grabbing a syringe from another drawer, I rush to Alex and hold it under his nose. "Need this too."

Annoyed, he's dragging me out of the pharmacy when a car pulls in the parking lot. Alex shuts the door behind us and peeks around the corner. "Cops."

Shit, we are officially screwed.

"We'll be fine," Alex whispers, feeling my trembling hands. When I hear footsteps approaching us, I doubt that.

"Now what?" I ask, unable to move.

He squeezes my hands to keep them from shaking "I'm sorry" is the last thing I hear before he pushes me against the wall and kisses me. Hard. Passionate. Desperate. I want to slap him, really I do. I also want to push him away and yell at him. Resist him, but I don't. Instead, I throw my arms around his neck and kiss him back. His lips are like sandpaper, grinding away every rational thought, leaving nothing but a burned out shell. With Alex, everything is in sync. Our jaws, our tongues, our breath, even our fucking heartbeats. God, I have been starving, and I didn't even know it until now.

"Guys," someone shouts. "Break it up."

What?

"Manda." Alex's forehead rests against mine. "Just play along."

Play along?

"Kids, this is a public space. Why don't you get a room?"

My hand in his, Alex smiles. "Sorry, officer."

Officer? I force my gaze away from his lips. Shit. Officer with flashlight. Flashlight with officer. God, I can't think straight.

He points the beam of light at the door, checking

the lock. "Just get out of here," Officer Friendly says with a grin on his face.

Alex nods and hauls me to the car. "You okay?" he asks sheepishly.

"Sure." I just need to attend an Anonymous Alex-aholic meeting. But, hey, could be worse, right?

Chapter 22

"This Kiss" by Faith Hill blares through the radio, getting on my last nerve. I change the fucking station, hoping to hear something less kissy and more angry, but all I get is "Poison" by Alice Cooper. That's just great. Wondering if the whole freaking universe is plotting against me, I switch the goddamn radio off and tighten my grip on the steering wheel.

"Hey," Alex bitches. "What's wrong with Alice Cooper?"

"Nothing." The dude is freaking amazing. Saw him live once, but how the hell am I supposed to concentrate on our mission if the radio tortures me with the memory of Alex's goddamn kiss?

God, I'm such a screw-up. I mean, why the hell does a simple kiss fuck with my head like this? Simple kiss? Nothing about that kiss was simple. Alex is an extraordinarily good kisser, but so are a million other guys on Planet Earth.

"Manda?"

"What?" I snap.

"You're not mad at me for kissing you, are you?"

When the fuck did he turn into mind-reading Edward freaking Cullen? A nervous laugh escapes from the depths of my soul. "Don't be ridiculous. Why would I be mad?"

From the corner of my eye, I see his suspicious

glare and the stupid grin. "Dunno. But you've been awfully quiet ever since—"

"You pushed me against a wall and treated me like some whore?" I know I'm being unfair, but it's either flipping the bitch-switch or telling him the truth, and I can't have this conversation with him. Not now, not ever.

"Manda," he starts, but is cut off by his ringing phone. "Damn," he mutters under his breath as he glares at his screen. "It's Carter."

Maybe the universe is taking pity on me after all. "You wanna just sit there and stare at the screen, or are you planning to take that call?" Apart from the need to end this kissing nonsense, we also need the info Carter promised to get us. Right after the pharmacy incident, he had called Alex back and given him the address of Walter's house at Lake Isabella. Alex needed more than that, though. He needed Carter to find out as much about Walter Griffin as possible and it seems like he'd struck gold.

A frown on his face, he touches the accept button.

"Put him on speaker," I order. To my surprise, he does.

"Whatcha got, man?"

"You owe me big time," Carter says. "Turns out the life of an agent before the Golden Age of the internet was pure torture. Had to dig through a ton of handwritten files to get this shit."

Alex shakes his head. "Cut to the chase, man."

Carter makes a *tsk*ing sound. "Your man Walter was never convicted of child abuse."

"Awesome," Alex mutters, running a hand over his three-day beard. "You could have texted me that."

“Whoa, hold on,” Carter says. “I said he had no priors not that he doesn’t have a file.”

Carter sounds one helluva lot like Bonnie, and I have a hard time hiding the smile tugging at my lips.

“Dude, are you trying to piss me off? Just tell me what the fuck you know.”

“You know no one likes Grouchy Smurf, right?” he counters.

“Carter,” Alex shouts.

“All right, all right. Turns out your dead witch filed a complaint against her ex-husband shortly after that Scarlet kid drowned.”

Curiosity gets the best of me. “What kind of complaint?” I never took Hedwig for evil, and this might be proof she hadn’t been playing us after all.

“Oh boy, is that Amanda Bishop?”

I grin. “In the flesh.”

“Can’t believe it. Damn, I’ve heard so—”

A hint of annoyance flickers across Alex’s face. “Dude, we don’t have all night. So, how about you just focus?”

“Right. Your girl Hedwig accused her husband of child molestation, and drum roll…” Carter taps his fingers against a table and imitates the sound of drums.

“You sure he’s FBI?” I ask.

Alex shrugs.

“Murder,” Carter bursts out. “She told the cops Walter killed John and was responsible for Scarlet’s suicide.”

Suicide? Hedwig thought Scarlet took her own life?

“Apparently, the kid drowned herself after she witnessed the murder of her father,” Carter explains.

Just like in my vision.

"Why was Walter never arrested?" Alex asks.

The sound of rustling paper resonates through the phone. "Some detective… Damn, what was his name again?" More rustling. "Titcher. Detective Titcher dismissed the complaint. He claimed due to Hedwig's unstable mental health, she couldn't be taken seriously."

"You've gotta be kiddin' me," I yelp, pushing the gas pedal a little harder. "There's no way Hedwig had mental health issues."

"She's right," Alex says. "We met the woman. She was pretty sane." The wheels in Alex's head turn, and after a short period of silence, he faces me. "Didn't you say Walter and Titcher were friends?"

Eyes on the street signs in front of me, I nod. "Yeah. That's what Detective Good-looking said."

"Sure as hell sounds like you two stumbled over a corrupt cop," Carter grumbles more seriously than ever. "Maybe you should wait for backup, guys."

Backup? I haven't even thought about backup.

"This is bigger than just one rotten cop, Carter. If Amanda is right, there's a whole organization behind them," Alex explains. "As soon as I find the kids and Jesse, I'll inform the LA field office. But until then, we'll do this on our own. We don't know who else is in on this."

"Just be careful, man. Can't lose you just yet. You'll be gone soon enough."

"Gone soon enough? What the hell is he talkin' about? Where are you goin'?" I ask, confused.

My gaze darts through Alex, and he instantly puts his guard up. "No idea what he's talking about."

“Oh no, you didn’t—”

“Carter,” Alex snaps. “Shut the fuck up, man.”

“But—”

“Gotta go.”

“Alex, you have to—”

He hangs up on Carter.

“Wanna tell me what this is all about?” I wish I sounded less worried and more pissed, but something in Carter’s voice rang all my alarm bells.

“I’m going to quit the job,” he says, as if it isn’t a big thing he’s about to give up the one thing that defines his life.

“What? Why?”

“Need a change.” The brightest pink ever surrounds him, but before I get a chance to tell him what a rotten liar he is, he points to the idyllic house at the end of the street. “That’s it. Paradise Point.”

An uneasy feeling settles over me as I pull into the tree-lined driveway. I’m not sure if that’s because of what Alex is keeping from me, or the fact that we’re about to face off with a bunch of crazies.

Killing the engine, I lean in. “I know we’ve had our issues, Alex, but I still care about you. So if you need—”

“Care ’bout me?” He laughs. “I’m curious, Manda. Did you also care ’bout me when you kept the crucial information that you’re a freaking witch from me?” He tenses. “Know what? It doesn’t matter, ’cause I don’t have any problems. Let’s just go back to the real issue, all right?”

No problems? Right. I bet that’s the reason why his pulse jackknifes against his neck, and his leg is trembling. Whatever. He made it clear he doesn’t want my help. Swallowing the anger boiling inside me, I clear my throat. "You're a jerk, Alex, but I agree. We should focus on Jesse and the kids. What's the plan?"

He looks through the windshield to the crescent blood moon that lingers above us like the harbinger of all things evil. "No plan. I'm going in, and that's that."

I stare at him. "You mean *we* go in."

"No," he says. "You don't have to do this."

"What are you sayin', Alex?"

"Jesse is my brother. My responsibility. You've paid your dues, Manda. We're even."

I've never walked away from my magical responsibilities, and the second I had an encounter with Scarlet's spirit, this became more than just a Rescue Jesse Mission. "You're delusional if you think I'll let you walk into this alone."

His eyes go wide and, I swear, for a spilt second he considers the *Invasion of the Body Snatchers* theory. "Manda, you said it yourself. Going against a bocor is suicide. Plus, we don't even know if the cure works."

I can read people like open books, but Alex is a mystery I'll never solve. One second he acts as if I'm the source of all evil, and the next he tries to keep me safe? His mood swings give me a fucking headache. "I can take care of myself, thank you very much. Now, if we're done here, I'd like to kick some ass."

He blows out a frustrated breath. "I forgot how fucking stubborn you are."

I grab the physostigmine from my bag and draw it into the syringe. "Perks of being a Capricorn."

"This better work," he grumbles.

I yank the door open and smile. "No risk, no fun. Remember?"

Millions of stars are sprinkled across the sky, and the scent of water and grass fills my lungs. It's quiet and beautiful out here, but I've learned the hard way it ain't all gold that glitters. The knot in my belly confirms this night is a fiasco in the making.

"You coming or what?" Alex whispers, Beretta in one hand, doorknob in the other.

I reach into my pocket, checking my belladonna root powder supply. If things go south, it might be our only shot at subduing Jesse. "All right." I wipe sweaty hands on my jeans. "Let's get this party started."

Stalking toward him, I say a little prayer, hoping the blood moon isn't meant for us, but for the bastard of a bocor.

Alex yanks the door open. Holding his gun cop-style, he blocks my path. "Stay here. I'm going to take a look around."

I'm ready to remind him I'm not one of the chicks in need of a savior, but Alex goes inside before I get a chance to open my mouth. In some bizarre Alex way, he means well, but no way in hell am I going to wait here like a chicken while he's having all the fun.

The scent of rotten meat tingles in my nose as I step over the threshold. It's a nasty, sour smell. I have to hold my breath to endure that shit. Stumbling through the gloomy house, I find myself in the center of a small living room. No doubt in my mind this is the place of my vision. Murder. Rape. Incest. These walls have seen it all.

Walking toward a small oak table, I scan the room. Old magazines, a moth-eaten daisy print sofa, decaying wooden floorboards—the place is a freaking mess. Judging by the thick layers of dust that cover everything, I'd say this house hasn't seen a broom in ages.

"What the hell?" I jump at the sound of Alex's deep voice. Spinning around, I find him in the doorframe with his Beretta pointed at me. "I almost shot you, Amanda. Couldn't you, for once in your life, do what you're told?"

"Sorry, dude. There are only three people I take orders from: me, me, and," I grin, "oh yeah, me."

"You're—"

"Awesome?" I wave my hand in the air. "I know, but we're not here to celebrate my awesomeness. Did you find anything?"

He shoves the gun into his waistband. "Other than a few rats, the house is empty. Are you sure this is the place? No offense, but there's not even a basement as far as I can tell."

There's a vase with red roses on the dining room table, and a burning pain rushes through my ankh tattoo. "They're here," I whisper, stalking toward the flowers. "I feel it in my bones."

Alex's aura turns insecure gray: he disagrees. "I've searched the whole house, Manda. Seems like no one has been here for a while," he says, pointing to the moldy yellow wallpaper.

He has a point, but sometimes you need to take a closer look. What the hell am I missing? "How about some spiritual assistance," I snap at the ceiling.

"Manda, I want to find them, too, but they're not here." Alex grasps my hand. "C'mon, let's get outta here."

The burning pain of the tattoo shoots up my arm. "Please, Alex, you've got to trust me. I know they're here. Look at the roses. They're fresh."

Asking him to trust me probably wasn't the smartest move, but despite his doubts, his aura changes into a soft I-want-to-believe-you blue.

Tracing along a drawer, Alex coughs. "Damn, this place is a shithole. Dust everywhere."

Dust. That's it. The magazines, the sofa, the table, everything is covered with thick layers of dust. Everything but the floor next to the filthy rug.

"What are you doing'?" Alex asks, perplexed as I get on my knees and pull the rug away.

"Don't just stand there," I snap. "Give me a hand."

He grabs the other side of the fabric and lifts. "Damn," he says, glaring at the trap door in the floor.

Knocking the dust off my hands, I get up. "Now do you believe me?"

He pulls the door open and reaches for his gun. "I have to admit, having you around has its perks." Throwing the flashlight my way, he meets my gaze. "Ready?"

I grin. "After you, Buffy."

He tries hard to look annoyed, but a smile tugs at his lips. "Careful," he warns, walking down the gritty steps. "The wood is rotten."

I switch the flashlight on and follow him down the rabbit hole. One hand on the cold, wet brick wall, I take each step with care, trying hard not to fall to my untimely death. Jeez, why the fuck don't I own shoes without heels?

Just when I've decided to buy a pair of Chucks, I stumble over a loose board and pitch forward. "Damn." Alex catches me seconds before I learn how to fly without wings.

It's so dark down here, even with the flashlight, I can't see a thing. I feel my heart beating in my neck when Alex stops me. "Wait." Finger on the trigger, he scans the narrow hallway. "Do you hear that?"

"Hear what?" I whisper.

"Sounds like sobbing."

He's right.

He continues down the corridor, then stops dead in his tracks. "What the—"

"What is it?" I ask.

No answer.

"Alex?" I push past him and freeze like a deer in the headlights.

Dog kennels. Tiny fingers. Iron bars. Brown hair. Blonde hair. Black hair. Jesus freaking Christ. The bitter scent of fear crawls up my nose, clouding my brain like an opaque mist. In a trance-like state, I step closer.

Soft whimpers penetrate the musty air. Heavy breathing vibrates in my ears. "Please don't." The broken voice of a little girl hits me like a fucking uppercut. "Not again," she cries, terrified.

Rushing to the first kennel in the line of many, I gawk at the child. She's barely ten. Cowering in the corner of her prison, she weeps silently. I'm not sure how I'm still able to speak, but I wrap my fingers around the iron bars and say, "Sweetheart, look at me."

Her nails dig into the ripped fabric of her oversized shirt. "No, no, no." Head resting on her knees, she rocks back and forth. "Please don't hurt me again."

I stare at her, a piece of my soul breaking each time she begs for mercy. "Baby girl, you gotta look at me. I'm not going to hurt you. I'm here to help."

Her head slowly moves. Blue eyes gaze at me. Half dead, half alive. "They're coming back," she whispers when she realizes I'm not one of them. "Please help us."

"I will," I assure her, fiddling with the lock on the kennel door. "Alex, how about a little help?" Jeez, what is wrong with him? "Damn, Alex." I look up. "Help me!"

Unable to move, he glares at me. No, wait. He's looking behind me.

"Alex, what the—"

The little girl's eyes go wide with fear as strong arms wrap around me, lifting me from the ground. I try to kick the bastard who holds me in a death grip, but I'm being crushed by a freaking ball python.

"L-let her go, Jesse," Alex stammers, hands shaking, gun pointed in my direction.

Gun plus trembling generally equals accidently pulling the trigger. Struggling to free myself, I reach for the belladonna root in my pocket, but Jesse pulls me tighter against him, suffocating me.

"Jesse, c'mon, man. Let her go," Alex pleads with him, but reasoning with a brainless zombie is pointless.

Gathering the last resources of strength, I push back into his chest. "Let. Me. Go," I yell, stomping on his instep

Completely unaffected, Jesse tightens his grip. Hell, I can hear my ribs cracking as a sharp pain slices through me. I think I'll need to see a doctor. If I survive, that is.

"This ain't you, bro'. You don't want to hurt her. She's your friend." Determination and worry sharpens Alex's voice.

"This isn't," I can hardly finish the sentence, "your brother."

Alex looks from me to Jesse. "What the hell am I supposed to do?"

"C…Cu…C…" I can't form a coherent sentence. I pant for breath, but it's useless. Kinda weird how we never appreciate things until we lose them.

"Manda," Alex screams, his index finger pressed against the trigger of his Beretta.

Our eyes lock. Fear swirls around him like a freaking tornado, and his eyes are darker than ever. "Manda, I—" His lips move, but the pounding in my ears drowns out every other sound.

My heartbeat slows.

I'm going to die *again*.

Damn, must be a new freaking record.

Chapter 23

A high-pitched sound vibrates through the corridor, and Jesse loosens his grip. I plummet to the ground like a bagful of old clothes. Agonizing pain shoots through every bone in my body as I hit the hard floor. The flesh on my kneecaps tears from the impact, spilling fresh blood on the cold cement.

"Amanda!" I barely hear Alex through the ringing in my ears. Gasping for air, I look up, vision blurred, head swimming from lack of oxygen. After blinking several times, Alex's worried face finally takes shape.

His warm hand wraps around my arm. "You okay?" He pulls me away from Jesse, hovering above me.

Cracked ribs, bleeding knees, and aching bones. "Peachy."

The barrel of his Beretta pointed at his obedient zombie brother, Alex's alluring eyes plead with me. "You gotta get up, Manda."

I look over my shoulder. Jesse is motionless. Red spots blight his once flawless skin. His pupils are dilated, and the white in his eyes resembles the colors of hell.

Pressing my right hand against my ribcage, I try to get on my feet, but fail miserably.

"Fuck," Alex cusses, never taking his eyes off Jesse. "Get on your feet, Amanda."

What the hell does it look like I'm trying to do? Under zombie-boy's scrutiny, I reach for Alex's shoulder and lift myself up. My ankh tattoo burns like crazy, but what really freaks me out is I feel the bocor. His presence fills the place with a dark, almost demonic atmosphere.

"He's here," I whisper, leaning against Alex to steady myself. "The bocor is here."

Like a hawk, Alex scans the room. "Where?"

Prolonged applause echoes off the walls. A fraction of a second later, a tall lean figure steps out of a shadowy corner at the far end of the corridor. "They were right," he says. The French accent is unmistakable. "You truly are gifted."

Alex shields me with his body. "Stay right there," he yells, index finger anchored to the trigger of his Beretta.

Disregarding Alex, Francoise or whatever the hell his name is, laughs the warning off and comes straight toward us. Creepy voodoo symbols cover his skin, but his white shirt and jeans make him look like a fucking physician. "A hunter protecting a witch, and here I thought I had seen it all."

Alex's jaw hardens. "Are you deaf? I said don't fucking move." No doubt lingers in my mind Alex will pull that trigger, but Francoise uses Jesse as cover and the possibility of accidently shooting his brother leads to hesitation.

Hiding behind Jesse, the bocor's barbarous laughter floats through the eerie corridor. "Do you really think I'm afraid of your gun? Puny creature, don't you know who I am? I am Baron Samedi. Death is my guardian." The sound of the bastard's voice makes kids in the kennels flinch. Their fear permeates the musty air.

"Yeah, well, for a guy who isn't afraid of guns, you sure as hell know how to put someone else in the line of fire," Alex says, pointing to his brother, who stands there like a living shield.

"Oh please, Monsieur Remington," the bocor says, resting a hand on Jesse's limp shoulder. "Don't be so melodramatic. I assure you, your brother thoroughly enjoys his new life." The bocor's black eyes lock with mine. "I'm curious, though. Tell me, Mademoiselle Bishop. Why would a reckless witch like you help a man like him?" He grins. "From all I've heard, you're the rotten apple in a line of powerful white witches. Not exactly a role model for selflessness."

Playing the family card, hm? That's pretty lame, even for psycho-voodoo-priest standards. Barely able to stand, I push past Alex and put on my best fake smile. "What can I say? I'm always up for some bocor ass kicking."

"I see." He tilts his head to the side. "Well, despite your attitude problem, you should hear me out. I'm going to make you a one-time-only offer."

"Your head on a silver platter?" I ask, the pain from my broken ribs making me sweat.

He throws his hands in the air and laughs. "No, chéri. I'm offering you a way out. Walk away from this, and I shall spare your life." His gaze moves to Alex. "You wouldn't risk your life for such a pitiful creature as him, would you?"

"Says the guy who works for a pedophile," I spit.

His eyes narrow on me. "I don't judge my clients, chéri. They pay. I serve. You of all people should know how this works. From what I've heard, you're much like me."

"I'm nothing like you."

"Oh really?" he says, running his bony fingers over Jesse's face. "That's not what your friend here said. You see, after I turned him into my puppet, he was eager to tell me all about the witch that," he makes quotation marks in the air, "ruined his brother."

Ruined. There's that word again. Why does everyone believe I fucked Alex up? I wasn't the one who pointed a gun at his head, threatening to blow his brains out just because he was a witch-hunter.

"They are hunters, chéri. They don't care about you or your life. To them, you'll always be a freak of nature, and to protect their own, they'll kill you without hesitation." His charcoal eyes bore into me. "Walk away and I will spare your life. You have my word."

"Don't listen to him," Alex snarls. "He's just messing with you."

"Am I?" The bocor laughs. "Then why don't you tell her how you really feel about her, Monsieur Remington? She is, after all, the reason your beloved brother is in this mess in the first place."

Jaw clenched, I face Alex. "What the hell is he talking about?" I haven't seen Jesse in ages, so how on earth could I be responsible for his zombie state?

"I don't know," Alex snaps. His pink aura says something else though.

The bocor, aka Francoise, points to the watch around his wrist. "I'm a very busy man. I need your answer, chéri. Will you fall with him or stand with me?"

I have no idea what the hell is going on, but no way

will I stand with a man who kills little girls. "You can shove your offer up your ass, pal. I'd rather be killed by him than pardoned by you," I snap and mean it. Being killed by a witch hunter sucks, but at least it's an honorable death.

Francoise arches his brows. "Mademoiselle Bishop, is that love I sense?"

Alex studies me. Although he keeps quiet, I can't shake the feeling he's eager for an answer to this question.

I gather my chi and force my spine into a straighter position. "Nope," I say, shaking my head. "You sense my desire to rip out your heart and feed it to the hellhounds."

Still hiding behind Jesse, he shrugs. "As you wish, chéri." He faces Jesse. "Get the gun," he orders.

Without blinking, Jesse stalks toward his brother like a freaking robot.

Alex stumbles back. "Stop, Jesse," he begs, but it's pointless.

Jesse seizes hold of the Berretta. Alex moves his left elbow, placing an uppercut to his little brother's jaw, but the boy doesn't even flinch. Pain obviously doesn't affect zombies.

Now or never. Taking a chance, I pull the syringe out of my pocket and aim for Jesse's carotid artery. I'm seconds away from penetrating his skin when a metallic clicking resonates through the damp dungeon.

"I wouldn't do that if I were you," someone new croaks.

Alex freezes like a deer in headlights and let's go of his gun.

The needle still pointed at Jesse's neck, I peek over

my shoulder to where Walter Griffin pushes a goddamn rifle against Alex's head. I didn't even hear him coming down the stairs.

Fan-freaking-tastic. At least a million thoughts bolt through my mind. What the fuck am I supposed to do, drop the cure and lose Jesse forever? Ignore Walter and get Alex killed? And when the hell did my life become so complicated?

I lock eyes with Alex, my thumb trembling against the syringe.

"Do it," he begs.

"Drop it," Walter yells.

"Think about it," Francoise says. "Do you really want lover boy's blood on your hands?"

My gaze glides from Jesse to Alex. "Fuck!"

"Amanda, look at me," Alex pleads. "You've gotta save Jesse."

Call me selfish, but there's only one thing I can do. "I'm sorry," I mouth as I drop the cure. "I can't."

Alex's aura lights up like a freaking traffic light. It's a weird mixture of disappointment, surprise, and confusion. "Why did you do that?"

Before I get a chance to explain my decision, French Connection folds a hand over Jesse's shoulder. "Pick up the needle and give it to me," he commands, and zombie boy obeys.

A knot in my belly, I watch as the bocor empties the syringe. Gone is every hope to get Jesse back.

"Thanks, Manda," Alex bitches. "You just killed my brother."

The bocor was right about one thing; Alex has melodramatic tendencies.

"Move!" Walter presses the rifle harder against the

back of Alex's head, pushing him forward.

Alex curls his hands into fists. He wants to fight, but one look at Jesse is enough to change his mind. Reluctantly, he walks toward the bocor.

"Get her," Francoise instructs Jesse.

Hands up in defense, I try to tell zombie-boy I can walk by myself, but he doesn't give a shit. He grabs me by the hair and drags me down the hallway like a piece of trash.

"Let the fuck go!" I dig my nails into his skin, but he's numb. "Jesse, you're scalping me," I scream as the pain in my chest becomes unbearable. "Let go!"

"I'm afraid, chéri," Francoise says, "he doesn't take orders from you."

Chapter 24

Jesse pushes me down on the filthy mattress of my vision. The scent of body liquids and rotten meat stings my nostrils. I try not to think about all the gross things that have happened here, but with Scarlet's picture hanging on the wall behind me, the omnipresent evil is hard to ignore.

On the other side of the room, Walter forces Alex into a chair. "Don't do anything stupid," he warns, not taking the gun off his chest.

We're officially screwed. The cure is gone. Alex has a rifle pointed at his heart. I'm badly hurt and, let's be honest, don't stand a freaking chance against all three of them. Long story short, I have no clue how to get out of this mess.

Considering our options, I study the room. Maybe Alex could take Walter down, but there'd still be psycho bocor and Jesse, aka zombie slave. The best thing I can do right now is buy us some time. Eyeballing the bocor, I clear my throat. "So, Francoise. I can call you Francoise, right?"

"I'd prefer Baron Samedi," he says, pulling the edges of his mouth down.

"Sure, Francoise." Straightening, I rub my scalp to ease the pain. "Now that we no longer pose a threat to you, how about telling us why the fuck you killed James McKenzie? I mean, he was the founder of your child pornography ring, wasn't he?"

Walter spins around. "How does she know?" he asks, his eyes almost popping out.

Francoise rolls his shoulders back and grins. "She's a witch, Walter." Amusement flickers across his face. "I told you she'd get to the bottom of this."

Kneeling next to me, Francoise looks me in the eye. "The second you unlocked Jamie's memory, I sensed you. After that, I had no choice but to eliminate the mayor. He posed a threat to the whole organization."

"And Isobelle? Was she a threat, too?" Alex asks.

"Yes," Francoise says, holding my gaze. "I never intended to kill her, but your little witch here gave me little choice." He leans closer, his breath raising the hair on my neck. "All you had to do was dig a little deeper." He grins. "You were so close to finding our location. Who knows, the girl might still be alive if you had been strong enough to endure her pain."

Rage runs through my veins like melting lava. The asshole knows how to play the guilt card.

"Bullshit," Alex hisses. "Don't put this on her. She didn't kill Isobelle. You're the evil bastard who preys on helpless kids."

"This is ridiculous," Walter shouts, his finger moving back and forth from the trigger. "Let's just kill them and be done with it."

Alex looks at me, a silent message in his eyes as he tilts his chin toward Walter. "Distract him," I read from his lips.

Assuming hunter-heroic has a plan, I do as he asks. "Killing us won't solve your problems, Walter." I press a hand against my broken ribs and get on my knees.

"C'mon, do you really think we came here without backup?"

His face hardens. "What?" Pale, he glares at Francoise. "You said we'd be safe here."

Francoise is about to say something, but I cut him off. "And you believed him? He's a bocor, Walter. All he cares about is saving his own skin. I bet he didn't even tell you the guy you're holding at gunpoint works for the Feds."

Fear swirls around him, changing his aura into a dark mess. "The Feds?" He steps aside, the rifle still pointed at Alex, but his eyes on Francoise. "What is she talking about?"

Francoise waves his hands. "Oh, for the love of death, she's just messing with you, Walter. That's what witches do."

"Am I?" I challenge him, brows raised. "Think about it, Walter. He said it himself: the second the mayor of Harpers Ferry posed a threat, he killed him. He'll do the same to you. It's just a matter of time."

Dark blue taints Walter's aura. His doubt grows like a nasty cancer. "She has a point, Francoise. How do I know you won't sacrifice me to save yourself?"

The bocor jumps to his feet. "Stop this nonsense, or did you forget who undid the curse your ex-wife put on you?" He lets out a sharp breath. "You'd still be popping Viagra if it wasn't for me."

And here I wondered why Walter had waited over thirty years to get back to his dirty business. "Hedwig put a no-sex hex on you?" I burst into laughter. "Damn, I hope heaven has a best spell award. She totally deserves it."

Walter stalks toward me with squinted eyes.

Mission accomplished.

"You think this is funny, witch?" With crazy written all over his face, he slaps the back of his hand across my face, sending my head flying to the side. "That bitch destroyed my whole life." He looks at the picture of Scarlet. "My little girl would still be alive if it wasn't for that goddamn mambo."

Francoise makes a calming gesture. "Easy, my friend. This isn't the time to…how do you Americans say? Lose your shit?"

Rubbing my jaw, I glance at Alex, who's slowly rising from his chair. I gotta buy him more time. "Are you serious?" I bark. "You blame Hedwig for Scarlet's death?" Shaking my head, I grin. "Dude, your granddaughter drowned herself because she couldn't stand you."

BAM. The butt of the rifle connects with my temple. "Shut the fuck up. You don't know what you're talking about."

Blood runs down my forehead, blurring my peripheral vision. "I know enough to be certain she hated you with all her heart," I say, wiping the crimson liquid off my cheeks with the sleeve of my shirt.

"Walter, stop. She's playing you," Francoise shouts as the pedophile douchebag kicks me in the stomach.

Damn, my brain feels like pudding, the seizures in my stomach are worse than PMS, and don't even get me started on my ribs. But if I want to get out of here, I have to pull it together. Rubbing my belly, I straighten. "What's wrong, Walter? Am I upsetting you?" I try to smile, but the muscles in my face won't move. "Little girls are easier to control, right? Hey," I say, batting my thick lashes at him. "Can you even get a boner when they fight back?"

I shouldn't have said that.

Walter's pale gray eyes turn midnight blue, and his facial expression reminds me of the *Evil Dead* chick who split her tongue with the bread cutter. Sweat drips down his forehead as he pushes the rifle against my temple. "I'm going to kill you," he yells like a lunatic who just escaped the loony bin.

Alex ambushes him from behind, tackling him to the ground before he can pull the trigger. The old man puts up quite a fight, but Alex is faster and stronger. He disarms him in no time, then beats the fucking crap out of him. After several punches, Walter loses consciousness, and Alex turns his focus on the bocor, who stands there dumbstruck.

"Jesus," Francois hisses as he realizes what's happening. "Kill him," he commands Jesse.

Zombie-boy rushes to Alex and grabs him by the collar of his shirt.

Using my last strength, I get on my feet. It's all or nothing. I reach in my pocket, grab the belladonna root powder meant to subdue Jesse, and throw it in Francoise's face.

Coughing, he falls on his knees. "What," he wraps his hands around his neck, "have you done?" Gasping for air, he tries to fight the poison, but it's useless. Belladonna is ruthless and quick. Within seconds, Francoise lies on the floor, jerking violently.

A victorious smile on my bruised lips, I stand over the asshole. Two down, one to go. My gaze glides to Alex, and all of a sudden, I'm not so optimistic. Jesse is sitting on top of him, delivering punch after punch. Alex's face is a canvas of blood. Instead of defending himself, he takes the beating.

"Alex, you've gotta fight him," I shout, but he's paralyzed. Shit, Jesse's going to kill him. I have to do something. Question is what? The cure is gone, and unless I turn into a superhero, I doubt I can take on super-zombie-boy.

Alex looks at me, his eyelids flickering. "Save him," he whispers as Jesse's fist connects with his jaw. Once, twice.

Save him? How? The real Jesse would never do this to his brother. If only he could remember. Wait, that's it. I just have to remind him who he really is. I'm not sure if I'm strong enough to break through the drug, but it's worth a shot.

I attack Jesse from behind. Pressing my forefinger against his third eye, I wrap my legs around his waist. "I know you're still in there." I close my eyes. "You just have to remember." Concentrating on memories of brighter days, I force him to feel and see what the bocor has taken away from him.

The first time we met.

The night we laughed our asses off because Alex got so wasted, he started imitating Taylor Swift.

The day he saved me from getting shot.

It all flickers across his mind's eye, but doesn't affect him at all. He reaches over his shoulder, seizes hold of my shirt, and tries to get me off his back.

"Hold him," I order.

Alex grabs Jesse's hands, securing them at his sides.

"C'mon, Jess. Remember." I focus all my energy on one memory, hoping beneath the brainless slave is still a part of the pre-zombie Jesse.

****

We had been sitting for quite some time, enjoying the calmness of the deserted piece of land while Alex tried to fix his beloved Mustang. A faint breeze carried the distinct scent of summer rain. I took a deep breath, wondering why Jesse had grown so silent all of a sudden. One second he told me all about his dream to travel the world. The next, his eyes had grown distant, and he glared at the sunset that cast a beautiful, coral light on the blossoming flowers.

I sipped my soda and studied him. "Why don't you just do it?"

He ran a hand through his styled hair and laughed. "You mean buy a ticket and travel the world?"

I nodded. "Hell, yeah. What's holding you back?"

Jesse's warm chocolate eyes found Alex. "It ain't that easy, Manda."

"It sure is," I said matter-of-factly. "Alex loves you. He'll understand."

The saddest, yet proudest smile crossed his lips. "I know. But he's my brother, Manda. We swore we'd never leave each other."

"Hey!" Alex waved Jesse over with the screwdriver he held. "How about you give me a hand, little brother?"

"See?" Jesse said as he got up. "The boy's helpless without me."

****

The weighty atmosphere in the room lifts, and Jesse relaxes. I did it. I don't know how, but I got through to him. I get off his back, and he rolls to the ground.

Alex pushes up on his elbows. Eyes wide, he stares

at his brother. “Manda, is he—”

Bang!

What the—

Something hits me hard in the chest. The scent of copper wafts through the air, turning my stomach as I tremble. Next thing I know, I’m lying on the floor, glaring at Walter with the rifle in his hand.

“You should have accepted his offer,” he says with a scary-as-hell grin.

“Manda!” Alex is next to me in an instant. Raw fear colors his aura the deepest blue. “Shit!” He presses his hand against the hole in my chest. “You’re gonna be okay. Do you hear me?”

I doubt that.

“My—” I try to inhale, but blood bubbles into my lungs.

“Shhh. Don’t talk,” Alex says, resting my head in his lap.

“Pocket. Pennies,” I choke out, feeling the crimson liquid crawling up my throat.

Alex gives me a weird look, but reaches in my pocket and pulls out the ferryman coins. Better safe than sorry, Grams used to say. I couldn’t agree more.

“Here.” He places the coins in the palm of my hand.

From the corner of my eye, I watch Walter approach us. His left eye is swollen and bruises cover his face.

I try to speak, but my voice is barely a whisper. Alex leans closer. My lips brush his ear. “Keep,” I gasp for air, “one. Throw…” I cough blood, and Alex goes white. “When over.”

Confusion paints his face. “What?”

Pointing the rifle at Alex, Walter grins. "Enough. I'm sure you guys can talk all you want in hell."

It takes all the strength I've got left, but I manage to throw the ferryman's coin to the ground and start chanting, "Ancients gods, I call upon thee." I cough more blood. "Set these tormented spirits free." I pant for air, choking on the coppery liquid. "Let justice be done and revenge come undone."

Violent winds blow. Static voices float through the room.

"Father?"

"My name's Isobelle! It's Isobelle."

"I hate you, Grandpa."

"What did you do?" Walter screams as the ghosts of his past surround him: Scarlet, Isobelle, John. They're all here.

"Karma serves what you deserve," I whisper as Scarlet's grateful eyes lock with mine.

"No. Please," Walter begs.

Man, I wish I could see his face, but the world around me grows darker.

"Manda, open your eyes."

I try. I really do. But my eyelids are so damn heavy.

"Don't you dare die on me, Amanda." I love the sound of Alex's voice. I'm glad he's the one singing me down.

Chapter 25

Beep…Beep…Beep… The goddamn sound drives me nuts. I wish I could throw a pillow over my head or press my hands against my ears. The thing is, I can't move. Can't even open my eyes. Surrounded by an eerie darkness, I try to remember how I got here, but the past is a blur. One minute I saw Jesse lying on the floor, the next I heard a loud *bang*, and now I'm floating through some kind of in between world, tormented by a centrifugal force that wants me to let go.

Is this the after-Limbo, where souls wait for heaven or hell?

"Don't be so melodramatic." My own voice thunders in my ears. "You ain't dead yet."

All right, I'm neither dead nor alive. So what the hell am I? Better question: why the hell do I hear my own voice, even though I can't move my lips? God, if I get outta here, wherever the hell *here* is, I will see a shrink.

"How about you shut up for a second and focus?"

On what? The beeping? The floating? The darkness?

"Just listen."

Drawing a deep breath, I center myself. A few moments later, a distant, but familiar voice rings in my ears. "Any changes?"

Why do I get the feeling of holding a grudge

against that person?

"She's stable, but hasn't come to yet."

Alex?

"How are the kids doing?"

Jesse? Damn, it's good to hear his un-zombie-like voice. At least something good came out of this mess.

"They are getting the best psychological treatment money can buy, but it's going to be a long process. One of the girls still swears Miss Bishop is a witch."

"Sure, and I'm Jason Bourne," Alex says. The sound of his voice makes my heart beat a little faster, and the annoying beeping gets a little louder.

Ignoring Alex's comment, the man clears his throat. "Mr. Matthieu is in solitary confinement. Just like you instructed."

"Good. Make sure he stays that way," Jesse says.

"Don't worry. He'll never see the light of day again, but we need Miss Bishop's statement. Would you call us when she wakes up?"

Stop talking about me in the fucking third person. I'm right here. Concentrating on my numb hand, I try to move it. The transmitters in my brain are obviously on holiday, though. I resist the centrifugal pull of the otherworld and anchor myself by focusing on the one thing that always made me feel alive. Alex.

"Are you kidding? The bullet punctured her lung. She has two broken ribs and is still unconscious. So excuse me if I don't give a fuck about your statement right now."

Bullet? So that's what that *bang* was.

"Calm down, man. He's just doing his job," Jesse says, but even he can't ease the poisonous anger heating his brother's veins.

"His job?" Alex snaps. "Let me tell you something. If he had done his job thirty years ago, Isobelle and Hedwig would still be alive. And Manda—"

Ah, that's why the voice sounds so familiar. The one and only Detective Bitcher.

"I had no idea what Walter was up to." Titcher sounds guilty. "You have to believe me, Agent Remington. I would have arrested him if—"

"Whatever makes you sleep better."

"Maybe you should come back later," Jesse suggests, knowing Alex is about to burst.

"I have a better idea," Alex says, his voice dangerously low. "How about you don't come back at all?"

Damn, why the hell can't I open my fucking eyes? I would pay a fortune to see Detective Grumpy's face.

"I really am sorry," Titcher mutters, and then a door slams.

"What is wrong with you?" Jesse asks. "Pissing off the local police isn't exactly a smart move. Carter already lost it because he didn't know how to explain Walter's super-freaking-natural death. I mean, who knew spirits could make such a mess, right?"

Spirits? Ah, right. That's the last thing I did before darkness swallowed me; I summoned a bunch of vengeful ghosts.

I feel Alex's hand on my forehead. Pretty ironic, considering I can't even feel my own legs. "That son of a bitch got what he deserved."

"Man, you sound less like you and more like—"

Me?

Alex cuts him off. "Just shut up, all right?"

"You act all tough, Alex, but deep down you blame

yourself for what happened to her. You gotta stop, man. Acting like a jerk won't ease the guilt."

He knows his brother too damn well, I'd say.

"Thanks, Dr. Phil. Anything else you'd like to add, or are you done shrinking me?"

"Alex, I'm serious. None of this is your fault."

Brushing a strand of hair out of my face, he sighs. "I should have never dragged her into this."

"Are you serious?" Jesse snarls. "Dude, we're talking about Amanda Bishop here. No one forces her to do anything she doesn't want to."

Alex's breath tingles on my cheeks. "I pointed my goddamn gun at her head and threatened to kill her. That's a pretty convincing argument, don't you think?" Taking my hand in his, he draws tiny circles on my palm. "You can say what you want, but the truth is Amanda would never have been shot if I hadn't forced her to help me. Her selfishness would have saved her from this."

Even after everything that happened, I'm still the selfish witch with a capital *B* to him? Way to go, Alex.

Battling the everlasting darkness, I picture a ray of light. Open. Eyes. Eyes. Eyes. Using Vipassana meditation usually helps. Not this time, though. My eyelids are just too damn stubborn to listen.

"For a guy who hasn't slept, eaten, or walked out of this room in the last four days, you're sure as hell trying hard to sound like a dick."

Four days? You've gotta be fucking kidding me.

"The only reason I'm still here is because unlike her, I don't just walk away from people. Now why don't you go and get some coffee or read another self-help magazine, 'cause I'm about done listening to your psycho-analytical crap."

The door creaks. "You know, Alex, I've put up with your she's-a-witch shit for way too long. That's still the girl you fell in love with lying there. The one who taught you how to live again. And yeah, she walked away from you. But you were the one who pushed her in that direction." Jesse almost never loses his temper, but boy, is he pissed.

The vibration of the slamming door rattles through my body. Moments later, the mattress sinks under Alex's weight. He lets out a frustrated breath. "I'm sorry," he whispers, caressing my face. "I know we weren't always on the same page, but you have to believe me when I say I never wanted it to end like this."

Oh, please. Is this going to be one of those cheesy Hollywood speeches that is supposed to make me feel all loved and cared for? Boy, next thing, he's gonna kiss me sleeping princess-style, expecting me to wake up and proclaim my everlasting love to him. What shit have I done in my past life to deserve this?

"I should have protected you, Manda. Should have snapped that son of a bitch's neck when I had the chance."

Excuse me, but I think I need to puke. Jeez, when will jerk-face finally accept I'm not a damsel in distress and I… "Don't need saving."

Did I just say that out loud?

"Amanda?"

I blink my eyes open, but the fluorescent light hurts like hell. Shit. So, that's how vampires feel when they stare into the sun, hm?

"Manda, can you hear me?" Alex says, voice

infected with hope.

Still battling the light, I open my mouth. It's as dry as Death Valley. "W—" I swallow hard, but my throat feels like it's been scraped with sandpaper. "Water."

Alex pours me a glass and carefully places it at my lips. "Slowly," he orders.

Taking tiny sips, I check out his fucked up appearance. His skin is dry. Eyes are red. The worst part, though: he still wears the blood-soaked clothes from that night.

"How do you feel?" he asks, putting the glass down. "Are you in pain?" He rests his hand on my forehead, checking my temperature. "Do you need anything? Can I… I don't know; get you another pillow? Or maybe I should get the nurse." He's looking at me, but I get the feeling he's talking to himself.

I would laugh my ass off if my jaw didn't hurt so badly. "I'm…" Every word is painful. "Fine." I point to the water. "More?"

I don't have to ask twice. The lukewarm liquid slides down my throat, easing the soreness.

Alex's gaze travels over my face. "You scared the living shit outta me. Don't ever do that again, or—"

"You're goin' to shoot me?" I tease.

The disturbed look on his face is priceless. "Not funny," he grumbles.

I try to take a deep breath, but inhaling feels like being stabbed in the chest. "Actually, it is," I say weakly. He threatened to shoot me twice. Now the universe has rewarded him with a taste of what it would feel like to lose me to a gunshot. Some would call that coincidence. I prefer karma.

Pushing my numb hands into the mattress, I try to

push myself up, but my body isn't up for it. "Take it easy," he commands, taking a seat next to me. "You've been hurt pretty bad." He runs a hand over his battered face. "You're lucky you're still alive."

"Hell isn't ready for me," I joke.

Alex carefully holds my head up and shoves the pillow a little higher. "I'm sorry, Amanda. I should never have dragged you into this."

Not again. "You don't get it, do you?"

"Get what? That I almost got you and Jesse killed?"

I don't know why, but I seize hold of his hand and rest it above my heart. "This wasn't about you or Jesse," I explain. "I was exactly where I was supposed to be."

Doubt and guilt darken his aura, but he knows better than to argue with me when I'm not feeling well. "I should get the nurse," he says, reluctant to leave.

"Go." I point to the needles and cables all over my body. "It's not like I could run."

His lips curve in a tight half-smile. "I'll be right back."

"I'll be right here waitin' for you."

Chapter 26

Daytime TV sucks, hospital pudding is disgusting, and the nurses are so damn sweet, I'll probably leave this place with diabetes. I've only been awake for two days, but it feels like an eternity. I seriously fear I'm going to lose my mind if I have to stay any longer.

I won't lie, though. It was nice to have the boys camping on chairs next to my bed. Jesse entertained me with crazy stories that would make the best *How Not to Treat Your One Night Stand* book ever. Alex was all guilt ridden and determined to read every wish from my eyes. But no matter how much I appreciate Jesse's Oprah act and Alex's newly discovered *I Dream of Jeannie* side, I need to get the hell outta here.

Knowing neither Jesse nor Alex would support my mission, I had them convinced they smelled worse than Swiss cheese. After a fairly heated even-Jacob-the-werewolf-smells-better discussion, they agreed to return to the motel to get a shower and some much-needed sleep, giving me enough time to sign the release papers. Goes without saying the doctors considered me brain-damaged goods, but what can I say? I'm stubborn like that.

I'm covering the black-and-blue bruises all over my face with plenty of concealer when my phone rings again. There's no need to look at the screen; I know exactly who it is. Melinda has assaulted my poor phone ever since jerk-face told her I had a gaping hole in my chest. I might not blame him for getting me shot, but I totally blame him for going through my phone contacts without permission and calling my upright, crazy-ass sister. I consider picking up, but I still feel like I've been hit by a truck and can't handle a lecture from Miss Perfect.

"Movie sounds good."

Jesse leans against the doorframe, loaded with coffee and engulfed by a lusty aura. Shit, why the fuck is he back already? It's only been an hour since they left.

Nurse Rachel's eyes light up like goddamn Fourth of July fireworks. "Great. My shift ends at seven. See you then?"

Don't do it, Jesse.

Eyes on her boobs he smirks. "Sure."

I sorta feel sorry for the poor, soon-to-be heartbroken girl. She was always sweet to me, partly because she has the hots for Jesse, partly because she has that genuine caring aura you often find around doctors, nurses, and teachers.

"Looking forward to it," he says, and once she's out of sight, he walks into my room.

Taking a last look at my battered reflection, I shove my pocket mirror in my bag. "Really, Jesse? Breaking the heart of yet another innocent girl?"

"I'd never—" His eyes go wide as he realizes I'm dressed and ready to leave. "Whoa, what the fuck do you think you're doing?"

Throwing my phone in my bag, I shrug. "What's it look like? I'm checkin' out."

He puts the coffee down on the nightstand. "Are

you crazy? You've got some serious injuries, girl. You can't just walk outta here."

I refuse to meet his gaze. "These," I hold up the release papers, "say I can."

Hands in his pockets, he strides toward me in typical Jesse fashion. "Does Alex know about this?"

I almost laugh. "It's not like he's the boss of me, Jess. I'm old enough to make my own decisions."

His warm eyes search mine. "I get it, Manda. You've been through some real bad shit, but I don't think this is such a great idea." He points to my packed bag.

I know he means well, but if I have to stay another day in this depressing shithole, they'll have to transfer me to the loony bin. "Look, I've paid my dues, Jess. The bocor is rotting in jail. Walter is dead. The kids are saved." I give him the biggest smile. "And you are back to your old, charming, heartbreaking self. It's time for me to move on. Start my new life."

He flings himself on the bed and studies me. "So it's true?"

"What?"

"You really are going straight?" he says, searching my face.

"Yep."

"Didn't believe Alex when he said you were headed to NYU. Couldn't, for the life of me, picture you as a girl who gives up her freedom for a normal life."

Careful not to make sudden moves, I sit on the bed next to him. "I guess I've realized it's time to grow up."

"Grow up?" he says suspiciously. "What happened to you, Manda?"

It's a good thing I'm no longer connected to the medical IV monitor. Otherwise, there'd be a massive spike in my heart rate. "Nothing happened to me, Jess. I just can't spend the rest of my life roaming the country, reading cards. That's all."

"Why not?" he asks, narrowing his eyes. "Last time I checked, it made you pretty damn happy."

"Yeah, well." I run my fingers through my knotty hair. "Things change."

"Maybe so," he says, holding my gaze. "But people usually don't. So why don't you tell me what's really going on?"

I wish I could be honest with him. He deserves the truth, but trusting him with my secret would affect his relationship with Alex, and I can't let that happen. So I turn the tables. "How about you tell me what's going on between you and Alex first?"

"I don't know what you're talking about," he says, staring at the wall.

Even if there weren't a shiny pink light around him, I'd know he's lying. "Oh please, Jesse. You guys barely speak to each other, and if you do, there's an unspoken argument hovering above ya. Quit fooling around and spill it."

His lips form a straight line. "I know what you're doing, Manda. Changing the topic to avoid my question. Gets old, don't you think?"

I make a face. "You quite literally almost crushed me to death, and I took a bullet because of you and your brother. So excuse me if I'd like to know what the hell is going on." I look him in the eye. "I had a hard time believing you'd run off without Alex to seek the help of a bocor. But seeing you guys like this, well, it makes me wonder if there's more to the story than you're lettin' on."

Playing with the buttons of his flannel shirt, he gazes out the window. "I was just trying to help out a friend." His aura turns gray. He's scared of something.

"Yeah, 'bout that. Must be one helluva friend if you take your chances with a malicious, backstabbing, voodoo-priest asshole."

"He is," he says matter-of-factly.

Gosh, these boys are tight-lipped about this whole bocor business. When the memories finally came back to me, I remembered the all-of-this-is-your-fault speeches from wasted Alex and asshole bocor. Every time I tried to ask Alex what this was about, he had to go to the bathroom or find a nurse. And now Jesse is acting just as weird.

I narrow my eyes. "He is? Is that all?" I grab my bag and shakily get on my feet. "Well, I can't force you to tell the truth, but if that's all you have to say, I'm outta here."

"Wait," he says, wrapping his fingers around my wrist. "You have to understand, Manda. I begged him to tell you, but—"

"What the fuck is going on here?" Alex yells, pissed beyond words.

Awesome timing. Letting my head fall into my hands, I brace myself for his wrath.

"Someone better explain why it looks like she's about to hit a club when she should be in bed."

Translation: little brother, if you don't give me a damn good reason why she looks like she's leaving the hospital, I will make sure every future one-night stand learns about your My Little Pony obsession.

Jesse raises his hands in defeat. "I tried to talk her out of it, I swear, but you know how she is."

"Oh please," I snarl. "Would you two stop it already? I'm fine, okay?"

A crazy look in his eyes, Alex stalks toward me. "Manda, this is—"

"My choice," I say. "And you can hate it all you want, but I need to get out of this town and away from—"

"Me?" Alex snaps.

I was going to say the shit that happened here, but whatever. "I—"

Alex's striking face turns to granite. "It's all right. No need to explain. I mean, that was the deal, right? You held up your end of the bargain. Now it's my turn."

What the hell is going on with him? I just want to get on with my life. It's not like he wants me in his anyway. "Alex—"

"You want me out of your life, I get that. But you could have just told me to leave."

"Alex," Jesse interrupts his rampage. "Why don't you let her explain herself, dude?"

A creepy smile crosses Alex's lips. "Explain what? That she's ready to risk her life because she can't stand me? Or that she's so full of herself, she doesn't even listen to the doctors?"

Enough. Who the fuck does he think he is? Cutting me off twice, talking about me in the third person when I'm standing right here. I've had it. "*She* isn't checkin' herself out because of *you*. I know that it's hard to imagine, but my world doesn't revolve around you, Alex."

He squints. "Yeah, right."

Asshole. I cross my arms and knit my brows. "Did you know the woman next door has cluster headaches, and her husband is so desperate because of her suffering he considers mercy killing? Or that the kid across the hallway has leukemia, and his parents know he will never grow up? No. How could you? You don't have to feel the despair, fear, and sadness of the whole floor, but I do, Alex. So yeah, I am checking myself out, and there's nothing you can do about it. Do I make myself clear?"

Alex's eyes widen. I bet he hasn't even considered the fact my gift can also be a curse, especially when I'm stuck in places like this. "I-I had no idea," he stutters.

"Clearly, you didn't."

"Okay, let's all take a deep breath," Jesse says, getting between Alex and me. "How about we take you back to the motel, you get some rest, and when you're up for it we drive you to New York?"

Always the peacemaker.

I shake my head. "No worries, Jess. I'm goin' to catch a bus."

"Of course she is," Alex mutters under his breath.

Stay calm. This is going to be one of the last conversations you ever have with him. I draw in a deep breath, or as deep as my lungs allow. "I don't wanna fight, Alex. As a matter of fact, I wanted to ask you for a favor."

"A favor? Why don't I like the sound of that?" he says, a smile touching his eyes.

"Probably because you know me too well." I answer honestly.

"What do you need?" Jesse sounds curious.

I pull pen and paper out of my bag and jot down a few things. "Can you get that for me?" I ask, passing him the note. I'd get it myself, but I still feel like crap.

Jesse skims my handwriting. "Twenty-one peppers, rum, a Cuban cigar, and," he gives me the WTF look, "a black diamond?"

"You've gotta be fucking kidding me," Alex yells, his eyes wide with fury.

Poor Jesse doesn't understand jack. "Someone care to tell me what this is all about?"

"I—"

"She's going to summon death."

I smile. The boy is a quick study.

Jesse frowns. "Say that again, 'cause I thought you just said she's going to summon death."

Alex's gaze glides from me to his brother. "Told ya. The girl has a death wish."

I lock eyes with Alex. "I don't have a death wish, jerk. But I always keep my promises, and I owe Isobelle."

"That's insane," Jesse says, hand fisted around a streak of his wild curls.

Alex faces me. "He's right, Manda. It's a crazy idea."

I shrug. "Not crazier than going against a bocor."

Jesse studies his brother. "You can't let her do that, man."

"Look," I say nonchalantly. "If you're too scared, I can do it on my own."

Alex eyeballs me. I can tell he hates the idea, but he understands why I have to do this. "Get the stuff, bro," he says, running a hand over his freshly shaved face. "We owe her that much."

Chapter 27

The night air blows through the open windows as Alex pulls over onto the side of the road. “This is as good as it gets,” he says, pointing to the deserted crossroad in front of us.

I gaze through the windshield. Ghostly trees line the unpaved street. Withered flowers and a crooked cross mark the death of some poor bastard, and an uncanny atmosphere poisons the air. Perfect spot to invoke a reaper.

“This is a stupid idea,” Jesse bitches, yanking the door of the Mustang open. “What if your summoning ritual pisses him off?” He hasn’t exactly been chatty since we got in the car, and judging by the look on his face, I’d say he’d rather go on a date with Lucifer than be anywhere near here. I don’t blame him. The whole zombie thing fucked him up pretty bad.

Digging my heels into the dusty ground, I get out of the car. “Guess he’ll just have to deal with it.”

Mr. Snappy looks over the top of the car and grimaces. “He’s a reaper, Manda. Dealing with it could very well result in a blood bath.” He clears his throat. “Our blood, I might add.”

Stalking to the trunk, I frown. “C’mon, Jess. You sound like your brother.”

“Knock it off, guys,” Alex orders. “The sooner we get this over with the better. So everybody just go to work, all right?"

"If you say so," Jesse hisses.

I grab a black bag from the trunk and walk to the center of the crossroad. Scanning the area, I make sure no one's around. Then I pull a book with voodoo symbols out, open the page with Samedi's sigil, and start drawing.

Jesse's gaze travels from the symbol in the book to my poor imitation on the road. "Your drawing skills suck, Amanda."

Maybe if I hadn't flunked all those art classes, my masterpiece would look less WTF and more like the sigil, but beggars can't be choosers. "Feel free to join in if you think you can do a better job."

Jerking the book and the chalk out of my hand, he goes to work. The boy has some real talent. "When did you become the new Picasso?"

Sketching the last lines, Jesse smiles. "Took a few classes in junior high. Chicks dig artists, you know."

"Of course they do."

"Guys," Alex groans. "How about we focus on the task at hand and save the small talk for later?"

He's right. There are a million things that could go wrong tonight. We better make damn sure we're prepared.

Leaning against the car next to Alex, I shove gum in my mouth. "Just so we're clear, under no circumstances will either of you enter that circle when I call upon him. Understood?"

Alex frowns. "I hear ya, Manda. No entering the circle because we might get gutted. Noted. Now tell me something." He bats his long lashes. "What are you going to do if he doesn't free her?"

Spit some insults at him? "What is it with the Remington brothers and pessimism?"

"Comes with the job," Jesse explains as he throws the chalk in the bag and grabs the juniper to make a circle.

I'm about to cross the juniper line when Alex reaches for my hand, spinning me around. My heart leaps in my chest when his malachite eyes find mine. "I know you're not scared of death," he says. "But I hate funerals and suits, so could you please try not to get killed?"

"Will do my best," I promise. "Hand me the rum." Jesse throws the bottle, which I stuffed with twenty-one peppers, my way. I catch it just before it smashes on the ground. "Dude," I yell, giving him the evil eye.

"What?"

"I know you have some serious doubts, man. But I need to know you guys have my back."

"Your back?" Jesse laughs. "It's not like we can kill death, Amanda."

"Relax," Alex says, placing a hand on his anxious brother's shoulder. "She knows what she's doing. It's not like she hasn't done it before."

Jesse tilts his head to the side. "Has she?"

Alex's eyes lock with mine. "You have, right?"

Lie. "Sure."

"Manda," Jesse warns.

I bite on my lower lip. "All right. Truth is I've never mixed voodoo with traditional witchcraft."

"What?" Alex snaps, his eyes almost popping out of their sockets. "Are you kidding?"

Jesse smites his forehead. "Holy shit, we're beyond screwed."

I make a calming gesture. “Would you relax already? I’ve got this.” How hard can it be to get a date with a reaper?

Walking into the circle with the rum in one hand and the Cuban cigar in the other, I take a seat in front of the sigil. “Let’s get this party started.”

Jesse crosses his arms and pulls a face. “I don’t see how this is a party, but whatever.”

“Just be careful,” Alex orders.

A silly grin spreads across my face. “Worried ’bout me?”

“You wish.”

Jesse frowns. “Some screwed up foreplay you guys have, that’s for sure.”

“Shut up,” Alex and I shout at the same time.

Jesse grins like the Cheshire Cat. “Don’t shoot the messenger. Just stating the facts.”

I ignore him and unscrew the top of the rum bottle. “Remember, don’t enter the circle.”

They both nod.

I get to my feet, pull the knife out of my back pocket, and throw the cigar on the sigil. I use the knife to draw a pentagram in each cardinal direction. Starting with the north, I work my way to the west and chant, “Uriel behind me, Raphael to my left, Michael across from me, and Gabriel to my right. Archangels, I call upon thee. Bless this circle and let no harm come to me.”

“What the hell is she doing?” Jesse mumbles.

Alex shrugs. “Beats me, man.”

“Guys, please. I’m tryin’ to work here.”

“Sorry,” they grumble.

Once I feel the protective energy buzzing around

me, I sit down and sip the spicy rum. Damn, that shit is hot. "*Messorem, messorem veni foras. Sit velantur parte saecula. Quacumque die invocavero te, orbisque mortis. Mihi in occúrsum hoc in bivio et perficiets volentem.*" A warm breeze wafts through my hair as I take another sip. "*Messorem, messorem veni foras. Sit velantur parte saecula. Quacumque die invocavero te, orbisque mortis. Mihi in occúrsum hoc in bivio et perficiets volentem.*"

Shit, why the fuck is it so hot all of a sudden? Sweat drips down my forehead as I repeat the spell one last time before spiting the rum on the sigil and slicing my palm with the knife.

Fisting my hand, I let the blood drop onto the white chalk. "Samedi, Samedi, I call upon thee. Samedi, Samedi, come to me."

A black mist surfaces in the middle of the sigil. While Alex and Jesse are busy picking their jaws from the ground, I'm fighting the fire that burns me inside. I've never been a fan of saunas, but nothing compares to the lava running through my veins. Instinct tells me to run, but the second I step out of that circle, I'll be without protection, and that could be fatal.

"Who calls upon me?" the mist asks, coalescing into a grotesque shape wearing an old-fashioned top hat.

C'mon, Manda, show some dignity. Under Alex and Jesse's watchful eyes, I straighten. "I do."

"What a surprise. A Bishop witch practicing the dark arts?" The energy around that thing is so strong it electrifies the air.

Waves of heat jolt through me, twisting my gut. "Cut the crap," I say. "I'm not in the mood for small talk."

Advancing toward me, the creature laughs. "I see. Let's cut to the chase then. How can I assist you?"

Stay focused. He can't harm you.

"Your friend, Francoise, banished the soul of a little girl to purgatory. I need you to release her." I sound pretty confident, considering his sheer presence freaks me out.

"Hmm."

The weird energy, along with the heat makes my head swim. "What's that supposed to mean?"

The thing closes the gap between us. From the corner of my eye, I see Alex reaching for his gun. What's he gonna do? Shoot a reaper?

"It means I have to think about it." The creature's voice is so otherworldly he could play a role in *Outlander*.

Rage pumps through my heart. "What's there to think about?" I say, sounding pissed. "Your shitty friend put an innocent girl in the realm of evil witches and demons. Get her the hell outta there or—"

"Don't threaten me," he warns, holding up a shadowy hand. "I'm not big on the whole *Pretty Little Liars* act, Amanda."

When reapers watch TV, the world must really be coming to an end.

I wave the comment off. "Threat? Me? You? Don't be silly. I might be insane, but I'd never threaten a reaper." I smile. "Hypothetically speakin', though, I would make him a promise."

"What kind of promise would that be?"

My lips curl into a mischievous grin. "The promise would involve a black diamond and a trapping ritual."

Black diamonds can trap spirits. Until a few seconds ago, I wasn't sure if they worked on reapers, but when he stiffens, I realize I'm on the right path.

"I see," the thing says, his hollow gaze gliding to Jesse and Alex.

Alex pulls the tiny black gemstone out of his pocket and holds it up. "A word of advice?" The creature groans. "Don't piss her off. She can be a real pain."

One side of Jesse's mouth rises. "I bet Francoise would agree."

Pacing the juniper line, the reaper considers his options. Damn, he needs to hurry the fuck up. I'm melting here. "What do you say?"

Stopping dead in his tracks, his non-existing eyes search my soul. "Your arguments are very convincing."

"But?"

He floats back to the sigil and picks up the cigar. "I'm aware you are no mambo, love. Surely, though, you know I am the only reaper who's in the service sector, right?"

"What's your point?"

"After everything Francoise did, I do think there must be some compensation. However, I am willing to grant you one wish and one wish only. After that, I will never answer any of your calls again, and there will be no chance for further assistance from my side." The cigar in his hand lights, and he takes a drag off it. "Do you understand my terms, Amanda?"

I wipe the sweat off my neck. "What in God's name makes you think I would call upon you again?"

Taking another drag off the Cuban, he points at Alex. "Why don't you ask your little hunter friend over there?"

What's this, a goddamn quiz show? I look at Alex and Jesse. "What's he talking about?"

Jesse averts his gaze.

Alex shrugs. "No idea."

The energy of the reaper messes with my ability to read Alex's aura. Apart from a few traces of gray and blue, which could mean anything, I don't get a clear reading.

The thing laughs. "Alexander Remington. Always concerned about everyone, but himself."

"Shut up," Alex hisses.

"Man, think about this," Jesse whispers. The look he gives his brother is one of pure desperation.

"Yes, Alexander," the creature says, amused. "Think about it."

"All right, that's enough," I yell, unable to endure the heat any longer. "Someone better tell me what the fuck is going on here, or I'll banish all of your asses into that diamond."

Silence.

I'm surrounded by morons.

Between the urge to rip my sticky clothes off, the cramps in my stomach, and the fact that I'm more than mad because no one gives me a damn answer, I make a decision. "Either someone tells me what this corrupt piece of shit is talking about, or *I'm* going to get Isobelle's soul out of Purgatory."

Alex faces me with a softness in his eyes that's both surprising and heartbreaking. "Do it. Get her out of there, Amanda."

Jesse pales, but when his lips stay sealed, I have no choice but to go through with it. Spinning around, I eyeball the reaper. "I want Isobelle's soul freed from Purgatory."

The creature tips his hat. "Very well then. Your wish shall be granted. Her soul will be shipped to Limbo, where the weight of her heart will decide her future."

In other words, depending on her lifestyle, she'll either be reborn, enter the everlasting light, or deported to hell.

"It was certainly a pleasure to meet you, love."

"Oh please," I bitch, throwing my hands in the air. "Spare me the false amiability."

Slowly dissolving, the reaper turns to Alex. "Until we meet again, Alexander." Then his shadow merges with the night.

We head back to the motel, a bone-crushing silence filling the Mustang. Alex drives, Jesse rides shotgun, and I sit in back, wondering what these guys are keeping from me. There's a big part of me that wants to torture them until they tell me the truth. The rational side of my brain, though, urges me to forget all about it and get on with my life. They clearly don't want my help, and after tonight, neither Jesse nor Alex will be my problem anymore.

****

The bus station crawls with people: grownups, kids, teenagers, fighting couples, loving couples. It's a chaotic mess.

Gawking at the TV screen that hangs on the wall of the station, I listen to the CNN chick. "Several members of the Prevent Crimes Against Children Foundation were arrested last night after the FBI found compromising material in their homes. The organization first came under the scrutiny of the agency when one of their members, a French citizen named Francoise Matthieu, was arrested for abduction, rape, and child pornography in Bakersfield."

Karma, without a doubt, is a ruthless bitch, but it never fails to deliver justice.

Breathing a sigh of relief, I walk toward the bus, typing a text to Bonnie.

Alex sneaks up behind me. "In case you get grumpy," he says, holding a doggy bag under my nose.

I spin around, a big smile spread across my face. "Afraid I might go crazy-witch-pants on the driver?"

Alex's lips curl up. "Pretty much."

I open the bag and stare at the carefully chosen supplies: lemon cupcakes, sandwiches, a package of onion and cheese chips, lots of soda, and Red Bull. "You know me well, Alex."

Jesse wraps his arms around my waist and rests his chin on my shoulder. "Never saw him do anything like it for another girl."

"Jesse," Alex warns.

"Just saying, man."

"Final call for New York," a middle-aged driver shouts, and people start lining up at the bus door.

With one swift move, Jesse spins me around. "So, that's it, huh?" he says, eyes locked on mine.

Call me sentimental, but the prospect of never seeing them again tugs at my non-existing heart. "I guess."

He pulls me into a bear hug. "Take care, Manda," he whispers, almost breaking another rib.

"You too, Jess." Stepping back, I shove the doggy bag into my backpack. "And no more zombie excursions, understood?"

His full lips curl into a big smile. "Aye, aye, Captain," he says, saluting me like a good soldier.

Throwing my backpack over my shoulder, I face Alex. "Take good care of him."

Alex nods, but won't meet my gaze. "Always."

For the last time, I drink in his God-like appearance: the ripped jeans that fit him like a second skin, the striking face that has always been so hard to resist, and the malachite eyes that offer an eternity of happiness.

Having second thoughts?

Does it matter?

I walk toward the bus. My stupid heart jumps at the sound of Alex's voice. "Manda, wait."

I look over my shoulder. "Don't tell me you already miss me," I tease.

He jogs toward me.

Cliché alarm!

Stopping inches in front of me, he looks me in the eyes. "I know I've been a jerk most of the time, but I just wanted to…" He trails off and drops his gaze to the ground.

I hate when people get sentimental. "It's okay, Alex. You don't have to—"

"Yeah, I do." He holds my wrists and stares at me. Something dark passes through his eyes, and before I know what's happening, his lips are on mine.

The people around us cease to exist. My heart pounds and excitement bubbles in my belly. I scrub my fingers through his hair. He pulls me hard against him. Nothing about this kiss is gentle or innocent. It's masochistic torture, but it's real.

He pulls away, out of breath, wide-eyed. “Thank you,” he whispers. “For everything.”

My senses reel, and I have a hard time catching my breath. There’s something about the kiss that scares the living shit outta me. It was almost like—

The end?

“Alex, what—”

“Hey, honey,” the driver, yells. “You coming or what?”

Stepping back, Alex smiles sadly. “You should go.”

Every fiber in my soul tells me to stay, but I can’t. “Goodbye, Alex.”

“Bye, Manda.”

I can still taste him when I get on the bus and watch the doors to my past close in front of me.

A word about the author…

A passionate reader and writer, addicted to the dark side of the craft, Nadine grew up with Marvel heroes and horror films. She loves stories that challenge gender stereotypes and religious beliefs and that tackle topics such as racism and cultural differences in an entertaining way.

Nadine has a BA in Comparative Religions and studied Creative Writing at the University of Oxford. If she isn't traveling the world, she's reading, writing, or watching movies.

www.ingramcontent.com/pod-product-compliance
Lightning Source LLC
Chambersburg PA
CBHW060531260626
47161CB00003B/847

* 9 7 8 1 5 0 9 2 0 7 3 1 2 *